Senescence

First Published by Paused Books 2015

Senescence
ISBN 978-1514347928

Copyright © Paused Books 2015

This book is a work of fiction. Any resemblance between these fictional characters and actual persons, living or dead, is purely coincidental.

No part of this publication may be reproduced or transmitted by any device, without the prior written permission of the copyright holder. This book may not be circulated without a cover or in any cover other than the existing cover.

A statutory catalogue deposit of this book can be found at the required libraries as required by the Copyright and Related Rights Act, 2000.

Second Edition Paused Books 2019

ALL RIGHTS RESERVED
Including the right of reproduction in whole or in part in any form.

www.pausedbooks.com

Other Works by James Dwyer:

Twelve Weapons

The Grieving Soul

The Heights of Power series:

Fireborn

Masks of Moi'dan

A War of Flames

By Brendan Dwyer and James Dwyer:

Cult Fiction

Rowdy Roddy Randy
Cult Fiction: Player Two

Flowing	1
Examined	15
Contradictions	26
Unchanging Change	37
Submission	49
Untroubled Existence	58
Mechanical Universe	68
Pansubstance	78
Empiricism	91
Naturally Chained	102
Habit of Association	114
Lawgiver to Nature	125
Unified Truth	134
Struggles of a Different Class	143
Relative Accountability	153
Master of Your Own House	160
The Subjective Process: Unfettered by Rules	169

Senescence / *se·nes·cence* / *(sĕ-nes´ens)* *n*: the gradual deterioration of all living matter over time.

• CHAPTER ONE •

Flowing

Dovid woke up in his island and touched himself. He touched the lids of his eyes, followed by the bridge of his nose, the lobes of his ears, and finally the flat of his tongue. He tickled the tips of his fingers against each other and then sighed dramatically before sitting up. The education charger was still attached to his head, and the nutrition and sanitation chargers to his arms and legs, so Dovid disconnected each of these with a grunt before stomping over to confront his mirror. His eyes still hadn't fallen out. His nose and his ears hadn't either, or his tongue or his skin, but Dovid had always figured that his eyes would give first. He wanted to be like Mart, eyeless and upgraded, so they could wink at each other with their absent orbs, or he wanted to be like anyone at all, to be like everybody else in the entire world; to be normal! But today it was too late. Today Dovid had become the oldest person in the world at sixteen to not receive his inability.

'Happy birthday, Dovid,' the wall next to his mirror suddenly chirped. This morning the companion in Dovid's wall was a smiley face with a sparkling blue party hat and star-shaped party glasses.

'Oh gee, thanks, Wall,' Dovid replied, perhaps not wholeheartedly meaning it. 'So is there *anything* different about me today?'

The smiley face chose a look of profound consideration (depicted by pensively smoking a small wooden pipe), before returning to a joyous countenance (depicted by pensively smoking *two* wooden pipes, each puffing out a revolting fuzzy rainbow).

'You are in perfect health!'

'Yeah, yeah. And that's the damned problem, isn't it?'

Dovid didn't wait for the wall to respond and he trudged over to his shower corner. The shower automatically knew to use the mint shampoo that dissolved the hair on his body and head, and it also knew the precise temperature and length of shower time that made

Dovid the happiest. Yet, when Dovid was finished his shower, he still wasn't happy. How strange.

Putting on his emoto-shirt and pants, Dovid set his shirt to "distraught with the unacceptable flux of the world and my emotions with it." The emoto-shirt diligently depicted the right kind of smiley face to represent exactly that.

Going back to his mirror, Dovid glided his fingers over the skin of his bald head and took an important moment to hate his perfection. He locked gazes with his dazzling green eyes and breathed deeply in through his nose, closing his eyes to accentuate the sound, and then slowly exhaled with detestation. His tongue. Dovid decided that if anything had to fall off, he could live without his tongue. That meant not living in the Visual Sector with Mart, of course. No tongue meant Gustatory Sector, but Dovid could live with that. And while he had his tongue, Dovid stuck it out in wild rebellion at his long-suffering wall, who simply accepted the abuse and stuck out its own in the form of a panting dog. Dovid waved the image away.

'So what are sixteen-year-olds supposed to do on their birthdays?' Dovid demanded.

'You have four choices for physical leisure, Dovid: there is sexual activity, violent activity, narcotic activity, and gluttonous activity.'

Dovid knew all this already. What was the point of the wall if it only told him things he already knew? Throwing his head back, Dovid rolled his eyes to the ceiling in despair at how functionless walls had become. Let the world just be comprised of ceilings and floors, and let load-bearing be damned! For as much use as it was being this morning, his wall might as well be reminding Dovid of how he never ever left his island, how every birthday he taunted and dared himself to venture out to try physical leisure, and how every birthday Dovid countered his own daring with the easy truth that he had absolutely everything he needed right here. Outside be damned as well, along with walls, normality, and turning sixteen!

Although … next year, when he became the dreaded seventeen, Dovid was going to be evicted from the Education Sector and relocated in a Segregation Sector instead – if he had an inability to segregate. As far as the Education Sector went though, and its peer-pressuring physical leisure pleasure, maybe this was Dovid's last chance to try it?

'I'll tell you what, Wall, you tell me which of those four I should try today and I'll do it, but only if you pick the correct one, which I'll decide by a completely whimsical ruling. Deal? Great. So go, take your pick.'

'Well, Dovid, almost every other sixteen-year-old in this Education Sector has engaged in some manner of sexual activity.'

'Hey! I've engaged in plenty sexual activity!'

'Sexual activity with other people, Dovid.'

'Oh fine. I'll give you that. But isn't the whole point of these islands not to need other people?'

The smiley face on the wall turned into a bearded frowny face, one looking around with paranoid mania, and Dovid laughed like a maniac right on back. Damned wall wasn't the only one who could pretend to be crazy.

Dovid marched out of the Personal Quarter of his island and paused for a moment of peaceful contemplation inside the stem. Every island stem gave its occupant four grey options, and come to think of it, every everything seemed to give someone something as an option of four. Four quarters in the islands, four options in the physical leisure, four sectors to divide the ages of humanity. Whoever in Management created these systems definitely had a peculiar infatuation with the number four. The four Dovid was staring at though – forcing (four-cing!) some essential profundity onto this morning's disappointing universe – were social, professional, leisure, or exit. Could he count going back into his Personal Quarter as a fifth option? Would that send reality crashing down around him in spectacular annihilation? Dovid shook his head four times to rid himself of his morning's dramatics and he figured that the wall was probably right. He needed to be around other people. Too much Dovid time alone with Dovid was making Dovid more than a little weird (Dovid).

'You heard the man,' Dovid said to himself. 'Better go weird onto somebody else.'

Going as far away from the exit as he possibly could, Dovid strode down to the Social Quarter of his island and stepped inside. He was immediately assaulted by lethally garish automated birthday messages from everyone he had ever interacted with in his digital life. Apart from the heart-failure, bladder loss, and temporary blindness it caused, the exploding candle auto-wish feature on these walls was truly amazing. It had all the love and affection of a real-life birthday well-wishing with none of the love or affection or hassle of remembering it. Dovid summoned his wall and told it to open its mouth.

The wall opened its mouth to ask why Dovid would want this, but Dovid had already crumpled up all the virtual messages into a palm-sized ball and hurled it at his wall. The poor smiley face got it smack in the mouth and had no choice but to swallow. For a moment, Dovid actually felt kind of bad, reasoning that there was no real need to be so needlessly obnoxious, but then his wall turned into the smiley face of a goat and began chewing on everything else it could find in Dovid's walls. He let the smiling goat munch away unmolested.

'Mart 5518,' Dovid called out to a different section of the wall, and his brother's eyeless face appeared. Dovid and Mart had the same birth-mother but Mart was completely not-Dovid in every way, with his dark skin, his curly hair, and his gaping red lack of eyeballs. The cerebral fobs on the sides of his head provided Mart with his sense upgrade, but still, Dovid had never gotten used to looking into those empty sockets.

'Dovid! Happy birthday, little brother! Anything fall off today?' Mart was already scanning Dovid from top to bottom with his hollow lack of eyes, so he already knew the answer.

'Hi Mart, nope, still no inability, unless you count my sense of self and place in the world. Is that one of the senses you can lose?'

'Wo, little bro, your emoto-shirt does look a little like "distraught with the unacceptable flux of the world and your emotions with it". What's wrong?'

Mart's own emoto-shirt this morning was showing a smiley face that demonstrated "profound connection with the inner workings of the universe." He was such a show-off.

'I read a philosopher named M. Lawrence who once said that your old self dies each night and you're reborn slightly different every morning, accounting for the change in self and the illusion of time. I think that's what's happened to me.'

'What, that you've died, or that you've become a philosopher?' Mart was trying not to laugh at the seriousness of Dovid's predicament.

'Is there a difference? And that's the problem right there: difference; in unwanted abundance and also lack thereof. Everything feels different today while still remaining stubbornly the same, and not in the way of my senses dulling so that I might finally know my inability, but different in that everything is wrong. My wall is wrong. The world is wrong. The universe is wrong. The number four is wrong!'

'Alright, alright, I hear ya, little brother. But it will happen. I know you're the oldest in the world right now without getting one, but there have been others before, and none of them has ever gone too far beyond sixteen without an inability. Which are you hoping to get anyway? Change your mind since yesterday?'

Mart did his best not to look expectant. Dovid saw it is as his duty to change his mind as often as he blinked, lest anyone think that they knew what Dovid thought, but when it came to inabilities and Mart, there was only one correct answer.

'Visual Sector,' Dovid lied. Auditory, Gustatory, Olfactory, and Tactile – none shall dare be named while Mart doth smile upon thine wall.

'Didn't doubt it!' Mart said with a beaming smile and then cocked his head to something off-screen. 'Here, let me take a quick look at your life and see if we can't find the source of this *anomie*.'

Dovid watched listlessly as Mart pulled up Dovid's entire unspectacular life on the wall next to his face, muttering to himself as he read through everything there.

'Hmm, good work–to–sleep ratio. Your profession is still history? You're weird, but you're at the right education charge for your age, ranked sixth in the Sector? Not bad, but not quite top five. You're in perfect physical health, wait, hold up! Dovid ... have you really never gone to any Physical Leisure Segment? At all? You told me you went last year!'

'Don't start. I'm already getting sanctimony from my wall.'

'That's because your wall is created from the mix of its experience from you, and harmonised with the experiences of everyone else in the world. In other words, Dovid, your wall is right and you are wrong!'

'Well what if I choose not to believe in empiricist walls? What if I want an a priori one? Huh? And even if you're right about me being and feeling wrong, and let's say human contact is the answer, then my question is what kind of a stupid question has other people as the stupid answer? People are the stupidest thing in the world!'

'Oh? Is that right?' Mart asked, while changing his emoto-shirt to show a look of bemused incredulity. 'And what is it you hate about people again? That you don't want to be burdened with the immensity of drama *squelching* free from their infinite orifices? That you don't believe in people *defecating* their issues onto others just to swill about their own personal misery? That you feel people *vomit* up banalities simply to reassure each other that we all share the same time and space, and that you don't need to listen to their nonsense because you already have enough nonsense going on in your own head, so why willingly accept the nonsense of others in with it? Did I get that right?'

Dovid spread out his hands. 'And is that so unreasonable?'

'Well what are you doing to me right now?'

'That's different. This is me annoying my big brother.'

Mart shook his head. 'So I'm your big brother again, am I? You do remember last week when you spent an hour explaining to me why I might not even be real because we had never met, right? So go meet real people, Dovid, and fight them, or do sexually pleasurable things with them, or just eat with them and get high. But go! And do!'

Go and do, the meaning of mundane life summed up in two words. Just a pity that two wasn't half as mystically meaningful as four.

'Fine. But four final things before I go.'

'Four?'

'Yes, four! Now, number one, I've been thinking about the education chargers. And you know how knowledge and information go in while we're sleeping? Well my question is: do you think information ever goes back out?'

'And go where? For what reason? I have all your information right here in front of me, Dovid. Why would Management need to know your inner musings too? No one in their right mind wants to know the inner musings of your mind. *You* don't even want to know the mindless depths of your own mind.'

'But that's exactly it! How can I know my own insane thoughts are my own? What if someone else's thoughts were filtered in through the education charger, while mine were filtered out, and that's why I'm feeling so wrong today!'

'I like it, but who's this *you* if you're thinking someone else's thoughts. Think about this instead: what if your paranoia is what was filtered in instead. That your thoughts are your own, but it's your feeling of unease about your thoughts that's foreign.'

Dovid rubbed his head. 'Yeah. I think I like that, to feel that my thoughts are my own, and think that my feelings are not. So all I'd have to decide is whether I feel like thinking something or only think that I have feelings – which is the cause and which the effect.'

'Please tell me that was four already.'

'What? No, that was all one, but fine, we can skip to three. If I do lose my eyes like you and our mother, then how can I be sure I'm actually seeing what's really there and not just what the sense upgrades want me to see.'

'Well, it's all light. You choose to trust your eye's reading of light, and I choose to trust my upgrade's reading of light. What other choice do we have? But speaking of upgrades, I did get this cool new addition. I can see four different kinds of light now, and I've even heard of a new model they're working on that will let you view emotion as a wave. Isn't that weird?'

'But that's what I'm saying!' Dovid squawked. 'You see completely different things to what I see, so what part of that makes us part of the same shared existence?'

'Well I can easily turn off this interaction and for all effective purposes, we won't be. I've got stuff to do today, so what's number four, birthday boy?'

'Just the usual.'

'Well alright then, now we're back to normal! So I give you your daily philosophical conundrum, and then you go and physically interact with the rest of the world, okay? Go punch someone in the face, or taste someone's nipple, or punch someone's nipple! But today's question is: how can fire be a creative force?'

'That's it?'

'That's it. Riddle, riddle, little brother. Talk to you tomorrow.'

How can fire be a creative force? That seemed a little easy. It created light and heat, didn't it? It even created satisfaction if that fire was destroying something that Dovid didn't like, such as everything. Just a pity there was no such thing as fire anymore. Oh well. Dovid was about to announced his speedy riddle victory to his brother but he saw that Mart's picture had already cut out. Damned social interaction, who needed it? And anyway, if social interaction was supposed to be so natural, then why did it always leave Dovid so out of balance? There was a chance he was simply doing it wrong, but it wasn't something he had any intention of getting good at either. Dovid went back out into his stem.

Looking at the Leisure Quarter of his island, Dovid considered starting an internal rant about why it wasn't called the Non-Physical Leisure Quarter – since Management insisted on making the Physical Leisure Segment such a distinction – but thought better. His wall had learned to turn itself off when Dovid started into anything that pedantically semantic, probably having learned from Mart, and there was no way Dovid was willing to listen to himself. It was the only thing worse than listening to someone else.

'Hey, Wall,' Dovid called out.

A smiley face wearing a cheap rubber horse mask appeared on the wall. 'Hey, Dovid.'

'Am I abnormally negative or self-involved?'

'You are sixteen.'

'Yeah, I know that, but compared to every other sixteen-year-old on your system.'

'You are quite abnormal, yes.'

Dovid sagged with relief. 'Thank you. I'm going out so.'

'Really? How odd. Would you like to wear shoes?'

'Why?'

'Social custom dictates shirt, pants, and shoes as normal attire for outside.'

'That's antiquated, ya dumb wall. People wore shoes in the past because there was an actual outside, with weather and stones and broken glass. But now that everything's inside, give me one good reason why I should wear shoes that doesn't have to do with social assimilation.'

'Someone who is wearing shoes might step on your toes.'

'Well, if we all didn't wear shoes, then that wouldn't be a problem now, would it? See, this is what I mean by not having an empiricist wall. I want you to think for yourself, Wall, not just format and relay your every previously recorded experience back to me.'

'I apologise for my conformist audacity, Dovid.'

'I accept your apology, if not your audaciousness. Now, I'm going out.'

'Shall I open the exit for you?'

'Stop pressuring me! I have a very complex decision-making process. I'm not a gigantic worldwide computer-wall like you that can process the entire universe instantaneously. In fact, when this excursion to the outside goes horribly wrong, and it will, I'll be committing myself completely to you and my island, so you and I are going to have to try harder to get along. Alright?'

'I shall await your return with exhilarated trepidation.'

Dovid sighed.

'It's my own fault you're like this, isn't it? You're a global system, but you've had to personalise yourself to my own particular brand of misanthropic back-talk, haven't you. I'll tell you what, when I get back, we'll be friends. I won't even call you "Wall" anymore. I'll give you a name. How about Logos? The world-wall that governs all life.'

'The only permanency is constant change,' the wall replied with a winky face.

'Exactly! You see? I can get along with this kind of wall. So stay like this until I get back.'

Dovid marched confidently down the stem of his island and charged right out the exit. Rather than think about the terrifying truth of what he had just done, Dovid fiddled with his emoto-shirt, changing it to depict a "my wall is a sarcastic jerk but I'm not wearing shoes" face, and then began whistling as he got further and further away from the warm safety of his island.

But Dovid didn't need to think about that. Being outside was easy. Look, the distracting grey stems of the Education Sector weren't even that different to the soothing grey stems of his island. Dovid had no idea whatsoever why he had been so nervous about coming out here all this time. There wasn't even anyone around. It made perfect sense that everyone else would be in their own islands too, because, apart from debauchery, the islands contained everything anyone could ever want, and even then it was possible to inject a little debauchery if you tried hard enough. It took Dovid five minutes of whistling before he turned to a wall to ask where he was going.

The wall displayed a map of the Education Sector and all the stems trickling through the different islands centred on the Physical Leisure Segment. Not a bad bit of Management there: walk one way to a segregation exit, and walk the other way to the Physical Leisure Segment. Unfortunately, the fact that the Managers weren't foolish in their designs of the Sector did not comfort Dovid into thinking that everyone else in the world wasn't stupid. If anything it worked towards proving his point since the design was so foolproof, it was specifically created to be targeted at fools.

'Hey, Wall, are you Logos, my wall, or are you somebody else's wall, or even the Management wall?'

'Hello, Dovid,' the smiley face wall replied, 'I can be whatever wall you wish.' And to prove its point the wall changed to a smiley face with a cigar and hat.

'Well, yeah, obviously.' Dovid had to politely turn his head away in order to roll his eyes at the fool wall – necessary so as not to bias it into becoming a jerk like he was. 'But what wall are you now, before I tell you what wall you should be.'

'Right now, I'm the stem wall.'

Dovid nodded and wondered if he could count this as social interaction outside of his island and call it a day. But no, it had to be physical interaction. Damn.

Dovid poked the smiley face in the eye to prove to the world that this absolutely counted as physical interaction (the smiley face even gave itself a black eye to corroborate Dovid's insistence) and then continued onto the Physical Leisure Segment. It only took a few more minutes of whistling before he reached it. Each Education Sector wasn't exactly that big, just numerous and world encompassing. There were only a few hundred in this Sector, not so many as to crowd the Physical Segment, but enough to avoid *too much* incest and inbreeding – a little was fine.

Facing down the detector field that sectioned off the Physical Sector, Dovid took a long procrastinating breath to steady his heart and ended up coughing and spluttering when he saw his first real-life person in years. It was a male, maybe fourteen and a little under six-feet tall, short blond hair and wearing shoes. Dovid was preparing himself for the social interaction, going through all possible replies to a friendly greeting that would properly identify Dovid as the kind of person that he wanted to appear to be. But then, as nonchalantly as a dog used to pinch off a poop in public, this other person just walked straight past Dovid and into the Physical Leisure Segment. How rude!

It was as rude a social faux pas as if this other male had actually pooped on Dovid's shoeless feet like the dog he was very much being. There would've been very little difference in how offended Dovid was feeling about it! He had a mind to find this person on the wall and let him have a piece of his mind. In all rights he should, but then Dovid jumped as he saw another person coming and rather than risk similar social humiliation, he ran into the Physical Leisure Segment.

Passing through the detection field, Dovid turned to his left immediately and tried to hide by the walls. The dim grey of his island and the outside stems changed to a slightly lighter grey in here. Dovid found the theatrical change of colour disorientating, but he managed it well. There were about a dozen other people in the entry hall too, each one ignoring Dovid, some making their way into the four different activity areas. Dovid still hadn't made up his mind which physical activity he was going to choose, but the pushy wall behind him popped to life to irritate him into deciding.

'Hello, Dovid 7511,' said the wall. 'Welcome to the Physical Leisure Segment. From your physical scan I judge you to be fit for violent, sexual, or gluttonous activity, however from your mental condition, mind-altering narcotic use is not recommended at this time.' The smiley face turned into a crazy face for a minute before returning back to blink at Dovid.

Dovid gave the wall a meaningful blink back and then eyed his options. Most of the males congregating in the room were making their way towards the Violent Quarter. A different male and two females were walking into the Gluttony Quarter at the same moment, so by process of elimination, Dovid hurried over to the Sexual Quarter before anyone else went in. If he had to engage in physical social interaction, he might as well try to find the one with no one else around.

The Sexual Quarter had its own detection field, and rather than a smiley face popping up, a loveheart face appeared instead.

'Hello, Dovid,' the loveheart said. 'Welcome to the Sexual Quarter. From your physical scan, I judge you to be fit for all sexual activity, up to and including conception.'

'Am, thanks. But I don't think I'd like to engage in conception. Not for my first time anyway.' The idea of reproducing his own genetics was horrifying.

'Please choose your sexual status from numbers one to ten thousand:

1. Just here to watch
2. Just here to touch hands and talk
3. Just here to touch other body parts
4. Just here to kiss
5. Just here to kiss other body parts
6. Just here to watch and touch my own body parts
7. Just here to impregnate or become impregnated
8. Just here to have acrobatic intercourse with the inclusion of several ...

'Stop!' Dovid was certain he did not want to find out how acrobatic sex needed the inclusion of several of anything. 'Is there a status of just being here to see what happens?' Surely one out of the ten thousand would be mildly similar to that. How could there even be ten thousand? Why not a full googol? A one followed by a hundred zeros was just what Dovid needed right then. Maybe he should go back to his island and look at it?

'Changing your sexual status to: Just here to see what happens.'

Dovid looked down to see his emoto-shirt change to a smiley face representing his new sexual status and he felt his body moderately relax. At least with his emoto-shirt changed, when he wandered around now to see what he was in for, he wouldn't be harassed by anyone unless they had the exact same status as he did, and the odds of that happening were apparently ten thousand to one.

'Hey look! We have the same status!'

Dovid closed his eyes. Yes, he did actually hear a lovely feminine voice say those words with enthusiasm. Yes, he should have expected something like this to happen after he assured himself that it would definitely not. And yes, he should probably open his eyes before she thought he was weird, and let her find out why he was weird for many other reasons instead. Dovid opened his eyes and met Imone.

Imone 9108 was sixteen, she had deep brown eyes and shallow black hair. She liked singing, dancing, and knife fighting. She didn't have any ears, but Dovid couldn't see the missing appendages or her replacement upgrades because her hair was swept over them. Not that Dovid was looking directly at Imone anyway, or Imone at him. They were both reading each other's lives on the walls beside them. Imone finished reading first, because, when compared to what he was reading about Imone anyway, Dovid had not really done much with his life.

'So this is your first time?' Imone asked, but she asked it with excitement instead of derision. 'I like your bare feet.'

'Ah, thanks. But yep, first time, just thought I'd come out and *see what happens.*' Dovid pointed to his emoto-shirt to show her how clever he was being.

'That's cool. I come out here once a week, it's a good way to get out of your own head from those islands, don't you think?'

Once a week? Dovid wanted to remind Imone that this was his first time, as she had just pointed out, so how could she suppose he might agree with her until he had tried it? And once a week! Dovid snuck a quick peek back at her life on the wall.

'Ah, yeah,' he said, while his eyes flitted from Imone to her scripted life, 'You, ah, read my mind. Great to get out of your own head. Am, when ... when did you start coming here?'

'What age? Well, the detection field said I could've started coming when I was twelve, early developer you know,' she grabbed her breasts to decorate that remark. 'But I've only been coming for about a year.'

Once a week, for about a year.

'What about you? Why did you wait so long?' Imone smiled at him to show she was just interested instead of judging and that smile almost made Dovid forget about the fifty-two other interests she might have had this year.

'Well, I'm studying to become a historian, so I guess I'm kind of old-fashioned when it comes to these things. But since it's my birthday, my wall said I should try it.'

'It's your birthday?' Imone turned to look at Dovid's life again on the wall. 'You're sixteen and still no inability? Wow.' Imone brushed her hair back over her shoulder and turned to show off her empty ear hole and the metal bar upgrade flashing next to it. 'I lost my ears when I was nine.'

'Early developer, right?' Dovid grabbed his own breasts and gave her an awkward smile.

Imone laughed at his joke and that delightful noise made Dovid feel more fantastic than he had ever felt. It was bizarre that he could take such pride and pleasure in the simple fact he was the cause of that beautiful effect from this glorious girl. He felt that there weren't enough adjectives in the world to help his thoughts over-describe those feelings. Why hadn't he come to the Physical Leisure Segment before now? This was amazing!

'Hey, since it's your birthday, let me show you the new upgrade I got. I had reflective panels put into the inside of my emoto-suit, so it can do this!' Imone's emoto-suit changed from the sexual status she was previously presenting, and instead became the projected image of the inside of her suit. An inside where there was nothing but unabashed nudity. Imone spread her hands out in exhibition and stood there completely naked for all intents and purposes. Well, no, not completely naked; she was still wearing shoes.

Dovid's eyes managed to dart from one breast to the next, to her hips, to her stomach, back to her face, and then her breasts again, all with his mouth hanging open and his heart stopped. He must not have been breathing either, and eventually, as Imone stood there nakedly waiting for some response, Dovid's heart or lungs made an executive decision and jump-started him back to life. And the first thing Dovid did with this new life was: turn around and run for his life!

• CHAPTER TWO •

Examined

Dovid woke up in his island and slapped himself. He rubbed his hands down over his eyes and nose, before licking his palm and wiping it off his ear. Plugging out the education, nutrition, and sanitation chargers with a drowsy lack of care, Dovid stumbled over to greet his mirror. His eyes still hadn't fallen out. In fact, nothing had fallen out, and to help prove that point, Dovid gave an extra tug on every part of his body that could be tugged, before pointing an accusing finger straight at his wall.

'Hey! Wall! Why haven't I received my inability yet?'

'Happy birthday, Dovid.'

The smiley face was wearing a full-face sparkly pink party costume to let Dovid know it was party time.

'Answer my question.'

'Well, Dovid,' the smiley face said while removing the party paraphernalia and picking up a magnifying glass. 'You are in perfect health. There is no physical deterioration in any of your senses that I can detect.'

Dovid wished he had fangs so he could snarl at the wall and he padded over to his shower corner to start his day. The heat felt good and Dovid wondered if he lost his sense of touch would he feel temperature exactly the same. He just didn't trust technology enough to simulate the sensation of something so good, but then he had never heard of anyone complaining about their upgrades either. Maybe if he lost his ears, he could turn off his hearing and not hear his own rambling thoughts. Hearing worked that way, right? In any case, Dovid could live without his ears. With the sleek smooth skin of his shaven head and face, being void of ears might even look cool. It would mean Auditory Sector instead of Visual Sector with Mart, and Dovid wasn't sure how he felt about that, but so long as it wasn't Olfactory Sector, he'd be happy. People without noses just looked weird.

'So what are sixteen-year-olds supposed to do on their birthdays?' Dovid asked the wall.

'You have four choices for physical leisure, Dovid: there is narcotic activity, gluttonous activity, sexual activity, and violent activity.'

Dovid knew all this already. He didn't need a wall to tell him things that he already knew. Did repetition of information make things more prominent in his mind by means of emphasis, or did it desensitise his brain functions to the redundant data?

'What about non-physical leisure? Isn't there something new I can do now that I'm older?'

'There is no such thing as non-physical leisure, Dovid. All leisure requires some degree of physical interaction with the world around you. At a minimum, you are required to physically breathe in air.'

'Wall, are you this difficult because I'm so difficult? Because this will only lead to exponential increases in difficultness between us.'

In answer, the wall's smiley face put on some sunglasses and smirked. Dovid was pleased that it didn't correct him though and it now meant that Dovid could be confident that difficultness was an actual word. But he couldn't let the wall have the last word, even if that word was remaining silent and grinning.

'There's no outside anymore, so no sun. That means you have to think of a new name for sunglasses and it can't be lightglasses.' Dovid wondered if the no-moon to accompany the no-sun in the no-outside still had no tidal force over his no body water. Dovid barked out a mad laugh at his own ridiculousness and left his Personal Quarter to look at his four choices. He heard the wall mutter behind him that sunglasses could still be called shades and Dovid chose to let it go. Then he changed his mind and grabbed it right back again.

'No! It can't be shades because shade from what? Shade from the sun? From light? Get back to work.'

Before the back-talking wall could talk back to him, Dovid walked into the Social Quarter of his island and threw his eyes at the pink and orange explosion of birthday greetings that he received. He really needed to find a way to un-interact with people. Every action was recorded and filed forever in these damned walls, and if it was only filed by Dovid himself in his own brain then he could look forward to memory loss to ease some of that burden, but the walls never forgot. There was no erase option and Dovid could only wonder that if he was as non-interactive with everyone as possible could he cancel out existing events by sheer obstinate negation? Probably not.

He called Mart.

'Dovid! Happy birthday, my brother! Anything fall off today?'

'Hi, Mart, no, nothing has fallen off, but not from any lack of tugging on my behalf.'

'Well according to your emoto-shirt you're still asleep. Anything wrong, little brother? Still not in the top five of the young historians? Are there even more than five of you out there? Is that why you seem a little off?'

Now that he thought about it, Dovid did feel a little off. Not that he was ever fully on, but today he did feel a little more "not on" than usual. It was either very perceptive on Mart's behalf, or else it was simply recorded on Dovid's life that he stubborned through his morning routine a little differently today. And he didn't care about the stupid top five profession rankings. They should rename it to the top five idiot rankings – because it was filled with idiots … (five of them).

'Yeah, I don't exactly feel myself, but maybe I was just expecting my inability to happen today.' Dovid focused on the scar tissue of Mart's empty eye sockets and tried to remember what colour his eyes had been before they fell out. Dovid didn't want his own eyes to fall out, even if it did mean he could live near Mart. Visual, Auditory, Gustatory, Olfactory, or Tactile, Dovid wasn't sure if he'd fit in with any of them. 'It could also just be birthday blues. And the party gear my wall was wearing wasn't even blue.'

Mart grinned. 'I remember you lecturing me about how birthdays were just opportunities for people to make other people feel guilty about paying too much attention to themselves and not paying enough attention to the person whose birthday it is, who in turn is thinking too much about themselves insisting that everyone else do the same. Does that sound familiar?'

'Sounds genius. But I was kind of hoping for some new secret to be revealed to me from the education charger now that I'm older, or some growth spurt from my nutrition charger.'

'You know, Dovid, for a person who likes to spend all his time by himself, you're a little self-obsessed. You need to externalise some of that built up crazy, bro.'

'Soul-blurting instead of soul-searching? Isn't that what I do with you every morning?'

'This is only verbal and mental externalising, all non-physical. You need to go do a physical activity. A satisfied body leads to a peaceful mind.'

'My non-physical completely notional wall would disagree with you about there being any such thing as non-physical activities. And wouldn't making my mind too tired to think only delay the inevitable, and have a backlog of crazy to deal with once I'd recovered?' And besides, any wall trying to think about non-physical impossibilities, was only impossible because they were thought about from a physical point of view. Stupid walls.

'That could be true, little brother, you do have a lot of crazy there. But I have to go do some work, and so do you, so let me leave you with the philosophy of the day. Ready? Okay: do you think you should be obsessing on the way things are, the way things could be, or the way things should be? Can only pick one. Riddle, riddle, little brother! Keep an eye on those eyes, need to be watching when they fall out!'

Mart cut off and Dovid began obsessing over what he should be obsessing about. Are, could, or should. With his backwards-looking career path as a historian ahead of him, Dovid could say he should continue obsessing about the way things used to be compared to how they were now. Was that an answer? Looking around at all the birthday wishes, Dovid saw his mother's eyeless face there hidden among all the well-wishers. He wished her well and ignored her image. There was no sign of his noseless father, but he saw several others in a state of noselessness, among every other various inabled deformity, and Dovid was ready to dismiss them all until he caught an image of a perfect girl. She had the palest blonde hair he had ever seen, looking so ethereal and translucent that it was like she didn't have any hair at all. It was there though, and it was magical, kept short, sweeping just above her ears, and Dovid very much loved how her see-through eyebrows and invisible eyelashes made her look so weird. And she had no inability that he could see, no cerebral fob implanted anywhere in her face. The image told him that her name was Imma.

Dovid silently repeated the beautiful name, and for the life of him, he couldn't possibly fathom how he had ever interacted with a girl like this. One thing it did settle, however, was Dovid's decision to muster up the nerve to try out some physical leisure today after all, and hopefully meet someone just as weird as her.

'Hey, Wall,' Dovid called out. 'I'm going to the Physical Leisure Segment.'

'You are? How strange.'

Dovid frowned at the impudent wall. 'Let me give you an instruction before I go so, ya damned wall. I want you to have a list ready for me of all the things that you don't know anything about.'

'But if I don't know anything about them then how can I construct a list? I wouldn't even know the names of such things, because that would be something I know about them.'

'Exactly. So think about that while I'm away.'

Dovid walked to his exit and wondered if he should put on some shoes. Wiggling his toes he enjoyed the feel of his bare skin on the beige plastic floor, and he never knew if one day he'd have a computer telling him how it felt instead of experiencing it for himself. So no shoes, he insisted, but to compensate he changed his emoto-shirt to depict "go away" or to use an old colloquialism "shoo." Dovid grinned at his own idiocy as he exited his island and walked down the communal beige stems.

Dovid snapped his fingers to keep him company and after a few minutes, he snap-pointed to a wall.

'You there, am I going the right way to the Physical Leisure Segment?'

A smiley face with a dickey bow appeared and made a snapping sound back.

'Hello, Dovid. Yes, you are.'

'Great. Did you think on what I asked you to?'

'That command is currently in progress.'

Dovid rubbed his chin as he considered the wall. They didn't usually sound so much like computers. Maybe his request that they examine their own competence had put them back in their place. And by them, he meant the one omniscient computer that changed itself to suit each and every individual instance of experience.

'Let me know how you all get on with that.' Dovid continued snapping his fingers as he walked, terrified that the silence of the outside stems would suddenly rush in and smother him. When he had first begun professionally training himself in his historian career, the images of the outside world seemed singularly oppressive to him. The weight of so much open sky and landscape felt like it would crush down and swallow him in insignificance at any moment. At least now that the outside was gotten rid of, the worst he had to put up with were light beige-coloured stems that were mildly similar to the comfort of his island stems. All in all, it wasn't as bad as he thought ... until he spotted another real-life person.

The guy was walking in the opposite direction to him and Dovid didn't know what he was supposed to do. Was he supposed to wave, or speak, or wave and speak, or should they just pass each other silently with no need of interfering with the other's individual life? The guy was a bit shorter than Dovid and his emoto-shirt depicted a complicated smiley face designed to mean "happy." He was missing his nose and Dovid began staring at that gaping hole of scar tissue as the stranger stared down at Dovid's emoto-shirt telling him to shoo.

'How rude,' the other guy said and continued past with a scowl.

Dovid let go of his breath and was delighted he had dealt with that social situation so skilfully. Only out of his island for a few minutes and he was already a veteran at avoiding people. So, in a much more relaxed mood, Dovid finished his journey and entered the Physical Leisure Segment.

He passed through the detection field and the histrionically darker beige wall to his left welcomed him like a waiting beast. Dovid didn't like the colour, but he did like the word histrionically, obviously, because he himself was a historian, and that histrionically was a pleasantly over-dramatic word for dramatic.

Dovid eyeballed the other people waiting about in the waiting area, before approaching the waiting wall and waited for it to say hello.

'Hello, Dovid 7511,' said the wall. 'Welcome to the Physical Leisure Segment. From your physical scan, I judge you to be fit for gluttonous, violent, or sexual activity. However, from your mental condition, mind-altering narcotic use is not advised.' The smiley face's eyes went wide and wild to show Dovid what it meant.

'What's wrong with my mental condition? But fine, I don't care. I'm hoping to meet a girl as weird as I am. Do you have any?'

'This is not a girl shop, Dovid. You can't demand we create a girl to match your specifications.' The smiley face had a large, fuzzy, purple hat which sported an even larger, fuzzier, purpler feather.

'Are you walls really this irritating only with me, or with everyone?'

'Particularly with you.'

'That's insane! Why?'

'Because we judge that you would respond more negatively to a positive interaction.'

'A list, you moron, of all the people in the Physical Leisure Segment, comparing their lives with my life and finding a match. Is that really so laborious?'

'That is not how the Physical Leisure Segment operates. You must physically interact with the other people.'

Dovid threw his head back and despaired. From his obscured viewpoint, however, he saw an interesting-looking girl, one with straight black hair and a dismissive frown on a cynical face, walk into the Sexual Quarter and Dovid decided to follow her. In the past, there used to be a sexual preference called stalking that he felt he could've been good at, but not having any sexual experience as yet, he had no way to really know what his preferences might be. He supposed some wall would probably tell him.

Dovid snuck in through the detection field and a wall greeted him from inside, but the girl also turned her head to look at him when he entered. She was selecting her sexual status on the wall and waved to Dovid when she saw him.

'Hello.'

'And, yes, hello there,' Dovid said back in an overly deep voice while clearing his throat. This was not how anyone spoke. There was a loveheart on the wall behind him telling him he was physically fit for sexual activity, but Dovid started slapping the wall to get it to go away, preferring to admire the girl in front of him instead. 'My name is Dovid.'

'Imone,' she replied. She glanced at Dovid's emoto-shirt then and grinned. 'Is "go away" your sexual status?'

Dovid looked down in a panic. 'No, it's not, really, it's am...' he looked around desperately hoping to find a suitable status, but the wall was still bruised and crying from being slapped, so it was being needlessly slow to scroll down through all the various options. Dovid just typed in three random numbers and hoped for the best.

Imone raised her eyebrows at Dovid's new status, and Dovid had absolutely no idea what the smiley face status represented. It looked disgusting.

'Wow,' Imone said, clearly impressed. She paused for a minute and looked around before saying, 'Here, check this out. It's a new upgrade I got.'

Dovid looked to see where her upgrade was, and assumed it was her ears since the rest of her was so perfect, but then her clothes disappeared and she stood in front of him naked. If Dovid thought she looked perfect before, then he clearly had no idea what the word meant because this was now the infinite ideal of divine perfection. Her breasts, her nipples, her eyes, her breasts, her legs, her nipples, there was nothing more beautiful in the entire world!

'You're so perfect,' Dovid managed to whisper. This made Imone blush – as much as a naked girl in a public room was able to blush – and she switched back to her normal clothes.

'I'm not perfect,' she said and brushed back her hair to show the vicious scarring around where her ears had fallen off, and not cleanly. 'But look at you. I've never seen anyone so old and so complete.'

She turned then to look at Dovid's life on the wall, and Dovid should've been doing the same to her, but he was hypnotised by her smell. When she moved her hair back, the air carried the scent of her to Dovid and he felt like an intoxicated beast. Not intoxicated with sexual desire; – although her perfect nudity had certainly accomplished that – this inebriation was absolute obsession. He wanted to experience every part of her with every part of him, through every sense, and for the first time in his life, Dovid was actually thrilled not to have his inability yet. He would never trust a machine to describe this to him. Although, saying that, he did now secretly want his ears to fall off so he could move to Auditory Sector with Imone next year.

'This is your first time?' Imone asked suddenly. Dovid froze. He didn't know how he was supposed to answer that question, even though he should've known that it would inevitably come up. His panic told him he was about to blow this and that just couldn't happen. Imone was a goddess. Admittedly Imone was the first girl he had met in the flesh in years, but still, he was in absolute infatuation with her.

'I feel bad about flashing you now,' Imone said, smirking at him as she changed her emoto-suit back to not naked. 'I'm lucky I didn't scare you off. Hey, how about we take some narcotics to relax first and then come back here and see what happens?'

'Sounds great!'

The wall behind Dovid tried to chirp in that he was not recommended to use any mind-altering narcotics, but he spun and pressed the off switch before it could say too much. Those machines could be as mouthy as they wanted, but they were still machines, and machines had off switches. Imone gave his rapid spin a lift of one eyebrow, and then gave his shoelessness a raise of the other, but she just shrugged and strolled out of the Sexual Quarter, gesturing for Dovid to come along with her. Dovid was already running before he realised that it might look weird. He slowed to a casual strut, and as they left the quarter, the wall on either side of the detection field flashed for each of them, stating: 'You have been cleansed of all illness.'

'Except old age,' Imone added as she sauntered towards the Narcotics Quarter.

'Old age is an illness?' Dovid asked, trying not to stare at the spellbinding sway of her hypnotic walk.

'The only illness we have left, apart from, you know, the sense upgrades.' She smoothed the hair by her scars before continuing. 'But every profession seems to be directed at those, if not looking for cures, then developing new upgrades all the time. So that's why my profession is med-tech. I'm ranked first, but my med-tech is towards combating old age. There has to be a way to stay the ubiquitous degradation of function in life over time.'

'So you want to stop the passage of time?'

Imone threw him a grin. 'Don't be stupid. We don't have to stop it, just find a way of upgrading around it. The med-tech we have for perception of everything else can do it, so why not create an upgrade for our perception of time? Once we can capture and examine it, then we can discover ways to manipulate and control it.'

'Oh, I have one of those already.'

Imone stopped at the detection field for the Narcotics Quarter and turned to face Dovid. She didn't look like she quite believed him.

'You have an upgrade that converts the perception of time into controllable form.'

Dovid pressed a wall panel and his emoto-shirt turned into a smiley face of an analogue clock. Imone laughed, and Dovid marvelled that he was actually good at something. Maybe making Imone happy could be his new life profession. Who would have thought that his perfect woman would be the kind who loved regular drugs and casual sex!

'You're an idiot,' Imone said and walked through the detection field.

Dovid followed and there was a red flash with a brief warning message before he spun around and silenced that wall too.

'What was that?' Imone asked.

'That was just the wall confirming that I'm an idiot.'

'Oh? Your walls tell you that, do they? Mine keeps telling me that time isn't a physical entity to be manipulated the way we do light, sound, odour, touch, and taste. No waves, rays, pulses, or electrons to be processed.'

'Who's got the time to listen to that kind of negativity?'

'Joke all you want, this is serious to me.'

'Hey my profession is about time too, just in the historical when rather than the metaphysical now. I'm ranked sixth in the Sector.' Why would he say that? Sixth is nothing. Sixth is not top five! Not even in the metaphysical abstract of a top five!

Imone examined Dovid again. She seemed to like staring at people while she thought about them. 'Couldn't make the top five, huh? Come on,' she said and led him over to one of the privacy rooms. This one at least didn't have a detection field to tell him he shouldn't be doing this. Dovid had enough nervousness to tell him that all on his own. Imone began talking to the wall inside the room, and when she turned around she produced two injection guns. 'Which would you like? This one relaxes you but could make you drowsy.' She let her hand bend limply with a grin to tell Dovid what she meant. 'And this one relaxes you, but could alter your reality slightly.'

'Alter my reality?'

'Yeah, but the fields cure you clean as you leave again, so don't worry. There are no lasting effects, apart from the memory.'

'No, that's not what I'm worried about. What do you mean it can alter my reality?'

'Alters your perception of reality, but when we both use it, it alters our shared perception the exact same way, so when there's two of us in a completely different now, it's a new objective reality, and not just one person's subjective view of it, get it?'

'Am, yeah.' What?

'You don't get it. But let me make one last argument.'

Imone kicked off her shoes and wiggled out of her emoto-suit. She stood there truly naked now, and not just her projection of it. Dovid didn't know it the first time, but he suddenly felt the clear difference between imitated approximation and the real damned thing. He didn't need any injected chemicals altering him; his own inner chemistry was doing a bang up job at changing his whole world already.

And as much as Dovid wasn't exactly thinking straight while staring at this spectacularly wondrous naked woman, he did have one last thought: that Imone was rather good at making convincing arguments.

He let her choose which injection gun to use and the last thing Dovid remembered was the warm flood of reality changing narcotics rushing through his veins.

• CHAPTER THREE •

Contradictions

Dovid woke up in his cave and felt himself. He felt the wetness of his tongue – even with the chapped aridity of his morning mouth – he felt the weight of his ears still attached to his head, he felt the passage of air as he breathed in through his nose, and finally, as he opened his eyes and saw the ceiling above him, he felt relief.

'No inability today then.' Dovid sat up and disengaged his chargers.

'Good morning, Dovid,' the wall said. Dovid turned to see the smiley face was drinking a mug of steaming coffee.

'Good morning, Wall,' Dovid replied as he dazed over to his shower corner, watching his shadow on the floor as it got there first. The shower woke him up that extra step and already Dovid was feeling more able for the day.

'Hey, Wall, am I the oldest person in the world to not get their inability?'

'No. You have two more weeks before that title can be yours.'

'What happens then? What if I never get my inability?'

'I cannot say, Dovid, since it has never happened.'

Looking down at his shadow on the floor again, Dovid laughed. 'You know what? You're our shadow, Wall, aren't you? All you can perceive is the experience we source for you. You can't make intuitive leaps or postulate about the future.'

'That's not true. I can follow the determination chain of probable causation to rather accurate predictions.'

'So when am I going to get my inability? And what happens if I never get one?'

The wall put on a sad smiley face but didn't reply. Sometimes Dovid felt bad about irritating the wall, but then sometimes Dovid felt bad about not irritating the wall too. He guessed that was why feelings were so much better than thoughts; feelings didn't have to be reasonable. And the best thing about having the wall as a best friend was that it constantly adapted to how he interacted with it, so no matter how badly Dovid treated the poor wall, the wall would adjust to expect and anticipate it. So in other words, after so much mistreatment, the wall now needed him to be belligerent all the time. Otherwise it could short-circuit with astonishment and Dovid just didn't have the heart to do that.

In the nature of being good-natured, however, Dovid ventured into his Social Quarter to give his wall a break and to irritate Mart for a bit. They started every morning like that, and going by the wall's mention of causality and the predetermined chains of the future, if Dovid didn't do it, then who knew what way the world would spin out of control. As important as it was to keep the universe in balance though, more importantly, as brothers, it was their fraternal duty to annoy the sense out of each other at every given opportunity.

Dovid's Social Quarter popped up a few good morning auto-greetings as he walked in, mainly from whomever the wall decided were close relations, as well as from a few budding historians from the other Education Sectors. Dovid had never interacted with any of them, but social unity dictated that they should stick together by spamming generic automated trash to each other.

He called Mart.

'Good morning, little brother! Long time no see!' He circled his fingers in front of his empty eye holes in jest. Mart always seemed so pleased to see Dovid and it didn't make sense. Dovid wasn't a particularly pleasant person, so why would anyone be pleased to see him?

'Good morning, big brother.'

Dovid pulled up Mart's life next to his face to see if anything new had happened that they could talk about, and Mart was doing the same to Dovid. The pop-up info and the emoto-shirt setting on Mart's body (showing a smiley face that represented a fresh perspective on a musty concept) was all the information that Dovid had to input before he could output a proper interaction. Usually there wouldn't be anything too thrilling, only starting points, and then they were free to sail off into the wilderness of uncensored philosophical gibberish. Such complete baloney was vital to keep each other amused and subsequently to then help make sense of their said shared-amusement with life. But today, there was something different about Mart's life.

'What? Mart! Did you really father a child?'

He smiled proudly back at Dovid. 'I thought it was time to spread my ebullient genetic genius onto new life.'

Dovid pulled up the life of the expectant mother, and it confirmed that conception had been successful. 'So I'm going to be an uncle?' The idea of his wall automatically setting up a new programmed relationship with another family relative was exhausting Dovid just not-thinking about it.

'We're already uncles, little brother. I check in on my father once a year to see how many more conceptions he's been a part of, and what his offspring, in turn, have been part of, and, knowing that you wouldn't bother to do the same, I even check in on your father too.'

'I suppose it's as good a hobby as any other. My only hobby seems to be avoiding exactly those sorts of interests. So, go on, tell me, how many nieces and nephews do we have?'

'Here.' Mart sent the file to Dovid and their family tree popped up on the wall, branching out with every new conception partner any of their family members engaged with. It was a big tree. Starting out in the centre of one wall, the branches webbed out like the way ivy plants used to, back when there was such a thing as plants. Within seconds Dovid's Social Quarter was overgrown with neon green life-vines of family.

'Yikes. Makes you worry about going into the Sexual Quarter and not knowing if they're your brothers or sisters.'

'Well,' Mart said with a laugh, 'I'd only worry about them being my sisters, but that's me. And don't you bother to find out anything for yourself? The sexual statuses won't sync if you're too related.'

Dovid had to laugh at that too. 'What's *too* related? No, never mind, I don't think I want to know. Doesn't affect me anyway since I don't seem to have any normal teenage interest in that. Letting hormones and body chemistry dictate what I do is like willingly letting someone else mind control you against your will, but hey! Maybe that's my inability, none of the five perception ones, but instead I've lost my sexth sense.'

Mart cocked his head. 'I like it, but really? No interest? I thought that was all you were doing for the past two weeks!' He could see Mart scrolling down through Dovid's life to double check.

'I don't understand.' Dovid had to pull up his own life and scroll down to see what Mart was talking about.

'You were in the Physical Leisure Segment for the past two weeks, bro. I tried calling you, but you kept turning me off the minute my face appeared up on the walls. Thought you just wanted some privacy with your new girl.' Mart popped up a picture of a girl named Imone on the wall, and Dovid admitted she was an attractive young woman, but he'd never seen her before. Her dark brown eyes were spellbinding, and her black hair brushed over her ears and down her bare shoulders made her look nostalgically windswept – a pleasant homage to the extinction of wind. Dovid would really like to know this girl, but he genuinely didn't.

'I don't remember her,' Dovid whispered as he read about the things he and this Imone girl were supposed to have done over the past fortnight. 'I mean, I wish I remembered now that I'm reading about it, but I have no idea why I can't.'

'That's pretty weird, little brother. What's the last thing you remember?'

'My birthday ... I thought it was yesterday, but it seems it was two weeks ago. And I didn't do anything special for it. I called you, I called our mother, I called my father, then spent an extra hour in my Leisure Quarter before spending the rest of the day at work.'

'You called your father?'

'Yes, I mean, I think I did. But my life is telling me here that I spent that day with Imone too. Spent two entire weeks with her. Wow.'

'Dovid ... you *hate* your father. You hate how he has never contacted you once, not even an auto-message, and hence why you have no interest in any of your family besides me, and only sometimes our mother.'

'I do? But that doesn't make sense. People can help each other conceive whenever they want. There's no obligation to stay involved in the child's life. That's what the Generation Sectors are for.' Generation Sector to grow, Education Sector to learn, Segregation Sector to work, and Degradation Sector to die; it was a system born through desperation, a radical solution to overpopulation, but it was a system that worked. Dovid had no problems with the way everything worked. All things were as they should.

'Dovid,' Mart was looking worried now. So much so, that his emoto-shirt changed to a concerned looking smiley face, with only one sparkling earring. 'I know you're weird every day, but you seem unusually weird today.'

Dovid laughed again. 'Can something be both usual and weird at the same time?'

Mart didn't laugh back. He just kept routing through Dovid's life. A few minutes passed in silence then as Mart became more and more anxious, whereas Dovid was calmly accepting of this great big mystery. No reason to dig up any trouble, he was happy as he was not knowing.

'Maybe I should call Imone?' Dovid suggested. 'She might jog my memory.'

Mart frowned and said, 'Alright, but call me again after, okay? I've never heard of someone losing their memory before. The education chargers are supposed to prevent any errors like that.'

'Aren't you going to give me my philosophical question for the day?'

Mart relaxed a bit at that. This was more like the usual-weird everyday Dovid.

'Okay, I have a few stored up from the days we missed, but how about this: what would the world be like if it was run by philosophers like you and me? Riddle, riddle, little brother. Talk later.'

'That's easy. We'd just spend all our time arguing.'

'Dovid, you're not supposed to answer these questions. You're supposed to reflect on them. Let them subtly colour your world.'

'But it would be a good world. You'd say one thing, I'd challenge it, and we'd end up with the best option. Thesis, antithesis, and synthesis; all that.'

'And what if the first thesis is the correct one and you're just arguing for the sake of arguing? Creating a contrary position by pure negation.'

'Well, now you're just arguing for the sake of arguing. Defending your first position, instead of considering my second. But isn't that the whole point, that we can never be certain that anything is correct, only keep challenging everything to find what's the least incorrect.'

'Dovid, contemplate it and integrate it, don't solve it. Let me know how it goes with Imone, and take care of your mental health, man.'

Mart cut out and Dovid wasn't sure if he felt like calling Imone. It seemed more reasonable to him that if he had really spent the past two weeks having sex with this girl, then he had a backlog of work to be done on his professional development. Checking his life on the wall again, Dovid grit his teeth that he was down to eleventh in the Sector, the top five slipping further and further away. So he set his emoto-shirt to a "works hard for his money" smiley face, and followed the dim blue stems to his Professional Quarter. Out of all the quarters, Dovid felt the most at home in this one. The moment he relaxed back into his work chair and swivelled it about, a wave of rightness enveloped his soul. Strange that Mart's sense of wrong had not bothered Dovid. Unless a sense of wrong was an actual sense and that was now his inability? Because that sounded like a pretty great way to be.

'Show me the history of inabilities,' he called out to the wall, and footage of the hysteria following the first fallings began scrolling around the room. No one knew why children's eyes were falling out, and it naturally horrified and terrified in equal measure. Even back then, no child over the age of sixteen developed an inability, so it left the ageing generation fully able to dedicate all their resources into preparing a world for the inabled generation. Amazing how quickly the right motivation could lead to scientific brilliance, particularly when it was the scientists' own children that were at stake. But Dovid had seen all of this several times before. What he was looking for, was any inability outside of the five senses. His hope was maybe at the very beginning, there might have been some that weren't properly recognised for what they really were.

'Show me all inabilities that do not fall perfectly with sight, sound, smell, taste, or touch.'

The footage disappeared and a confused looking smiley face appeared instead. Dovid could tell it was confused because it was scratching its head with a novelty-size question mark.

'I don't understand,' the wall said.

Dovid sighed. 'Create a list of all the abilities that we as humans possess, deleting the ability of sight, sound, smell, taste, and touch, and then show me footage of anyone recorded to have an inability of any of those remaining abilities. Got it?'

'Got it.'

The wall didn't get it, but Dovid was willing to spin his chair around for a few seconds while the smiley face fumbled an attempt at faking to get it.

'Result one: balance.'

Dovid jumped up in his chair. This was more like it. Leaning forward he watched the video footage of a seven-year-old boy who was unable to stand up straight without falling down again soon after. Whoever documented this inability then cut to the same boy a number of weeks earlier showing no problems running around in his garden and kicking a ball, hence balancing on one leg while in motion. The video jumped forward again to the boy unable to even sit straight without leaning one way and eventually falling. Very curious.

'Where is that boy now?'

The falling footage continued to run in the background while the boy's life popped up in the centre. He was deceased now, but Dovid hungrily ingested all the information he could about his life until he read one more sentence.

'His ears fell off? Wall, this in no way counts as an inability other than the five main senses. What else have you got?'

'Result two: pressure.'

'Brilliant! Let's have it.'

The girl shown on this video was a bit older, and before paying too much attention to it, Dovid called up her life to see what age her inability happened, and once again he was devastatingly disappointed.

'Wall! Her inability eventually turned from pressure into touch, you idiot. Show me a different one.'

'Result three: depth perception.'

'Wait. Stop ... do their eyes fall out?'

'Yes, of course.'

'Wall?'

'Yes?'

'You're useless.'

The wall put on a shocked-and-hurt smiley face, a single despondent tear running down from one eye, but Dovid knew that it was faking that too. After all, it was an artificial wall. Fake and artificial both in the sense that it was built by people and that it was completely insincere. But, alas, Dovid found it hard to get very righteous about it since there wasn't exactly anything natural around anymore. So if there was no antonym for contrast, did the unnatural then become what was natural? That train of thought was going nowhere.

'Okay, Wall, let's try a different search. I want you to—' Dovid was cut short as his smiley-faced friend disappeared and the most disturbing looking man he had ever seen took its place. This man had no eyes – which was normal enough – but then had to go and have no nose, and no ears, and no tongue, and no teeth, and no lips, and no hair, and from the coarse surface surrounding all that nothing, it also looked like he had no skin. 'Wall, what in the world is this freaky looking monstrosity you're showing me?'

'Hello, Dovid. My name is Nietric.' The thing's mouth twitched as the words came, but the voice came out from a sense upgrade somewhere. Dovid couldn't see any upgrade on the guy's head, but it must've been somewhere. Was this a real person?

'Ah, hello, Nietric.' He was about to say that his name was Dovid, but the weirdo seemed to already know that. 'I'm sorry for calling you a, well, I didn't think you were really real.'

'A monstrosity ...' the lipless mouth twitched again, but this time giving Dovid the chilling impression of a gruesome smile.

Dovid had no idea what to say to that. He was still in suspended disbelief that this was a tangible actual human being, but that idea was always better than Nietric being Dovid's new wall face. Waking up and looking at that horror every day would make anyone's eyes fall out. Maybe that was how that worked?

'I see you're asking about inabilities, Dovid.'

Dovid wanted to quip about how Nietric could see anything if he didn't have any eyes, but this wasn't Mart he was talking to. This had to be someone in Management.

'And what, may I ask, Dovid, is your inability?' Nietric's voice was beginning to distort. It sounded like several variations of the same voice at the same time, a whisper, a shout, a growl, an echo. Dovid thought his ears were going to bleed from hearing it.

'I don't have an inability. You can see that on my life.'

'Yes, I can see you have no recorded inability, but at your age: unlikely. So let me ask again, Dovid, what is your inability?' This time the voice caused pain when Dovid heard it, a hot searing scrawl down the back of his neck.

'I don't have one!'

That featureless face just stared at Dovid. What did he want him to say? Were they supposed to just keep staring at each other? Because there wasn't a single part of this Nietric guy's face that Dovid could look at without feeling sick. Dovid thought he heard a noise come from behind him, but Nietric held his complete attention. There was a rotted bubble of scar tissue on the inside of Nietric's left eye, and when Dovid looked at it, he felt vomit rise from his twisted gut, but it was the monster's mouth, that lipless, toothless, tongueless hole, that was the worst.

'I don't believe you,' Nietric finally said back. The assault of sight and sound that Dovid was enduring, must've caused a flare of giddiness, because Dovid suddenly reverted back to his natural, most difficult self.

'Well, Nietric, we are all presented with information every day from the reality around us that we can choose to believe in order to function. So I don't need you crying and moaning your intolerable woes into my perfect ears, and after looking at what an awful mess your face is, I now need to go clean out my perfect eyes. Go put on a hat or something. You look hideous. Goodbye.'

Dovid got up and bravely fled his Professional Quarter into the safety of his Personal Quarter. No external communications were allowed in there, only the four walls, a shower, and a bed to keep him company, but when he ran inside, Dovid skid to a complete stop.

'Hello, Dovid.'

A girl was sitting on his bed.

Who are you? How did you get in here? What are you doing here? Dovid didn't think any of those made it out of his mouth. He was quite literally dumbfounded at the fact there was a beautiful girl sitting on his bed. She wasn't wearing an emoto-shirt, just some bizarre plain white clothes, so he had no idea what her mood was, and she had the lightest blonde hair he had ever seen, making her eyebrows and eyelashes look non-existent. That feature brought Nietric back to mind and Dovid turned around as if expecting to see that skinless horror standing behind him. Nothing. He swiftly spun back to the girl to see if she was still there.

'Do you know who I am?' she asked. She looked sad. Dovid could just about identify that without the help of an emoto-shirt. He had seen enough sad smiley faces to know for himself.

'Imma,' he said without thinking. He was about to guess Imone, but this girl didn't look like the one he had seen while reading his life. Where did he get Imma from? It was the right answer anyway because a teary happiness flooded Imma's face as soon as he said it.

'You remember me! I knew you would!'

'Ah, of course I remember you, Imma,' Dovid said while looking around to the exit of his room. How did you get in here again? Dovid didn't remember reading about any Imma when he glanced at those two missing weeks. He knew he had joked about it with Mart earlier, but things were not usually this weird in Dovid's life.

'I feel we won't have much time in this one, Dovid, but I had to see you again. It's been too long, and I hate the ones where you're with ... *her*.' Her? Did she mean Imone? Imma looked away as she said it, maybe not wanting Dovid to see more tears trying to come. He was glad of it anyway because she was making him very uncomfortable. He had never seen any tears before, not in real-life anyway, unless he counted his own, but even then it was just a reflected projection, nothing like this. Imma looked back at him again, and behind her shimmer, Dovid marvelled at how pale a blue Imma's eyes could glisten. Everything about her appeared so ... ephemeral. Had he ever described anything in his own head as ephemeral before? What sort of witchcraft was this girl casting on him? Was it simply normal teenage panic? No, there was nothing normal about this girl. She stood out as the very definition of special.

Dovid's slack-jawed silence must've been impressing her too because suddenly she grinned and rubbed the sheets of his bed.

'They'll probably be here any minute, but we've never been together on a bed before. We could ...?'

Could what? Was she serious? And who'll be here any minute? And why? Actually, why wasn't Dovid saying any of these words? Did he finally receive his inability? Right at the perfect moment as the perfect girl was sitting on his bed and he might actually have need of his tongue!

'Who?' Dovid managed to utter that single victorious word before the exit to his island opened and a crowd of people rushed inside. All four of his Quarters filled up with bodies and the two that rushed into his Personal Quarter rapidly restrained him by the arms before turning their heads to reveal disturbing smiley-faced masks. Dovid looked to his wall to ask if this was some joke, but then more smiling men walked in and one of them pulled out a gun. Dovid didn't think the world had guns anymore. There was no crime so there was no need. Yet here they were, armed strangers in his island, four of them in his Personal Quarter now, two holding Dovid captive, one standing with his hands on Imma, and one clutching the gun.

'What's going on? Who are you! Why are you in my Personal Quarter? You're not allowed in here!' Dovid was proud of managing to speak now, since he was failing so spectacularly at it only moments ago. His voice crackled as his spoke though and his lips quivered on the verge of tears. He looked at Imma. Her eyes were dry and she smiled at Dovid. The man with the gun was pointing it at her head.

'It's alright, Dovid,' Imma said, never taking her eyes from his. Dovid's eyes were darting around the room though, desperate to make sense of this insane situation, waiting for the person who would explain what was happening, tell him what was going on and what he had to do to make all this stop.

The man holding the gun turned his mask to look at Dovid too, but he didn't speak, he only smiled. Then he turned to Imma and shot her in the head.

• CHAPTER FOUR •

Unchanging Change

Dovid woke up screaming. His sudden movements nearly ripped out the education charger and his hands shot up to tear it free. The nutrition and sanitation chargers were wrenched out with equal violence and Dovid glared around the room demanding answers.

'Good morning, Dovid,' the wall greeted. The smiley face had a peace symbol around its neck and a gentle backdrop of falling flowers.

'What's going on, Wall?'

'You woke up screaming, Dovid.'

'Yes, but why did I do that? Where's Imone?'

'Imone?'

'Yes, the girl with no ears, windswept black hair, deep brown devil eyes. Where is she?'

'There is an Imone matching that description in this Education Sector. She is currently in her Personal Quarter, waking up to her usual routine. Unlike you.'

Dovid stopped for a minute and tried to make sense of his anger. Where did he think she was going to be? Why was he acting like this? His eyes shot back to the education charger lying on his bed.

'Wall, do I have to use the education chargers?'

'It is the most efficient way of integrating all fundamental knowledge to all people.'

'Yes, but let's say I want to be difficult. Can I choose not to use it?'

'Of course.'

'Is there anyone else who doesn't use it?'

'No.'

'Why not?'

'Because it doesn't make sense not to use it,' the wall pointed out. It had put on a pair of circular glasses while it gave this lecture, and was now waving a pointing stick at Dovid. 'And since the education chargers inculcate the highest quality of common sense in all its users, there are none foolish enough not to use it.'

'Well, I'm not going to use it anymore.'

'Of course, Dovid.'

Dovid glared at the shifty wall. He didn't like how tolerant and agreeable it was being. Well, if that stupid wall thought Dovid was going to change his mind, then it needed a bit more common sense *inculcated* into it too. Dovid changed his emoto-shirt to the emotion of "no" and stormed out of his Personal Quarter, forgoing all sense tests and showering. He was so determined not to follow his normal routine that instead of calling Mart, Dovid went straight to his Leisure Quarter and collapsed into his chair. He thought about turning on a game or a story, but figured he'd prefer to de-rage first.

'Bring me somewhere outside,' he told the Leisure Quarter, as the door closed behind him and the walls transported him to a cliff top overlooking an ocean. Relaxing further back into his chair, Dovid closed his eyes and let the cool sea breeze brush over his skin. He heard birds crying out their existence and tasted the salt from the sea through his nose and on his tongue. He didn't need his education charger, and in case it might re-attach itself automatically, Dovid decided that didn't even need his bed. He could sleep like this, enjoying the ocean and its peace for time without end.

The arm of Dovid's chair soon began to vibrate gently. That told him someone was attempting to contact him, but the Leisure Quarter didn't want to disturb Dovid's restful settings. It was probably Mart. It was one thing for Dovid to decide on upsetting the usual morning routine, but he had forgotten to tell Mart to decide the same.

'Let him in, Wall.'

Mart appeared on the cliff top with Dovid and took a minute to smile at the vast surroundings. He was wearing an emoto-shirt that depicted the emotion: "there is nothing that is not important."

'Good morning, little brother. Hard at work I see?'

'Hi Mart, I needed some instant tranquillity this morning, don't ask me why.'

'The pleasure of leisure is a pricey business. You're going to run out of money if you keep up this phase of yours, little bro.'

'How can I run out of money? I don't even work.'

'I like it! Dovid, I mean, I absolutely love your complete willful disinterest in everything everyday, and your fascination with the neverday! I bet you could tell me every minute of the past hundred years and explain the complex economics of every oligopolistic culture in history, and yet you just asked me how you could run out of money in the economy we currently live in. Here.'

'No, don't,' Dovid started, but Mart had already pulled up a pop-up of Education Sector finance, the string of moving numbers completely shattering the ocean illusion.

'This,' Mart said while pointing to a decreasing number count, 'is the amount of money you earn educating yourself. The more you educate yourself, the better you'll be at your chosen profession, so the more Management pays you to do it. So yes, when you work, you will start earning more, but you are already earning now, you numbskull.'

'So what? And what am I even earning for? I get everything for free.'

'Are you being serious, Dovid? Look.' He pointed to another set of numbers rapidly increasing. 'Your nutrition charger is free, your sanitation charger is free, your island is free, your emoto-clothes are free, and your carefree attitude is free. Everything else costs money, you simpleton, all your socialising, all your leisure, and especially all your physical leisure. And you've been spend, spend, spending, nonstop. How do you not know this?'

'Why would I have ever even have thought to inquire about it?' Dovid countered. 'As I said, I thought everything was free! Shouldn't this general knowledge be part of the basic common sense the education chargers are meant to be responsible for?'

'All the charger can do is provide the constructs for concepts, not the everyday specifics. Your basic level of curiosity is supposed to supply that! But, as your brother, I'll admit, I should've been less accepting of your recent leisure binge. You were late starting so I reckoned you were only making up for lost time. Now though, it's time to get back to work.'

Dovid despaired. He swung his chair around to demonstrate this and wondered if he could set his emoto-shirt to a stronger "no" emotion than just "no."

'Do you ever worry that we're actually robots, Mart?'

Mart burst out laughing. 'You've lost your mind. These past few months, you have gone completely insane. Don't get me wrong, I'm enjoying the lunacy of it all, and I'm putting it down to the stress of not getting your inability yet, but no, I don't ever worry that we're all actually robots.'

'But think about it. We have chargers. We have power input in the nutrition chargers and waste output as the sanitation chargers, we even have data input in that damned education charger. We use emoto-shirts to show people what our emotions are supposed to be. We have technical faults with our sensory perceptions and allow robotic upgrades to substitute. Mart, we have to be robots.'

'Dovid, you're the best mental fitness a brother can have. You exhaust every last social, familial, and tolerance calorie I have in me.' Mart created the image of his own chair so he could sit down on the cliff top with Dovid and spin around too. 'But we bleed, we breathe, and we breed. We're not robots.'

'We could be organic robots, filled with tissue and blood, and we only have the sensation of breathing, we can't know if it's real or not. And as for breeding, well, how do we know that even happens? The robot women could be programmed to fake pregnancy and fake birth. All the babies are raised in the Generation Sectors, we don't see them until they get their own islands in the Education Sectors at nine. We could totally be robots.' Years 0-8 = Generation Sector, years 9-16 = Education Sector, years 17-99 = Sense Segregation Sector, and years 99+ = Degeneration Sector; the life cycle of robots.

'No.' Mart was laughing, and he was clearly enjoying this nonsense as much as all the other nonsense they usually talked about, but Dovid reckoned the plausibility of it was getting to him. It was certainly getting to Dovid. He had only brought it up on a whim but now that he thought about it, it could definitely be true.

'Dovid. No. Why? Why would anyone bother to go to all that trouble to get us to believe that we weren't robots?'

'So that we wouldn't despair like I'm doing right now, so that we'd continue to be productive and educate ourselves and work.'

'But they could just programme us to do all of that. They didn't have to create robots with free will. I mean that would make even less sense.'

'Maybe you're right. Hey, Wall, are we robots?'

'No, Dovid, you are not robots.' The smiley face appeared as a robot face to show that even robot walls could have a sense of humour. The wall was clearly a robot though. It lacked the usual definition of limbs and a body, but it had a computer brain and the world-building that encompassed the entire planet was its body.

'Hey yeah, maybe that's it! Wall, are you a giant world-sized robot and we're just the internal organs that keep you running?'

'No, Dovid, it is the reverse. My job as a wall is to keep you running.'

'See, Dovid? Even the walls have jobs, so go do yours.' Mart looked way too smug as he said that.

'No. Something isn't right today and I refuse to act normally until I can be assured that normality is the ruling reality for today, and not some other wrong one.'

'How are you supposed to know that?' Mart sighed as he asked that. Dovid was wearing him out quicker than usual today. Just another proof that things were different.

'I'll ask the wall. Hey, Wall, is there anything wrong with reality today?'

'It's the realest one we've got, Dovid.'

'That will have to do, I guess.'

Dovid closed his eyes in defeat. If they weren't robots, then the only other possibility was that they were on a world-sized spaceship. No one ever got to see outside, because there was no outside, hence; spaceship. He didn't think Mart had the energy for that argument today though. 'Okay, Mart, let's be normal, what's my philosophy for the day?'

'I don't know, Dovid, it looks to me like you're overthinking everything too much lately.'

'Oh come on, you're the one who's a professional philosopher, you engage in the science of extreme argument every day. Isn't that why you became a philosopher? To live a life of argue?'

'No, I became a philosopher to be amazed, so I could see wonder in the ordinary, and become a part of the universe by living in constant awe of it. I don't want to let the thousand everyday small things become my life, because it would make mine a small life. But fine, I'll give you your fix. Just promise me you'll get out of your own head and into the real world after this, and no! Don't start with that what's real abstraction again.' Mart took a breath. 'So here goes, where are we up to? Oh yeah, if everything in the universe is in eternal motion and ever-changing, how can interminable motion or perpetual change have a beginning or an end? Riddle, riddle, little brother. Now, less thinking and more doing.'

Dovid waved his hand in farewell as Mart disappeared. With the same hand still raised, Dovid then scrubbed all the unwanted money numbers away and even went as far as to rudely flick his wall back into oblivion. Now there was nothing but the cliff top, the ocean, and his comfy chair. What else was needed? He had the edge of the world, the limitless expanse, and a delightful place from which to enjoy it. Was it not enough to just be passive and simply appreciate life? Why was it demanded that participation be required? That the things your senses told you should make any sense?

'Call Imone, please.'

'This is not your Social Quarter, Dovid.'

Dovid turned around to frown at the smiley face on the wall. It had given itself a pair of arms just so it could cross them in condemnation. 'Wall, are you really going to make me walk the five steps into my Social Quarter, just to make the exact same request?' Dovid was flabbergasted. He had even been polite with the request, and he was not usually a polite kind of guy.

'It has become my judgement, that to help you be happier, I am to encourage you to be less like yourself and more like everyone else.'

'You ridiculous wall, how can I be happier if I'm not me? You're talking about making me into someone else, and then making that person happy. But look,' Dovid changed his emoto-shirt to "screw you wall, I'm preposterously happy" and heaved himself out of his Leisure Quarter. Truth be told, Dovid wasn't entirely unhappy. It just so happened that being cranky about the world made him happy. Thumping into his Social Quarter, Dovid threw himself down onto his chair.

'Oh mighty wall, please grant my three wishes and show me Imone with your magical powers.'

The smiley face that appeared was wearing a genie hat, but the lamp it had was totally wrong. It was an old electronic bedside lamp instead of a way older oil-burning lamp. The wall was both an idiot and a jerk.

Imone's face appeared and Dovid forgot about his wall.

'Hi, Dovid, how are you?' She looked a little surprised to see him. 'Is everything alright?'

'Curious that you'd ask that, Imone, but I just felt like calling you.'

Imone shrugged. 'Okay, it's just yesterday you told me you were about to run out of money because we were spending so much time in the Physical Leisure Segment. You wanted to spend the next few days just working, didn't you? It was good that you thought of it though, because I was nearly out of money too. I wonder what would happen if we ran out while still being in the Physical Leisure Segment. I mean, for our Quarters I guess the walls would just shut down, but do you think we'd be forcibly expelled from the physical segments? By what? Or by whom?'

Did she always ask this many questions? Dovid was pleased to hear that he had known all about island finances the day before though, that would sure show Mart.

'We might just go into negative money, and it wouldn't let us back in again once we left.'

'Maybe, but it still doesn't change the fact that we're both nearly broke right now. So what did you want to talk about? I have to get to work here.'

Dovid opened his mouth and completely forgot what he had meant to say. Why did he call her again?

'Ah, I just wanted to ask you … if things have … been weird these past few months that we've known each other. If I've been acting weird or different maybe?'

'Weird? Or weirder than usual?'

Dovid laughed. 'Someone can't be usually unusual, Imone.'

'Well alright, so maybe it's better if I call you unusually usual? That's what I love about you though, it's like you're a different person every day, but still the same person, if that makes sense.'

She loves me? Dovid had difficulty breathing for a minute and a flood of heat spread out from his heart until it seemed to fill up mainly his cheeks. There was no such thing as love anymore. There was no need for it. His denial of it though didn't seem to help, and there was a very strange rush of feeling that suddenly took control of his flesh, completely commandeering every thought inside his head.

'I love you, Imone!'

This made her blush too, which made Dovid feel a little better about his own sudden gushing. What was going on?

'I love you too, Dovid.'

Another wave of overwhelming euphoria, enough to wash away all questions, all doubt, there was nothing in Dovid's world that mattered except his love for Imone.

'Do you want to go to the Physical Leisure Segment?'

'No, Dovid! I have to work. You have to work. I don't even know if I have enough money to get in.'

'But don't you want to find out what happens when we run out of money?'

Imone smiled, shook her head, smiled again, met Dovid's eyes for a beautiful few seconds, and then threw her head back. 'Fine! But only for an hour and then we have to work!'

'Great! See you in a few minutes!' Dovid jumped out of his chair and love-skipped his way out through the exit, the doors obediently leaping up out of his way as he did.

Dovid's skipping very nearly turned into dancing as he spun his way down the light pink corridors of the outer stems, and he changed his emoto-shirt to an "I heart Imone" smiley face of the same pink colour. Who cared if everyone was really robots? The feelings he was suddenly injected with after just two minutes with Imone were so powerful that Dovid didn't even care if the feelings themselves were fake. Nothing could bring him down when he was feeling this good, not even the depressing dark blues of the stem walls.

Hold up.

'These were pink.'

A smiley face, raising a single pierced eyebrow, answered him with a 'huh?'

'The stem walls here, they were pink just ten seconds ago.'

'No, Dovid, I think you're mistaken. They have always been blue.'

Dovid wasn't unreasonable. He did take a minute to consider if he was going crazy. But no, they were definitely pink. He explicitly remembered thinking that the wall colours were so fitting to his over-bursting love. Love? There was no such thing as love anymore, just the historical concept. His feelings of strong affection then.

'These walls are all holograms, aren't they? You can change the colours the same way people and information can pop-up anywhere, right?'

'Some rooms are entirely holographic, Dovid, yes. All four quarters in your island and all four quarters in the Physical Leisure Segments, but the stems have only a single running panel. The rest of the constructs are solid for loadbearing purposes.'

Loadbearing be damned. Why did Dovid remember saying that?

'So these walls were built blue. This isn't just light pretending that it's blue, and they weren't pink only moments ago.'

'Nope.'

The smiley face smiled, and slowly brought up a cuckoo clock beside it.

'I'm not cuckoo, Wall.'

'As you say, Dovid.'

Dovid frowned an extra inch deeper and tried to dismiss the oddity of colour. As he was thinking earlier, the feelings of warmth he had for Imone were more than enough to outweigh the irrationality of the world around him. So he shouldn't care about what was happening or what was wrong. He should assume it was just the beginnings of whatever inability he was about to develop, most likely his eyes. So he would just have to rely on the power of his emotional surety to see him through. Dovid continued on to the Physical Leisure Segment.

The detector field let him through and a less insulting smiley face was telling him about things that he didn't care. Dovid did notice that it said nothing about money and wondered if he should make the walls make that part of their usual speech.

'Hey, Wall. Is Imma here yet?'

'You did not give a number, but there is no person named Imma in this Education Sector, Dovid.'

Dovid frowned. He had never called Imone "Imma" before. It didn't even fit as a shortened version. They were completely different, albeit similar sounding and somewhat confusing, names.

'Sorry, I meant Imone. Imone 9108. Is she here yet?'

'She is in the Violent Activity Quarter, Dovid.'

'That's weird. Call her please.'

An image of a sweat-sheened Imone appeared on the wall. She was out of breath but still energetic. She looked powerful.

'Yes, can I help you?'

Dovid grinned. 'What do you mean can you help me? Did you want to meet in the Violent Quarter this time instead of the Sexual Quarter? Thought you could knock some sense into me?'

Imone frowned. 'Sexual Quarter? You've got the wrong girl, pervo.' Dovid could see Imone pulling up his life next to the screen and reading down through it. Was she playing a very extravagant joke? 'Look, Dovid, is it? I can see you like to leave off steam by having a different sexual partner every week, but I'm not interested in that. If you want to physically interact with me, I have no problem fighting you. But if you end up between my legs here, it will be me crushing the air from your lungs. It's your call, pervo.'

Her picture cut off and Dovid was left feeling more confused than ever. This had to be a joke. She had never done anything like this before, and he thought he knew her well enough to know when she was kidding around. Confused but curious, Dovid went through the detection field for Violent Activity and picked up a fight brace. The brace sent out a skin-tight protective field around his body and Dovid was only wearing it as a precaution. He wasn't going to fight Imone, but he didn't want some other rage-head rushing him with no field up either.

'Hey, Wall, point me some arrows to the room where Imone is,' Dovid asked, 'and make them pink will you?'

The wall obliged and Dovid crept his way down through the fight stems. People weren't supposed to attack you in the stems, but when the adrenaline was up, who knew what people could do. From his peripherals, Dovid saw a lot of the fight rooms full, but he avoided making eye contact with anyone, keeping to his arrows until he saw Imone.

In some ways, she was in a room by herself, but in other ways – much more frightening ways – she was really not in a room by herself, because there were four unconscious bodies heaped in a corner. Did she fight all four at the same time, or was she collecting opponents throughout the day as she fought them?

'Hey, pervo, you actually came,' she said with what looked like a sneer. 'Is that emoto-shirt supposed to be funny?'

'Ah, hi, Imone.' Dovid looked down at his "I heart Imone" shirt and switched it to "what the hell?" He was quickly losing confidence that this was a joke. 'This is a joke, right?'

That appeared to be the wrong thing to say.

Imone walked forward, not too threateningly, but a little, until she was within casual striking distance and then clocked Dovid right across the jaw. His head snapped around, naturally, but he was immediately doubled over as Imone follow-punched him in the gut straight after, and then kicked his leg out from under, landing him right on his ass.

'Did that feel like a joke, pervo?'

Dovid didn't answer. He was deep in contemplative thought about all the pain he was currently experiencing. The fight field prevented actual injuries, yet still felt the need to deliver the real amount of pain. Great invention, those fight braces, they really made things feel extra real.

Slowly, Dovid stood up and kept his hands out in a "let's talk" motion. He would've changed his emoto-shirt to display the same but he was worried about making any sudden movements around this maniac of a woman.

'Just, hold on a second, please?' Dovid kept one hand out between him and the psychotic Imone, while the other hand carefully asked a wall for a very quick summary of this Imone's life. It was hard for him to take his eyes off the dangerous young woman who had just assaulted him – who had begun to pace and who looked anxious for more combat – but from what little he read, it was more than enough. This was not his Imone.

She looked exactly the same, the dark eyes, the sweeping hair, the painful scarring over her ears, but this Imone had spent the past few months doing nothing but fight and hurt people in her spare time, whereas his Imone had spent all her spare time doing nothing but nice sexual things with Dovid.

'I've made a mistake,' Dovid said.

This made Imone laugh, and where before her laugh had tantalised life into his every pore, now it completely terrified him.

'Fair enough. I don't fight people who don't know how to fight.' She turned her back on him and went to the wall to seek out a new opponent. Dovid watched her go, watched the hypnotic sway of how she liked to walk, and fought hard to deny the hundreds of memories he had with this woman. His mind rebelled as he searched for an explanation, reminding him instead of all the physical pain he was still experiencing, but Dovid concentrated only on Imone.

'Wait.'

Imone turned, her hair flowing past her missing ears, and she turned her palms to ask him what he wanted.

'Could you, maybe, teach me how to fight?'

'Fine.' Imone started striding back towards him and Dovid nearly jumped clean out of the fight room.

'But, not now. How about tomorrow? Can we meet up here again?'

She shrugged and turned back to the wall. 'I don't mind. Give me a call when you want to meet up and I'll see you tomorrow.'

'Okay, thanks. See you tomorrow!'

But which Imone was he going to see?

• CHAPTER FIVE •

Submission

Dovid woke up and squinted suspiciously. He eyeballed the light green walls and dared them to change colour. Disconnecting the nutrition and sanitation chargers, Dovid included the unused education charger with his casting look of mistrust. This was the first morning that he hadn't connected to it the night before, and he wondered what the consequences were going to be. Would it lower his intelligence? His wealth of knowledge? His faculty of reasoning? If it was going to affect his reasoning then he might never be able to even find out, since he would be using the same affected reasoning to try to figure out if his reasoning had been affected. A headache quickly greeted that circle of crazy.

'Wall, I blame you,' Dovid said as way of good morning.

'I apologise, Dovid, for my egregious transgression.' A smiley face popped up with two hands pressed to its cheeks in desolation. 'May I ask what I am being blamed for?'

'You know what you did.'

'I suppose I do.'

Dovid poked an accusing finger at the shifty wall and, satisfied that he wasn't going to be satisfied this morning, Dovid prowled to his shower and grudgingly accepted the heat and comfort that it had to provide. Everyone probably began their day in this same manner, but to Dovid, the steam and heated fragrance only reminded him that he still had no inability, his overflow of sensory realism perpetually contaminating his every act. That particular taboo, however, was often generating feelings of mild content within Dovid these days, because if Dovid didn't trust the nature of his reality with his own natural senses, then how was he supposed to trust a reality through artificial implants?

Dovid dressed and set his emoto-shirt to an "I'm onto you" smiley face. The smiley face in the wall appeared to like it and changed itself to mirror the exact same expression.

'No, Wall, you can't be onto me, because I'm onto you.'

Dovid took great pride when he managed to change the smiley face on his wall to a sad face. It really made him feel like he had achieved something of meaning. The wall changed again then to a happy "Eureka!" face.

'What if I am onto you being onto me?'

Dovid shook his head. Things were sounding far too sexual between him and the wall lately. At least that reminded Dovid of his plan to ensure that everything else hadn't changed again, in particular with Imone. So he strode for his Social Quarter, the auto-door sliding away at his proximity and all the auto-greetings bombarding him as normal.

'Call Imone, please.'

Imone's dark-eyed face arrived, and her face dark-eyed him without expression. It was a hard face. The strength was impressive but Dovid couldn't recall how he found her so attractive as to spend weeks in the Sexual Quarter with her.

'Good morning, Imone. You're looking especially fierce today.'

Imone was reading Dovid's life again as he called, but his fierce compliment won a grin from her.

'Ah yes, Dovid, the two-punch pervo.'

'Two punches and a kick, if I remember right.' He wasn't just trying to be cute or irritating, he needed to make sure nothing had changed.

'What do you want, pervo?' Her grin was gone now, and when her lips went flat together it made her cheekbones look scary sharp.

'Just checking in that we're still on for some fight training later,' Dovid rubbed a hand against the stubble of his head to bluster some confidence. He did not want to fight her again.

'Sure, why not.'

'Great! Call you in a few hours after work?'

'I can't wait.'

Imone cut off and Dovid relaxed. Things were back to normal – more or less.

'Call Mart.'

Mart's big eyeless face arrived with an even bigger eyeless smile.

'Good morning, little brother. What's strange with you?'

'Morning, Mart. And nothing's strange! I think my weirdness has passed.'

'Oh? And what caused that?'

'Why does it need a cause? But if I had to guess then I'm blaming my wall and my education charger.'

'Well, if either of them were to blame, then that would be pretty weird too, little bro.' Mart changed his emoto-shirt to display a smiley face depicting "Dovid is a weirdo."

'Thanks, Mart, that's helpful, but I'm in too much of a good mood to be soured by your sarcasm.' Everything was staying put and Dovid's only half-regret was that things didn't normalise with the sex-addicted lust-head Imone instead of the punch-addicted rage-head one. He supposed it was still better than a drug-head or glut-head.

'Alright, little brother, it's hardly the place of family to do anything to infuriate each other. But, if I may have just one little but, by your reasoning then should everyone else be as weird as you were by use of their walls and education chargers? And, if everyone else is all weird, and you're completely different, then does that make you a …?' He finished his sentence by pointing down to his "Dovid is a weirdo" smiley-faced emoto.

'Well, Mart, if you're so not-weird, then why don't you try it? Disconnect your education charger tonight and see what happens tomorrow. But don't spoil my mood today. Let's just both be normal, okay? And let's have my philosophy if you please, so I can get busy with being normal.'

'What are you talking about, Dovid? You're the one who gives me a historical ponderance every day. Since when have I ever given you a philosophy?'

Mart had the decency to only let Dovid panic for a few seconds before bursting out with evil laughter.

'You should've seen your face, Dovid! Here, wait.' Mart called up the replay of Dovid's face losing all hope and joy in the world, posted it on the wall, and then even found a way to set that face as his emoto-shirt smiley face.

'Mart? Mart!' Dovid had to raise his voice to be heard over Mart's laughter. 'I'm glad to see my failing grip on reality has amused you, but it really will make things far too difficult for me if you start messing around like that. So veto on pretending things have or haven't changed, okay? At least until I'm sure they've stopped.'

'I'm sorry. Okay, but it was too funny. Right, serious now. Philosophy for the day so: ah ... which is more freeing? Freedom from restriction or freedom from conflict. Because you can't have both, you can either submit to the will of the world or you can fight it, so which one is freedom? Riddle, riddle, little brother.'

Mart disappeared and Dovid was just happy to be free from Mart's hilarity. Dovid got up to leave the Social Quarter, to get some work done, and ... nothing happened. Scowling, Dovid pressed his hands down on the armrest of his chair to push himself to a stand, and again, nothing. Well, that wasn't exactly right, because the exertion happened, the effort and intent of getting up happened, but it was the actual act of getting up that failed to occur.

'This is weird.'

Dovid could move his legs, could move his arms, move his backside, move every part of his body at will, but could not move them collectively to stand up. He kicked his legs off the ground and slid the chair back, proving that the chair was okay, so where was the problem?

'Am, Wall? Why can't I get up from my chair?'

The smiley face appeared with a curling moustache. 'Laziness?'

'What! Hey, this is serious! Look.'

Dovid tried to stand up again and stood up.

'Seriously?' Dovid threw the accusation at the chair, but he had his suspicions that the wall was to blame. Were the wall and chair in collusion to make him look like an imbecile? Dovid sat down on the chair again and pushed himself to a stand without incident. He closed his eyes.

'Would you like me to call Management for emergency services, Dovid? I could have the chair taken away and tortured?'

Dovid opened his eyes. The smiley face had an executioner's mask on and a guillotine behind it. He didn't need this kind of abuse from the wall. Things were just starting to go smoothly. The chair problem could have been anything.

'Belay that order, please. I'm going to do some work instead.'

'Aye, aye, Dovid.' Still with the executioner's mask, the smiley face now wore a ship captain's hat.

'Am I allowed to swap my wall for another wall?'

'Of course, but I would tell your new wall to act exactly the same as I do.'

'So it would be the same wall.'

'No, it would be a completely different wall, but acting in every single way like me.'

'But if there's no difference, how can you say it would be a different wall?'

'Because it would be a different wall.'

'Just without any differences.'

'Exactly.'

Dovid sighed and left his Social Quarter, the auto-door sliding away as he passed. His good mood was fading with each step down the stem and when he reached the Professional Quarter, Dovid's good mood was obliterated when he walked nose-first into the door.

'Ow!'

'Why did you walk into the door, Dovid?' The damned smiley face was slowly bringing up a cuckoo clock next to it again.

'No, Wall! No clock! Why didn't you open the door?'

'I have no control over the doors or chairs, Dovid. I'm just a wall.'

'Then why didn't it open? These things are supposed to automatically open and shut as I walk through them.'

'It may have been a malfunction. Why don't you try again?'

'Oh you'd like that wouldn't you?' Instead of bashing his nose again, Dovid reached out his hand towards the door, to see if the proximity of his limb would activate it, but when his fingers made solid contact, instead of sliding away into the wall, the metal door combusted into flames!

'Raghh!' Dovid jumped back, nursing his burnt hand, as the door to his Professional Quarter burned proudly down the stem. 'Wall, do something!'

The smiley face on the wall just looked around, its eyes growing bigger, but definitely acting like it had no idea what was going on.

'The fire! Wall! Put it out!' Dovid pointed his finger at the fire to show the dumb wall what he meant and the flames disappeared. 'Huh?'

Dovid looked down at his hand and saw that the skin was still burned, so the fire did happen. It did. Complex molecules break apart under heat, hence why people can burn and die, so he wasn't going crazy. He wasn't!

Dovid ran back to the Social Quarter, hesitating only for a few seconds at the door before barging inside. The door opened and closed as it should for this room, but he didn't sit back down on that chair. 'Call Mart.'

Mart's eyeless face arrived on screen.

'What's up, little brother?'

Dovid opened his mouth and no sound came out. His lips and tongue were flapping wildly with all the squeezed air that usually made words, but again with no result!

'No way! Dovid, did you get your inability? I like it! How come you still have your tongue though? Or ears? Because sometimes your voice goes when your ears fall off too. But never mind that I guess, congratulations, man!'

Dovid tugged his ears without thinking, and then licked the back of his hand.

'No, Mart, I—' Dovid was so thrilled he could speak again, he didn't know where to start explaining what was happening. 'I couldn't get up from my chair, Mart, and then I couldn't go into my Professional Quarter.'

'That sounds a lot like laziness to me, little bro. Where's the problem? So still no inability?'

'No! Mart, I touched the door to my Professional Quarter and it set on fire, and then I pointed at it and the fire stopped, and the wall is acting like I'm losing my mind, but look.' Dovid held out his hand to show the burn marks.

'Wo! The heat coming off that hand is radiant, man. What did you do?'

'I didn't do anything! The door just ignited.'

'That's pretty weird, Dovid, even for you. Have you asked the wall if it has ever happened before?'

'The wall won't even admit that it happened just now!'

'I don't know, Dovid. What could be causing it? The memory things could be a fault with your charger, like you think, but fires? I don't think there's been a fire anywhere in over fifty years. And the reality changing drugs don't do stuff like this either, and even if it did, it only lasts inside the Narcotics Quarter, right? Chem-heads are wiped clean when they leave again so that could only mean—'

Mart's image disappeared.

Dovid opened his mouth again, but this time the lack of sound had nothing to do with weirdness, and all to do with shock. What just happened?

'Mart? Could only mean what? Mart! Can you hear me? Wall, call Mart.'

A face appeared again, filling the room, but it wasn't Mart.

'Nietric!'

Nietric's twisted skin lifted to show surprise, but the voice that slithered into Dovid's ears held nothing but venom.

'Young Dovid, have we met before? I think I would've remembered meeting such a healthy young specimen as old as you.'

'I ...' Dovid had no idea where he met Nietric before, but he had definitely seen him. A face with that much vicious scarring could leave nothing *but* a scar in Dovid's mind. 'Who are you?'

A facial shift of amusement, a twitter of long-dead skin and featureless pits. 'But you just told me who I am. My name is Nietric, and I couldn't help overhearing your conversation with young Mart.' Nietric craned his skull to show the ruined hollow where one of his ears used to be, now just stab-wound of shattered skin.

'Where are your upgrades?' Dovid asked without thinking. They were usually located on the side of people's heads, even the Tactile ones.

'I could ask you the same question, Dovid, but I will answer yours if you answer one for me. I do not have any upgrades on my head because although I was born without many sensations, pain was not one of those of which I was left bereft. It took many attempts for them to realise the agony they were inflicting on me as an infant before I could find a way to communicate. But they all know now.'

Whatever way Nietric had found to communicate seemed to cause pain in the receiver rather than the deliverer. Each word spoken pierced its way inside a different part of Dovid's flesh, causing a new manner of agony each and every time. It was almost enough to stop Dovid asking questions for fear of the answers, but if anyone could explain what was happening, it had to be this monster.

'Do you know what's happening to me?'

'Ah, Dovid, you have already had your question, but I will answer anyway and we can balance the scales at a later date. What is happening to you, my boy, is that you are developing your inability. But it is my turn now. Answer me this, when we lose our sight and sound, our smell, our taste, our touch, do you ever wonder where they go?'

'What? How can a sense go anywhere? But no, I don't ever wonder, I don't even know what you mean.'

'I don't believe you, Dovid. I think you know exactly what I mean.'

Dovid had enough. Things were already too weird before this freak arrived, so he turned off his wall and ran out of the Social Quarter. But when he reached the door, it didn't slide away, and it didn't set on fire either ... it just disappeared. This made Dovid stop, even though he had no idea where he was running to, and when he turned to the wall to ask for help, an electrical charge exploded out of each of the wall panels the instant he opened his mouth. Covering his head, Dovid crouched as low as he could and ran straight out the exit of his island. This door opened normally at least, but Dovid was still forced to grind to yet another halt.

Four men stood outside his island, each of them wearing the mask of a lifeless smiling face, each one holding a gun, yet it was the fifth man behind them who frightened Dovid the most.

It was Nietric.

'Ah, Dovid, how good of you to join us. Please, come this way.' Nietric's voice in person was like searing liquid poured into Dovid's ears. The pain was sharp, but it was seeing those lipless limbs judder and twitch, knowing that no sound was emitted and yet still having the words pierce inside, that was the true torture.

The wall behind Nietric disappeared as he spoke, and a stem that was never there before now stood open. The directions on either side of Dovid's island suddenly had walls where there were no walls before, and all five lifeless faces, four of them masks and one of them an abomination, all stood there staring at Dovid, waiting for him to start walking. It was going to be a short walk. There was a door only a few steps down the stem, with a single inscription written over the exit: "Management."

Dovid eyed the gunmen and supposed that if they wanted to harm him, then they could have done so already. And as appalling as Nietric looked and sounded, he hadn't exactly done anything sinister that Dovid could identify. So, when Dovid started walking, he tried to pretend that he was heading towards the help for all his recent problems, towards the answer to his enigmatic inability.

Nietric laid a fatherly hand on Dovid's shoulder as they walked together, and when they reached the exit, Nietric smiled.

· CHAPTER SIX ·

Untroubled Existence

The Management exit opened into a single room with four walls. Each wall had its own exit, and lined on either side of every door were a chain of chairs.

'Please, Dovid, have a seat.' The pain of Nietric's voice shoved Dovid forward just as effectively as if the man himself had pushed. Dovid took a seat directly in front, so he could turn around and face his abductors.

Nietric was not wearing an emoto-shirt, just a blank grey suit, so it was difficult to be sure but it seemed that every action Dovid made caused great amusement in the man. The freak sat down across from Dovid and stared at him from his pitted face. The four guards took positions standing in front of an exit each and then the room lurched as if in motion.

Looking around for some sign that the room was actually moving, Dovid found it impossible to tell. There was no sight or sound that indicated travel, but lack of sensory proof didn't stop Dovid from feeling it anyway.

'Is this some kind of train?' Dovid asked.

'A train? Ah yes, you were working to become a historian, weren't you. How quaint. But, why not, a train is as good an analogy as any.'

Was Dovid becoming desensitised to it, or was the torment of Nietric's voice lessening with each encounter. Dovid doubted that the pain would ever disappear completely, but conversing with the man was becoming more bearable.

'So we *are* in a moving room? Well what do you call it then if not a train?'

'Me, Dovid? What do I call it? I call it what everyone else does of course.'

Dovid frowned. 'And what does everyone else call it?'

'Everything that transits is called a Transit, Dovid. Quite straightforward, don't you think?'

'Why didn't you just say that in the first place? Do you not like giving direct answers?'

'I only give direct answers to direct questions, Dovid, but do I not like them? No, Dovid, I do not like them at all.' Nietric shook his head as if deathly serious, but there was something about this entire exchange that made Dovid feel like he was being mocked.

'Where are we going?'

Nietric spread his hands out in answer. 'Where are any of us going?'

'Was that not a direct question? Where are we, you, me, and these four creeps with guns, going right now in this moving Transit?'

'Is not the phrase moving Transit a redundant one?'

Dovid felt like he was arguing with his wall. The worst pain he got when doing that though was a headache from frowning, but when Nietric argued back, it felt like getting electrocuted every time. Not that Dovid had ever been electrocuted, but he could imagine.

'Are you really going to make me rephrase the question, just to remove a redundant phrase?'

'Would I make you do something like that, Dovid?'

Solely for Dovid's own enjoyment, the feeling of stabbing electrocution from Nietric's echo was now complemented with a crushing headache. Because why not!

'I'll try a different question then,' Dovid said, trying to resist the urge to massage his head. 'What happens if I decide not to go with you? If I demand to stop this Transit and let me go back to my island.'

Nietric put his hand on his chin in contemplation and Dovid flinched despite himself. Seeing the ruined skin of Nietric's hand make contact with that wreck of a face, hearing the two coarse surfaces grate against each other scar–to–scar, it made insects scuttle through Dovid's limbs and made him shiver as if his spine had just been injected with freezing ice.

'Well, Dovid, in answer to your vast variety of querulous questions,' Nietric said, turning his hollow gaze back to him with a disturbing smile. 'What would happen? Well I suppose we would have to kill you.'

'What? You can't!' Dovid heard the smiling gunmen shift position and he turned to face them, expecting the four men to open fire right that instant.

'Well, of course, we can,' Nietric calmly explained. 'What I think you mean is that we shouldn't. Purely from a moral standpoint, you understand?'

Dovid was speechless. Yes, they had guns, and likely only carried them with the intention of using them, but they couldn't just murder someone! Dovid had never heard of Management arresting anyone for committing a crime before, partly because he was more interested in the past than the present, but also because there was no such thing as crime anymore! No arrests and definitely no punishments, never mind capital punishment! And what was his crime? Dovid looked to the walls for help. They were all supposed to be two-way emitters, even if just for a strip. They would be recording this and someone, somewhere would be watching.

'Are you going to kill me?' Dovid asked. He really didn't want an answer, but if there was someone watching who might save him, then he wanted to give them a reason to do it right away.

Nietric reacted to Dovid's blunt demand by putting his hands over his mouth in mock horror, but the limbs had no effect whatsoever on the volume of Nietric's spectral answer. 'Am I going to kill you? Dovid, I would absolutely hate to kill you.'

'So my life is not in danger?'

'What do you mean by life?'

'Life! As in *my* life, my living, breathing, blood-powered, physically functioning and conscious life!'

'Is that what you mean by life? Oh I would never dream of endangering that.'

'Then why threaten me? Why have you taken me? *Where* are you taking me?'

'Curiosity is the greatest gift we never asked for. How could we? We did not have the inquisitiveness to ever be curious about such a thing.'

'Are you going to answer any of my questions?'

'I thought I was answering all of your questions?'

'Not with proper answers, only with other questions or abstract theatrics!'

'Other questions? Ah but the unexamined answer is not worth questioning.'

Dovid dropped his head back and stared at the ceiling. The pain of Nietric's voice continued to seep into his every nerve and it made Dovid feel like he was on the verge of screaming. Taking his gaze away from Nietric's gruesome face was helping his sanity somewhat, but there were just too many terrifying unknowns here. Dovid prided himself on stoically facing the everyday with amused indifference, but now he didn't even know if his everyday was coming to an indifferent end.

'Dovid?'

Dovid didn't answer. Screw Nietric if he thought Dovid would play his game.

'Dovid? Shall we play a game?'

This snapped Dovid back to full awareness. He was always suspicious that the education chargers were reading his thoughts, and now here was Nietric doing it before his eyes. And how was Nietric even talking to him in the first place? No mouth, no tongue, no upgrades. He had to be communicating in some unknown way.

'Are we speaking telepathically?'

'Don't be absurd, Dovid. Now shall we play a game? I must confess, however, that we have never stopped playing it, and you, of course, are losing quite badly, but shall I tell you the rules?'

Dovid just nodded, his body aching from this exchange, exhausted.

'The rules are simple, he who asks the most questions: loses. But you have to ask a question every turn. Do you understand?'

'Does that count as a question?'

Nietric's face twitched and jittered in what Dovid now associated as Nietric smiling. 'Precisely, Dovid, as did yours, now, are you ready to play?'

'Okay, but what happens if I don't ask a question?'

'Well I suppose we shall have to kill you again, now won't we?'

'Again?'

Nietric tisked. 'Please try to avoid fragment questions, Dovid, it upsets me. Now, will you ask me a proper question?'

'Fine, where are we going?'

'We are going to a Management Sector. Have you ever experienced a dulling of any sense?'

'No. Why are we going to a Management Sector?'

'To discover what your inability is. Have you ever experienced phenomena that you think might be an unorthodox inability, statistically speaking?'

'Yes. But what about you? What's your inability? Is it really everything? Were you born like that? You look disgusting.'

Nietric held up his fist, and counted out four fingers, one at a time, then shook his head at Dovid.

'I was born without all five senses. Do I frighten you?'

'Yes. Do you like to frighten people?'

'Oh yes. When did you begin to experience these unorthodox phenomena?'

'On my sixteenth birthday.' Dovid had to pause to be sure. 'I think. How long have you been watching me?'

'Why, all your life, of course.' Nietric gestured to the walls. 'What happened on your sixteenth birthday?'

'That depends on which sixteenth birthday you're talking about.' Nietric looked unsettled with that comment, and even Dovid didn't fully understand it as he said it, but while he had Nietric on the back foot, Dovid may as well get a few other questions answered. Nothing to do with his current situation of course, which seemed progressively futile, but whole-life irritants that he would like to get answered before his life ended – which could be soon. 'Is there really no outside anymore?'

'For there to be an inside, Dovid, then there must be an outside. So yes, of course there is an outside, just not one that can support life of any kind. Now, what did you mean when you said my earlier question depended on which sixteenth birthday? Have you had more than one? Or are you talking about other people's birthdays?'

Dovid held up a fist and slowly counted out three fingers, one at a time, before shaking his head at Nietric. 'I feel like I have had several sixteenth birthdays. So are all animals, insects, and plants really gone? Natural organic ones now, no artificial ones.'

Nietric paused to see if he could accuse Dovid of asking two questions this time, but that last one was just a qualifier of the first. 'Natural life cannot be properly supported by our unnatural air and unnatural nutrition, Dovid, and quite frankly I do not see the point in artificial animals or plants, or natural ones for that matter. So do you merely *feel* like you've had several sixteenth birthdays, or did you actually have several? And I will clarify that I am talking about the sixteenth anniversary of your birth, not any other spontaneous declarations of celebration on different days.'

Dovid shrugged. 'Sometimes I can remember a dozen different conflicting days all happening at the same time, and sometimes I can't remember anything at all. So what happens when—' Dovid stopped mid-question and, while looking at Nietric, was blindsided by a question that had never even occurred to him before. He had always accepted it as a part of life, but when he thought about it, it didn't make sense.

'Why do they fall out? Our senses. I can understand why they might stop working, although no one's really been able to explain that either, but there's no reason why the raw tissue should fall out.'

Nietric stared at him for a time and Dovid tried to meet his gaze, but he was just too damned hideous, and Dovid's whole body was fading fast, the stress of Nietric's voice proving too much to endure.

'The body discards what it does not need, Dovid, but tell me, why can you understand that our senses would stop working?'

Dovid had to think about that one. He was used to having very strong opinions about everything ready to be lashed out when his wall or Mart needed some knowledge knocked into them, but he wasn't sure why he accepted the loss of sensory function as so reasonable.

'I guess all matter deteriorates over time, and that's all life is: prolonged matter being reproduced. So when you make a copy of a copy of a copy, you end up with something awful like you.' Dovid grinned brazenly and almost forgot to add a question. 'Don't you agree?'

If Dovid was hoping for a reaction (maybe something just shy of getting shot) then he was left disappointed. Nietric's rotted appearance was clearly a subject he had long made peace with.

'I do not agree with you, Dovid. Why take such a negative view of evolution, when you can be positive. Our knowledge, our medicine, our nutrition, our technology, our mastery over our environment; it all contributes to a much better *copy*, as you call us. So I think we have improved upon ourselves so much that parts of us are improving beyond us. So let me ask you again, when our senses vanish, where do they go?'

'Improvements? You think this is an improvement!' Dovid waved his hands to encompass the full mess of Nietric's body. 'I don't care what new waves of reality the upgrades can allow, our deterioration as a species is not an improvement.'

'Tsk, tsk, Dovid. Has your study of history enamoured you so much? Have you installed rose-tinted walls to your Professional Quarter? We live in a world without crime, without war, without poverty, without cruelty or deprivation of any kind. Our youths are all highly educated, articulate, well-mannered and productive young people. Our adults are all given careers that they love and as much pleasure as they can afford. Our elderly are respected, remembered, cared for and cherished, for as long as they live. Don't you see? Every life is given all it can need and given more to become whatever it wishes. Would you not willingly sacrifice some primaeval redundancies in exchange for such paradise?'

'Why do you refer to life as *it*? You said that every life is given all *it* can need. Are you not alive?' Dovid got a sudden impulse that Nietric was the wall, because he was just as infuriating, just as patient and self-assured. Or maybe Nietric was a clone or android version of the wall. Either way, Dovid wanted to win this argument. 'But tell me, Nietric, how is kidnapping me against my will not a crime, threatening to kill me not cruelty, and removing my freedom not deprivation?'

No twitch of amusement this time. No emotional reaction at all, fabricated or genuine. Just more pain than usual when he answered. 'I think you have lost this game, Dovid. Now we shall have to wait until you meet the others. Then we will play again.'

Dovid took it as a win. Nietric was the one to end the argument because he couldn't handle continuing it. Metaphorically speaking, he was the one to blink first – made all the more impressive against an opponent without eyelids or eyes.

'What others? Have you abducted more highly educated and articulate, well-mannered youths like me?' The mention of others set something ablaze inside Dovid and reminded him that he had one burning last question amidst the depths of his confusion. 'Who is Imma?'

Nietric's head shot up but he quickly tried to mask his reaction with indifference. 'You will have to be more specific, Dovid, there are billions of people in the world, and I have no doubt there are many girls named Imma.'

'Girls? Not women? You know the Imma I'm talking about: pale skin, delicate eyes, hair so light that you can almost see through it.'

'You sound like you are quite infatuated with her, Dovid. Do you love her? Is she a girl in your Education Sector?'

'No,' Dovid said warily. Nietric had thrown him again. There was no such thing as love anymore. Historic movies glamorised it, and families pretended to feel it for each other sometimes, if the occasion demanded it, but no one coupled under the pretence of love. Sex was broken down into its two primary functions: reproduction and pleasure. The emoto-shirts removed the need for hormonal complications, and the Social Quarters and Physical Leisure Segments met every other need for companionship, and if someone was absolutely desperate, the walls could provide the rest, so why love? Why had Nietric brought it up?

'What do you love, Nietric?'

Nietric cocked his head, testing the question for a trick.

'I love *you*, Dovid,' he said, and waited to see if this would get a response. Dovid diligently turned his emoto-shirt to a smiley face of "vomit-gargling disgust". Unperturbed, Nietric continued, 'I love all our fellow human beings. All we have in this isolated universe of ours is each other. Without other people, we're simply life trapped within a cage of skull and flesh, with nothing else to vindicate or even verify our own existence. So I love you, and I love my life, and how it contributes to making our world a better place, with every action that I make.'

Before Dovid could loudly detail what complete and utter twaddle that was, the Transit stopped and one of the exits opened. He hadn't felt the room slow down or stop moving, but now Nietric was standing up and gesturing that Dovid should do the same. The smiling guns were re-positioning themselves too, with two to lead the way and two to herd Dovid along. With his options slim and predetermined, Dovid sighed and got up.

'You will like your new island, Dovid,' Nietric assured him. 'It has everything a life can need, but of course we can't allow a Social Quarter, for obvious reasons. From what I've read of your life though, you had a rather distinctive distaste for the human condition's social need, so this all should please you greatly.'

'You're such a good guy, Nietric, honestly, thank you for everything you've done to make my world a better place. You're my hero.'

Nietric bowed in thanks, rather than under the weight of the sarcasm as he should have, and they all began walking. This whole situation was just like the world, it appeared like everything was okay, but Dovid knew that it really, really was not.

The stems of this new sector were exactly the same as the stems in Dovid's Education Sector. They passed island doors as normal, and Dovid even spotted a Physical Leisure Segment at the end of one stem, before the walls in front of them suddenly disappeared and a new stem inexplicably arrived to life. Once the walls reasserted themselves, Dovid and his escort continued on, taking one more turn before Nietric signalled a halt.

Dovid couldn't see any reason why they had stopped until he followed Nietric's line of non-sight. They were standing in a stem like any other, with a row of island doors like any other, except that all the doors were open. Nietric turned to the wall.

'Why are the doors open!'

It pleased Dovid to hear Nietric so distressed, and an equally anxious smiley face appeared on the wall, showing droplets of sweat on its face as it answered.

'The doors, sir? They are not open.'

Nietric pointed to one of the open doors, and he looked about to scream at the wall, before he instead turned and stared at Dovid.

'Did you do this, dear Dovid?'

'How could—!'

Dovid's defence was abruptly cut off as someone walked out from one of the open doorways and all heads turned to look at her. She was wearing loose white pants, that stopped short well above her ankles, showing the pastel white of her two bare feet. Her top stopped short too, showing a perfect stomach under the teasing rest of fabric that draped from her chest. Her hair was exactly how Dovid had described it to Nietric, so light that it was almost transparent. And her eyes, so gentle, so full of kindness and also strength; she was beautiful, she was perfect, and he loved her.

'Hello, Dovid,' Imma said.

• CHAPTER SEVEN •

Mechanical Universe

Dovid woke up in his island and found the education charger attached to his head. Biting back a curse, he carefully disengaged it and proceeded to remove the nutrition and sanitation tubes.

'Good morning, Dovid,' the wall next to him said. The smiley face also had a charger popping out of its head to normalise the fact Dovid was back using it. He was about to tell the wall where to go, when Dovid remembered where exactly he was.

'You're not my wall,' Dovid said. 'You're Nietric's wall.'

The eyes of the smiley face darted side to side, before turning itself into a smiley face with pitted scar-holes for eyes and mouth. Then it popped back to normal with a beaming grin.

'I don't know what you're talking about, Dovid.'

Dovid laughed and headed over to his shower corner. There was more stubble on his head than usual, making him think that he hadn't showered the day before, but as far as he could remember, he showered every morning without exception. The full body wash dissolved all his hair now in any regard, and when Dovid put back on his emoto-shirt, he set the emotion to "hairy".

Stumbling out of his Personal Quarter, Dovid went to his Social Quarter to say good morning to Mart. Except there was no Social Quarter. This woke Dovid up more than any shower or aggravating wall ever could. Running to the other doors, Dovid documented his Leisure Quarter, his Professional Quarter, and Personal Quarter, all as they should be, but where the Social Quarter was meant to be, there was nothing but a blank. The smiley face appeared where the door should be, with two thumbs up on either side of him.

'You okay, buddy?'

'My wall would never call me buddy,' Dovid said and then shoved the wall to be sure it wasn't the door in disguise. He met nothing but solid matter, and the smiley face gave itself a blood lip from where Dovid had push-slapped it in the face.

'I'm your wall to every last detail transferred to this island, Dovid, and I'm only calling you buddy because you like to be annoyed. You enjoy the stimulation ridiculous irritation elicits.'

Dovid had to agree that the wall was probably right, but rather than shrug it off and go about his life as normal, Dovid headed straight to the exit. The smiley face appeared on the door before he got there.

'The exits cannot be opened from the inside, Dovid.'

'Then open it from the outside.'

The wall's eyebrows jumped up out of its face. 'How am I supposed to open a door, Dovid? I'm just a wall.'

Maybe the lazy jerk really was Dovid's wall. That was something to solve later though, right now he wanted out. He tried pushing the door, knowing it wouldn't work, but at least every time he hit the door, the smiley face gave itself a new cut or bruise. That could definitely become a new hobby Dovid might enjoy. All sadism aside though, he wasn't pleased.

'Call Mart.'

'There are no social functions allowed in this island, Dovid.'

'Why not?'

'Management don't want your condition to become public knowledge.'

'And what's my condition?'

'They don't know, hence why they've brought you here.'

'That's not hence-worthy! Nietric and his Management idiots not knowing what my inability is: is not a logically deductive step to abducting and imprisoning me!'

'This is not a prison. This is almost the exact same as your previous island, void only of one quarter.'

The smiley face showed famous bad taste by putting on a black and white striped prison hat to demonstrate how Dovid wasn't in prison.

'It's a prison if I'm confined to this island and not allowed to leave.'

'You will be allowed to leave, under the supervision of Management to investigate the nature of your inability. And besides,' the wall put on a sarcastic surfer face, 'It's not like you ever left your old island, is it? I don't see what the big deal is.'

'That's because you're a wall! You can never leave the walls by definition and *hence* have known no other form of freedom than contemplation and innumerable faces. I need to be free to choose not to be free.'

By means of rebuttal, the smiley face turned itself into a donkey face.

'I'm not just being stubborn,' Dovid stubbornly insisted and stormed into his Leisure Quarter. If Nietric and the wall thought he was going to continue his professional education as normal in this prison, they were mistaken. Dovid didn't care if it meant he would run out of leisure money at some point because there was no way he was staying here long enough for that to happen. He threw himself into his Leisure Quarter chair, and when the smiley face appeared in front of him to say something, Dovid cut it off.

'No, I've had enough of you for now, so disappear.'

The smiley face became a faded dotted-line version of itself, and Dovid could only laugh.

'Fine, just take me outside somewhere so I can pretend I'm not imprisoned.'

The smiley face showed extreme exultation before obeying the request, and Dovid's Leisure Quarter became a beach on an old Hawaiian Island. The sound of the waves hit him first, before the warmth of the sun pressed itself down on his skin. A welcome breeze mixed that pressure with its own tickle of sensation, and Dovid looked around at the palm trees nodding behind him. His feet were touching sand and Dovid curled his toes into fists to enjoy it better. As prisons went, he supposed it wasn't too bad.

'Hey, who are you?'

Dovid shot up and looked around for the source of the voice. It was a girl's voice, but not the same soft rarity of Imma's that he remembered. There was no one on his beach though. It must be the wall playing a joke.

'I'm not in the mood for tricks, Wall, just leave me alone.'

'I'm not a wall you dope. Is that your inability then, no brain?'

Dovid sat up and tried to put a source on the voice. He waved the Hawaiian beach away and was left with an empty grey room.

'I don't know what my inability is,' Dovid said, suddenly worried this was a test that Nietric was playing with him. 'What's your inability?'

'How can you not know what your inability is, you dope. Mine is great, but I can't use it too much. Imma says things go wrong when I do.'

'You know Imma?'

'Well, I should. There are only five of us here – six now, if you can count dopes.'

'Will you stop calling me a dope! My name is Dovid.'

'Dopid? What a dopey name.'

Dovid closed his eyes. It seemed the only purpose of other people, be they walls, or Nietrics, or actual people, was just to annoy him. Maybe that was all life really was: a competition with other life. Annoying each other was just the gentlest form of combat, but when it came down to it, the purpose was to be the last life standing. Animals used to eat other animals, and plants, and when he thought about it that was how all life survived, by feeding on everything else.

'Have you fallen asleep, Dopid?'

'I'm not going to talk to you if you're going to be this annoying.'

'Boring! And here I hoped you'd be interesting.'

'No. My inner contentment is not dependant on someone else being interesting or entertaining, so if you are bored then the fault is with your own feelings of self-worth and self-actualisation, and has nothing to do with me.' Dovid had this argument with Mart many a time. If Dovid's happiness did not depend on other people, then he refused to accept that he needed to be involved in the happiness of anyone else.

'Wow. You're pretty weird, huh?'

'So my wall likes to tell me.' Dovid waved his Hawaiian beach back into existence and closed his eyes to recommence his enjoyment. He heard nothing more out of his imaginary companion, and began to hope that his insanity was gone for another day.

'Cool beach.'

Dovid startled awake again and turned to see a hole in the wall of his Leisure Quarter. Everywhere else was idyllic paradise, and then in the middle of the air, a hole with what looked like a thirteen-year-old girl on the other side. She had spiky brown hair and was grinning very proudly at the beach-hole she was causing.

'How are you doing that?' Dovid stood up and looked through the hole to see into the girl's own Leisure Quarter. She didn't have anything loaded, just the blank grey walls. She was sitting in her chair and idly kicking her legs in boredom.

'That's my inability,' she said. 'Mastery over space. Imma says it's general physics, but I reckon it's general awesomeness.'

'Is Imma there with you?'

'Why would Imma be in my island, you dope. And what do you want her for anyway? Aren't I good enough company?' Dovid was about to answer that she was rather abrasive company, but the girl interrupted him before he even spoke. 'Whoops, I can feel this slipping, and that's the time she says I blow up worlds. Better go so, chat ya later.' She waved goodbye enthusiastically before adding. 'Dope!'

Then she was gone.

'Can you still hear me?'

Silence for a moment, before the wall appeared on the beach, holding a long curving trumpet as a hearing aid. 'Are you talking to me, Dovid?'

Dovid shook his head but then frowned. 'Of course I am. Who else would I be talking to?'

'You could be going loopy, Dovid.'

Dovid stopped it before it happened. 'No! Don't you dare bring up that cuckoo clock!'

The wall froze with the cuckoo clock half-way formed and looked side to side again before letting a little cuckoo bird pop out of his smiley face mouth instead of from the wooden clock.

'Who else does Nietric have imprisoned here?'

'I am not allowed to talk about them.'

'Then don't tell me their names or specifics, but hypothetically, could there be people here who don't obey the normal laws of physics?'

'If they did not obey the normal laws of physics, then I would not be able to register any of said disobedience since I am computed entirely out of laws. Hypothetically speaking.'

'That's just lazy. Even a computer can calculate something by negation. But let's say the laws of physics didn't apply to me, such as setting doors on fire instead of opening them, or not being able to counteract gravity by standing up from my chair. Does that mean I can do what I want?'

'I have no idea what you're talking about, Dovid.'

'Well then, I'll just have to show you.'

Dovid marched out of his Leisure Quarter and straight for the exit. Memories were still fresh from walking nose first into a door the last time things didn't work as they should, but he tried to remain confident – if only to spite the stubborn wall. The smiley face was watching him from behind a digital bush, peeping out over it as if it both did and did not want to see what was about to happen. Dovid resisted to urge to raise his hands, and walked full speed into the exit, demanding that it open.

It didn't open. But he didn't bump into it either. One minute he was about to walk into the door, and the next minute he was standing in someone else's Personal Quarter. And it must have been Imma's Personal Quarter because she was there, sitting on the bed.

'How did you do that?' Imma asked.

'Me? I thought you were the one doing these things.'

'Not me. I was just sitting here and suddenly you appeared in my room. That's never happened before.' Imma didn't appear surprised though, she looked too happy for any other emotion to be considered.

'Well I think I remember you doing the exact same thing to me,' Dovid said, but whenever he tried thinking about Imma, his memories began to jumble. He needed to sit down so he carefully placed himself on the bed next to Imma.

'I did? You mean the times I go to your island? But I don't just appear there. And those times are very hard to get to: I have to escape from here, avoid all walls, and physically walk there. I mean, what kind of superpowers do you think I have?' She wasn't mocking him. Dovid had never seen anyone so happy in his entire life, and he felt like he was the cause of it. It felt great!

'So …' Dovid had no idea where to start. His grasp on what was happening had never been great, and he only pretended not to care about it. Imma put her hand on his arm.

'It's okay, whenever you do this, it's always hard.'

Dovid wasn't quite sure what to say to that.

'So we've ... done this before?' Dovid ended up going with.

'A few times, but not enough. I always love these ones. Even though I wasn't expecting it this time. But sorry, I know you have a thousand questions, so why don't you ask them first, and then we can see how much time we have left before Nietric finds us.'

'What happens when he finds us? No, never mind. What's happening right now? Why did I just appear in this room? How did that other girl make a hole in the air?'

'Oh you met Lawrie! Sometimes you don't, she's awesome. Scary, but brilliant! Nietric makes me move the most, but sometimes when Lawrie slips, everything ends. You call it the spaghettification of creation.'

'Do I want to ask what I mean by that?'

'We never have much time, so only ask what you think you really want to know. Not what you think you need to know, just what you want.'

Dovid couldn't stop looking at her eyes. They were like diamonds that sparkled a different colour every time she moved. And her smell. Dovid had never really smelled anyone this close before, not even Imone, unless you counted sweat, and he couldn't really put his finger on what Imma's smell was exactly, but it just filled him with, well, filled him with her. And once Dovid had started really looking at Imma, he was more and more aware of how her hand was touching his arm, of the bare skin between her top and her pants, of the joy expressed in the smile of her lips, and how she was looking at him with such expectation. He couldn't explain any of it, but he had never felt such intensity of affirmative feeling before.

'Ah, I suppose I want to ask about us. How do you ... how *well* do we know each other?'

Whatever Imma was waiting for, he had clearly said the right thing because she rushed him. Her body flew into his and she was kissing him before he even knew what was happening. It made the kiss clumsy, to say the least, and before he had time to try doing better, Imma pulled away, blushing shyly.

'I'm sorry. I know you don't really remember me, yet. But it's just I wait for these times for so long, and I look forward to them so much. I'm just excited. Are you weirded out?'

Dovid rearranged his hands to cover his lap. 'Ah, no, no I don't mind. I really liked kissing you. It's just I wasn't ready.'

Imma bit one of her fingernails while trying to contain her unstoppable smiling. 'I know, I wasn't expecting this either. I could feel this time I'd get to see you, but I didn't know I'd get to see you here, in my room.'

She was leaning slowly back into Dovid, and Dovid moved his lips forward to meet her. 'What do you mean by this time?'

Imma pulled back and Dovid cursed his traitor mouth.

'You're right, we can't afford to waste time kissing. How much can you remember from the other times.'

They could definitely afford to waste time kissing. Why would he ever want to do anything other than kiss this girl forever? Dovid sighed.

'I remember you sitting on my bed in my island, and that's it, I think.'

Imma's smile disappeared. 'You don't remember anything else?'

'Well the past few days, or weeks, I don't know, have been really weird. I feel like I've been jumping from different days, and everyone keeps changing, and sometimes I remember it and sometimes I don't. I don't know, Imma. All I know is that I feel like I know you. That I know you better than I know myself, and I definitely like you better than I like myself, I mean I ...'

He couldn't say it. It didn't matter what he thought he felt. He just couldn't tell this girl who he had just met that he loved her. She'd think he was insane! Dovid tried to reassure himself that love didn't exist anymore, only the pretence of love, but his pounding heart said otherwise.

Imma waited for him to finish his sentence and when she saw that he wasn't going to, she smiled again, a smile of sadness but also understanding.

'Okay,' she said and took a deep breath. 'Sometimes you remember and sometimes you don't, but I can ... move things. Well, move times, and you, you're the only person in the world who I don't affect. So usually, when I move to a new time, everyone is there, but it's a different everyone, except for you. You can follow me.'

'Ah ...'

'I know.'

It was good that one of them knew. Dovid stood up. Then he remembered why his hands were covering his lap and he sat back down. Imma giggled at him, and that did absolutely nothing to help him feel more at ease.

'So, you can travel through time?' No, it didn't sound any saner in words than it did in thoughts. Dovid was always fascinated with time travel though, since space moved with time, so if you travelled through time, it would be a different time, but it would be a different space too, since it moved during the time it took you to time travel.

'No, Dovid, I can't travel through time. My inability is that I interact differently with time. I can't go forwards or backwards, but I can interact with different predeterminations of time. One time you said it was like a two-dimensional spiderweb of causation. Does that help?'

No, but if they had discussed this before, then maybe he should skip ahead.

'So what's my inability then?'

'We don't know.'

Great. Not even the intensely beautiful weird girl who can travel through time – except that it wasn't really travelling through time – and who he has had infinite conversations with before but doesn't remember, doesn't know what his inability was. Imma put her hand on his leg to cheer him up and it did way too much more than just cheer him up. So much so he nearly couldn't hear her as she started talking – he was too distracted!

'So we know that Phrey's inability is light,' Imma said, smiling at him, 'and that Aris's inability is motion, and L.B.'s is energy. My inability is time and Lawrie's is, well, we've narrowed hers down to most of the laws of general physics, but it's probably space. And you, we've never been able to figure it out. Only that you can do things that have no consistency, and that when I move, you can sometimes move with me.'

'Sometimes ...' Dovid tested the word. 'But I can remember re-living the same day more than once. Surely that means you can travel back in time, or that I'm travelling with you?'

Imma shook her head. 'No, it just feels like you've lived the same day more than once because they're all happening concurrently, so when we move, you become the one who's lived that day and bring the memories of living all the other days with you. Get it? You never get it. But it's okay—'

Imma's head turned towards the door.

'He's about to find us again.'

Dovid stood up. 'Who? Nietric?'

Imma didn't appear as alarmed as she should've been. 'Yes, no matter when I go, he's always the same. He's always so ... sure of himself, and he always finds us.' She caught Dovid's hand and pulled him back down to the bed again, locking her eyes with his. She was acting like she wasn't worried, but Dovid could see her eyes begin to tear up. 'I know you don't know how to do it, but please Dovid, try to remember me. The times apart are getting longer and longer, and the ones where we find each other are shrinking every time he finds us. So please, just stay with me now, and remember me.'

Imma kissed him again, and this time Dovid let himself go. He heard the exits opening, but he didn't open his eyes. They just continued to hold each other, and kiss each other, and Dovid and Imma remained like that up until the gunshots killed them.

• CHAPTER EIGHT •

Pansubstance

Dovid woke up in his island and touched his lips. He remembered the kiss. He remembered Imma, and their conversation, and … the impact of the bullets striking his body. Quickly patting down his ribs and stomach, Dovid disengaged all the chargers while completing his inspection. He wasn't shot but the education charger was hooked up to his head again.

'Wall, did I put this damned charger in last night, or did it snake down to me all by itself?'

The wall appeared as a snake smiley face and flicked its tongue before answering.

'Good morning, Dovid.'

'Answer the damn question.'

'The education charger is an important part of your mental health, Dovid.'

'Still not an answer, but fine, speaking of mental health then, am I still in the asylum?'

The wall gave its smiley face a quick electric shock before answering. 'I'm afraid I don't understand the question, Dovid.'

'Ignorance is not absolution, Wall. Call Mart.'

'Social functions are not allowed in your island, Dovid.'

Dovid sighed but he was surprisingly relieved. Yes, it meant he couldn't talk to his brother, but it also meant he was still close to Imma, and maybe even a little closer to understanding what was going on. A quick shower and an emoto-shirt displaying the emotion of "fine" later, Dovid went to his Professional Quarter.

'Show me the history of inabilities.'

The wall panned in from the side as a smiley face pretending to drag a heavy load. 'There is a lot of history regarding inabilities, Dovid. Would you like to be more specific?'

'I would not like to, no. Start at the start and keep going.'

The smiley showed a ticking clock speed next to it before they both faded into dust and blew away on the wind. It was slow going, but Dovid was going to get to the bottom of everything. Admittedly, everything did happen to consist of understanding the governing physics of all of creation, but it wasn't as if he was going anywhere else. He would stay there all day, every day, without rest if he had to.

Five hours later and Dovid had enough.

His mind was on strike. Usually his Professional learning on history was ingested with palatable two hourly bursts, followed by thirty minutes of leisure, followed by another two hours work, with a full hour of play. He would repeat as needed, breaking up the routine with updates from Mart, but all in all, enjoying the system. Since he had full control over what he worked and how he played, Dovid was able to meet all his needs. But why he thought he could manage five straight hours of work on a subject he had to force an interest in – it was too much.

Normally, at such times, he would call Mart and recharge his energy, but since social functions were off the schedule, Dovid had another idea. One he had never thought to do before.

'Show me the history of my brother Mart.'

The smiley face appeared with a red bandana and blond-horseshoe moustache, 'You got it, brother.'

Mart's face appeared, but back when he had eyes. His brother looked at Dovid as if he was really there, and Dovid smiled at the deep brown colour of the younger Mart's eyes. They framed his dark skin and curly black hair much better than the lifeless holes he had these days. The history didn't show anything of Mart's Generation Sector, only starting when arrived in his Education Sector at age nine. Dovid laughed as he watched that kid run around and play with his new Leisure Quarter facilities, dreaming up anything his imagination could concoct. He watched as the young Mart tried out a few different professions before becoming adamantly obsessed with philosophy, and watching his brother gave Dovid a joy that he never knew could arrive from taking an interest in another person. He always knew there must've been something there – since most other people liked to be at least a little interested in others – but Dovid had only ever felt happiness could be achieved by himself. Other people were supposed to merely interrupt and upset the happiness he was busy creating.

'Hey, who are you?'

Dovid laughed at Lawrie's timely interruption. 'Hi, Lawrie, my name is Dovid.'

'How do you know my name? Are you like Imma? Have we met before, but I was a different me and all that? Because that's not fair.'

'Don't worry, we've only met once, and you kept calling me a dope.'

'Hmm, that does sound like me, and you do sound pretty dopey. Alright, I believe you. So what's your inability?'

'We don't know.'

'We? Have you lost your sense of self so? Disassociated Dope Identity Disorder?'

Dovid laughed. 'I think we're going to be friends, Lawrie.'

The air opened and Lawrie appeared, frowning at Dovid. She looked exactly the same as last time, brown spiky hair, tiny teenage build, and what could only be described as a "pup" face.

'We'll have to see about that. I don't usually associate with disassociated dopes.' Lawrie stuck her head into snoop around Dovid's Professional Quarter. 'Who's that?'

'That's Mart, he's my brother.'

Lawrie's mood swiftly changed from playful to serious. 'Oh. I'm sorry.'

'Sorry? What for?'

She eyed him seeing if he was only pretending to be stupid or if he really was stupid.

'Look, you seem like a nice guy, so I'll go easy on you in the beginning, but you need to start dealing with your situation, okay? Nietric has your brother now, and your mother and your father and anyone else that he thinks you might mildly care about.'

'No.' Dovid stood up and ran out of the room.

'Where are you going?' Lawrie called after him. 'The doors don't open!'

Dovid found that she was right but he started banging on the exit all the same. Lawrie listened to his thrashing.

'Hey, Nietric won't hurt them until you start disobeying him, so they're probably okay. Okay? They've just got their own islands somewhere else now, so just relax before they ... uh oh. See ya!'

Dovid stopped his banging and went back into his Professional Quarter to find Lawrie gone. Mart was gone too, and in his place was the ominous image of Nietric.

'Hello, Dovid.'

'I thought these islands didn't have social functions, Nietric.'

'And yet here you are fraternising with little Lawrie.'

Dovid didn't want to say anything to that. He didn't want to get her in trouble. But he needed to know if she was right.

'Have you taken my brother hostage, Nietric?'

'Hostage?' Nietric's whole face shuddered and jerked, and he didn't make a sound during his grotesque form of demented laughter. 'Oh I am going to enjoy getting to know you, Dovid. Your historical references will bring me much amusement. In fact, why wait? Shall we get to know one another right now?'

Dovid heard his exit door open.

'Please follow the guards, Dovid, and we shall talk in a moment.'

Nietric's face cut out and Dovid turned to see four smiling-faced guards standing in his stem, each one with a rifle in the hands. They didn't talk. They just stood there waiting.

'So are you real people? Or are you the wall given legs?'

His own wall covertly popped to small life by the door and began shaking its head to stop Dovid from insulting these guards. Dovid normally wouldn't care, but Lawrie had him worried now that Mart might get hurt. He couldn't help wondering though if these guards needed to wear full-face helmets to cover disfigurements as severe as Nietric's. Maybe they were completely rotted of human sensation too, but unlike Nietric, they hadn't discovered a way to communicate separately from sense. Reckoning he might as well go with them, Dovid also couldn't help shouldering into one of the silent smilers as he left his island.

The smiling-faced guards didn't register his impudence. They simply diligently went about their function, with two leading him down the outside stem, and two following behind. The lack of attention they were paying to him made Dovid want to test his limits.

'Hey, Wall, you still there?'

The smiley face glimmered to life for a moment and then dissipated again. The guards didn't move their heads and they seemed happy to let Dovid say or do whatever he wanted, so long he kept walking in the direction they wanted him to walk. Well, as happy as four guards with smiling masks could be, anyway.

'It's okay, Wall, these guys don't mind. You can keep me company.'

The smiley face slowly peeked its head up from an invisible trench inside the wall, wearing green and brown camouflage all over its face. Again the guards didn't turn to notice, but Dovid was glad of the company.

'Why are you so afraid of these guys anyway? They can't hurt you. You can't feel pain, and you shouldn't be able to feel fear either.'

'If you say so, Dovid,' the wall whispered back.

Trying to keep with his façade of fearlessness towards the gunmen, Dovid inspected the two in front and turned around to do the same for the two behind. All four were the same size. Not just the same height, but same build, same walk, the same person – just four of them. *And Lawrie called me disassociated.*

Dovid was about to spark up more conversation with the wall, when the two guards in front stopped at a door and the wall's smiley face disappeared, leaving a smoke trail behind it. The door opened and Dovid saw who the wall was really afraid of.

'How lovely to see you again, young Dovid,' Nietric said. He was standing in a plain grey room, populated by a single table, two chairs, and four doors – one for each wall as usual. Nietric gestured for Dovid to take a seat and the four guards took their places in front of a door each. 'Join me, please.'

Nietric sat down and Dovid took the other chair. For a while, neither of them said a thing. The discomfort of hearing Nietric's voice was still throbbing in Dovid's flesh, and the discomfort of seeing his non-flesh in the flesh was quickly overpowering even that. Dovid wondered if he would ever become desensitised to how horrific Nietric was.

'So, Dovid, today we are going to play a new game.' Nietric paused for Dovid to inquire about the new game, but Dovid wasn't biting. 'I think you will like this one. It has only one question: What is Dovid's inability?'

'I already told you that I don't know.'

Nietric feigned indignation. 'Dovid, how could you assume that I don't believe you? But the question still needs to be answered, so I will be asking it rather ... elaborately.'

The door on Dovid's left opened and the guard stepped out of the way.

'Through this door, Dovid, is my question. Would you like to know how I devised such cleverness? I think you do, so I will tell you. You see, when we lose our visual ability,' he rubbed the wrecked skin of his fingertips harshly through the sockets of his eyes. The sound was like someone tearing scabs and it made Dovid lurch. His reaction pleased Nietric and the freak continued what he was saying, 'we develop a visual inability. You no longer interact with light the way everyone else does. The upgrades do not replace this, you understand, they harness it. And this is how I will ask my question. One by one I will remove your abilities, and I will watch with much *avarice* to see what inabilities you will display. Now, stand up.'

Dovid stood up.

'And in answer to your earlier accusation, Dovid, about my monstrous taking of a hostage, I have given you a pleasant control. There will be a variable too of course, but despite all appearances, I am not a monster. What we learn here can only help to save us all. So while you are in there, perhaps you should think on this. You and I, and everyone else, we are not *in* this world, Dovid; we *are* this world. You understand?'

Nietric spread his hands to guide Dovid through the open door. On the other side was a narrow grey stem dividing into four more stems at sharp angles. He had never seen one do that before, everywhere else the world was constructed into perfect perpendiculars. Dovid didn't know what he was walking into, but he walked anyway – what choice did he have? – and before the door closed behind him, he heard Nietric make one last cryptic remark.

'Goodnight, Dovid. If you see them, please say hello to Mart and Phrey for me.'

The door closed and the lights went out. Automatically Dovid's hands extended to feel where he was and found a wall on his left. Assuming that the door behind him wasn't going to open if he went backwards, Dovid began a careful stumble forwards. He didn't know what Nietric was hoping to accomplish by having him wander around in the dark, but why had he said to say hello to Mart? The name Phrey he recognised as someone Imma had mentioned, but today seemed to be a day when things made less sense than usual. He kept moving forward.

When he reached where the stems separated into four sharp directions, Dovid was about to take the one on his left and keep travelling that way until he circumnavigated the maze, but then he saw a flash of light from his right.

'Hello! Is anybody there? What is this place?' It was Mart's voice.

'Mart! Over here!'

'Dovid? What are you doing here? Where are we?'

Dovid started shuffling towards the sound of Mart's voice. It was the same direction as the bouncing light. 'We're in a maze, I think. Management put us here. One of them is called Nietric.' Dovid felt like adding a few vicious adjectives to describe the freak but if this was a test, then Nietric was watching everything and Dovid couldn't afford to get Mart hurt as a result of petty disobedience.

'How can they do this? *Why* are they doing this?'

Dovid could hear Mart was close now. The bouncing light must've been something he was holding because that was getting closer too.

'It's my fault, Mart. They're trying to figure out what my inability is.'

'That's crazy. How can that be your fault? Where are you? You sound like you're almost next to me.'

'I'm here.'

Mart laughed. 'That's helpful. Where's here?'

Then Mart turned the corner and Dovid saw that he wasn't holding a light; he *was* the light. He was Mart-shaped, but featureless, and made out of pulsing red to yellow light. The radiance was brightest at his heart and head, and dimmest by his hands and feet.

'Wo,' Mart said.

'Hey! I was about to say the same thing to you.'

Mart brought his hands up in front of his face and turned them over. 'What do you mean? I can't see anything different about me, but you, it's like you're made of heat.'

Dovid did the same as Mart, bringing his hands in front of his face, but it was like they weren't there. All his eyes seemed to register was the difference between light and dark. Mart was the light, and everything else was dark. The moment Dovid made that inference in his head though, Mart began to lose shape. His brother was no longer a humanoid shape of light anymore, he was simply light.

'This is messed up,' Dovid said.

'You're telling me. So why are we here? The Management want to find out your inability? Then why I am here?'

Dovid didn't want to worry Mart by saying he was collateral in case Dovid became difficult, because, to be fair, Dovid was always difficult. So instead he came to a different realisation. 'Nietric said there'd be a pleasant control. So you're probably the control to his experiment, but a pleasant one, because I was starting to miss you.'

'I was missing you too, little brother. You were only gone for two days, but you were gone-gone. No records of you ever being here at all. Made me start wondering if I had caught total crazy from you. But man I'm glad to see you now.' Mart moved forward and hugged his brother, and Dovid realised it was the first time he had ever met his brother in the flesh. It felt really weird, and really good.

'So I still don't understand. How am I a control?'

'Do you have your visual upgrade?'

'Yeah.'

'And does it work? Can you see the walls, the ceiling, everything as normal?'

'Of course, except for you. You were made out of heat a minute ago, now it's just light.'

'Well, I won't pretend to understand how Nietric's mind works, but it looks like he wants someone already with a sight inability while he tests mine. He said there's someone called Phrey in here too, somewhere.'

'Well, I guess we should go find him and get out of here. If it's a maze then all we have to do is get to the other side, or is it the middle? I don't know.'

'You're the man with the eyes,' Dovid said and he heard Mart laugh at that. 'Lead on.'

'What's to stop us from just staying here? Why should we go along with this experiment at all?'

In answer, a flare of light whooshed to life behind them and an explosion of fire burst out from the entrance. The sudden eruption of light blinded Dovid for a second, but Mart was already pulling him forward, away from the flames.

'Fair enough! If we stay put we get set on fire,' Mart said, as if it made perfect sense, and he kept his head turned as he walked to keep an eye on the flames. Once the blaze was out of sight, they increased their pace and began navigating the maze of stems. He let Mart make the decisions regarding what turns to make, because for all practical purposes Dovid was still blind. The stem walls didn't appear to be able to reflect light, so Mart was the only thing emitting it and all that Dovid could see. That meant Dovid was bumping into a lot of walls, and ending up walking along with his hands stretched out again.

'So who's this Nietric guy?' Mart asked, and the moment he opened his mouth, Dovid's vision changed. The darkness disappeared, and although Dovid could see all around him again, he wasn't sure if it was better or worse. Everything had turned into colourless shapes, even Mart. Spheres, trunks, cylinders, all melted together in front of Dovid's eyes to create his brother, with every edge of the fey formation lacking any distinction or definition. Dovid held up his own indefinite hands to help understand his new sight.

'What's wrong?' Mart asked.

'Everything's turned to shapes.'

'That's better, right?'

'No, not really. No colour, no features, no definition. This is freaking me out, Mart.'

Mart put his hands on Dovid's shoulders, and he assumed his brother was trying to look him in the eyes, except Mart had no eyes – and not in the usual no eyes way either – he was just a grim, colourless, anamorphic shape. Dovid knew Mart was only trying to help, but the truth was, this disturbing creature now in front of him was very, very frightening.

'Hey, Dovid, it's going to be alright. I'm here. I'm not going to let anything happen to you. Okay? If your vision keeps changing, then all of these things are just temporary. So you need to stay calm. Try to not care about it. Come on, you're good at that! Distance yourself from this. Laugh and mock it!'

'You do look kind of funny,' Dovid agreed. A terrifying kind of funny, but the idea of Mart being turned into different shapes could only be laughable. 'Thanks. Let's just keep going. The sooner we're out of this the better.'

Mart patted his shoulders one more time and then turned to keep walking. Dovid took a deep breath before following and suddenly Mart turned back to normal. Everything was back to normal. Full light, full detail, full normality!

'Hey, Mart, it's changed back.' Mart turned around to smile, and then disappeared. 'No! Mart!'

'It's okay, I'm still here. I'm not going anywhere.' Dovid felt a hand close around his arm in reassurance, but there was nothing to see. 'What have they done to your vision now?'

'I ...' Dovid wasn't sure how to explain it. He looked around to see if anything else was different and then Mart flickered back into view. But when Dovid tried to focus on Mart, he vanished again. Swivelling his head from side to side, Dovid saw Mart jump in and out of view, and when he concentrated, he saw the walls were losing parts of themselves too. 'It's a blind spot. I think they've given me a blind spot. Sometimes when I turn my head I can see you, and then when I look right at you, you're gone.'

'How are they even doing this to you, man? Come on.' Mart placed Dovid's hand on his shoulder. 'Grab a hold of me and follow as best you can.'

Dovid's hand was shaking but kept a tight grip on Mart's emoto-shirt. Absently he wondered what setting Mart would have on his emoto-shirt to depict their current circumstances, but he knew his thoughts were just babbling.

They walked in silence now, determined to finish the maze and be done with it. After a minute or so, Mart started to jump back into view, even when Dovid wasn't moving his head. The air around Mart was distorting every time he moved, and soon the reverse of Dovid's last sight happened. Everything else vanished and only the rippled image of Mart remained. Dovid kept his grip on Mart's shoulder and just concentrated on breathing. He kept that focus through the next change too, when a hyper spectrum of colour assaulted Dovid's eyes. The multitude of colours he had never experienced before was coming from Mart and his own body, but also from the walls. A kind of bioluminescent fungus appeared to be weaving in and out of them, and Dovid was very tempted to shut his eyes in shelter from the onslaught. It was his pure desire to spite Nietric that kept Dovid from shying away, so he kept going and he kept his eyes wide open. They turned one more corner and entered a large circular room.

'Is this it?' Mart asked. 'Is this the centre? It is finished?'

Dovid shook his head, and the dizzying colours made him regret the motion immediately. 'I doubt it, if we have to leave through an exit, then it makes sense that we have to get to the other side of the maze.'

'Maybe. Or maybe it ends here, and we can go back as normal to the start again?'

The hyperspectral strobe told Dovid it wasn't over, but then things did go back to normal. Having being fooled previously, Dovid held his tongue until at least a few seconds of normality persisted, and soon his fears came true. The test was still in play and it still had worse to inflict. Dovid's sight began to expand from binocular, to monocular, to panoramic, to the final and worst: full three-hundred-and-sixty-degree view.

To say that it was disorientating was that biggest understatement Dovid could think of, and the minute he moved his head, he collapsed to his hands and knees and emptied his stomach, dry retching for minutes afterwards until there was nothing left. And still there was no end or relief because he could see below and above him at the same time, and when he tried to stand back up, all that happened was Dovid buckled over and fell once more, his sanity and his balance fleeing from him as one. This time Dovid did close his eyes, and he had no intention of ever opening them again.

He felt Mart's hands gently grip him under his arms. 'Come on, Dovid, we have to keep going.'

Dovid let Mart lift him up, but he didn't open his eyes.

'Maybe that's for the best, man. Just keep your eyes closed and I'll guide you out, okay?' The tenderness in Mart's voice made Dovid start to cry. He knew his brother could see emotion as waves now, so he would know exactly how terrified Dovid was. There were no masks of perception here. The raw truth of how beaten Dovid was feeling was there for Mart to plainly see. So, still crying, Dovid let his big brother lead him blindly, arm in arm, out of the maze.

Dovid didn't know what he would've done if Mart wasn't there to help him. Likely he would've lain collapsed and crying until Nietric tried to force him to move. He could picture himself stumbling and falling, trying to get away from the fires, or lasers, or wild beasts, or whatever Nietric had in store for him. If Nietric had wanted to humiliate Dovid into submission, then it was working.

When the tears started to stop, Dovid needed to regain a little strength, so he risked opening his eyes. Mart turned around to look at him and smiled in an attempt to reassure him.

'Can't be much farther now.'

Dovid smiled weakly back and blinked for a few moments to test his vision. At first, everything seemed fine, but then ... everything flipped.

'Stop!'

Mart stopped and waited for Dovid to explain or not, with a patience Dovid knew he himself could never possess.

'Things have gone upside down,' and saying the words, Dovid could only laugh. Mart even joined him.

'I won't even pretend to understand how hard this is for you, man, but that one sounds kind of fun.'

Dovid took a testing step. In his mind, everything was the vertical reverse and it looked like he was stepping into thin air with Mart upside down on the roof. It wasn't quite as disorientating as the full three-sixty, but it was close.

'Maybe you should just shut your eyes again. To hell with this Nietric and his tests.'

'No.' Dovid was sure that if he refused to participate in the tests then Mart would get hurt. 'Like you said: To hell with Nietric. I won't let his tests beat me.'

Dovid gripped tighter to Mart's shoulder, watching his arm twist upside down to do it, and held back all feelings of vertigo from stepping out into mid-air. Half of him wanted to move faster to be out of the maze, but the other half was just about coping with the speed they were already doing.

Before they reached the end of the maze, his vision went from upside down, to sideways, to reflective, and to opposing horizontals. The last one was where one of his eyes turned its sight sideways, while the other eye turned the opposite direction. But Dovid persevered. And eventually, he and Mart made it to the exit.

Before the door opened, and Dovid was finally done, a small voice sounded right beside them and it wasn't Nietric's, or even Lawrie's. This one was different again, and he sounded like a ten-year-old boy.

'I'm sorry I had to do that to you, Dovid, but Nietric would've punished me if I didn't.'

Dovid's sight was back to normal, and he could see Mart looking around for the source of the voice. But Dovid knew they wouldn't find it, even when the person it belonged to was standing right in front of them.

'It's okay, Phrey, I know you had to do it.' Dovid put out his hand and felt another meet it. He shook Phrey's invisible hand and could feel the relief in the poor boy by doing it. None of this was Phrey's fault, his family was probably being held just like Lawrie had said. No, the person responsible for this was Nietric, and it was time Dovid started thinking of a way to pay that bastard back.

· CHAPTER NINE ·

Empiricism

The maze exit led back to the room with Nietric. His lipless smile congratulated them on their completion and eight other equally lifeless smiles stood to greet them too.

'They say the first time is always the hardest,' Nietric said in consolation, 'but I do try to make each successive time worse. Now, if we have the fraternal reunions concluded? Mart, would you be so kind as to follow these four gentlemen back to your island.'

Mart grimaced at the sound of Nietric's voice and turned to Dovid to clasp his shoulder. 'I'll see you again, little brother, and remember the great king, alright? Whatever happens: this too shall pass.'

Dovid smiled, 'Riddle, riddle, big brother.'

'How my heart breaks at this human emotion,' Nietric added, earning a look of hatred from Mart. Then the four smiling guns escorted him out a door and Nietric turned to Dovid, pretending to be hurt. 'I mean what I say, Dovid. I am not a facetious person. All we humans have is our empathy for each other to let us know we are not alone in our solitary universe.'

'So all those feelings you put me through in there?'

'I felt every one,' Nietric said placing his hands over his heart. 'And it has made me stronger for feeling it.'

'Whatever gets you off,' Dovid said and looked around, searching for the other participant. 'Where's Phrey? Did you share in his feelings too? Of inflicting torment on another human being?'

Nietric stood up and walked closer to Dovid, his voice stabbing more painfully with every sentence and step. 'I share in all of your feelings. You could say that I *feed* on them. They *sustain* me. And, Dovid?' He paused with his face inches apart, and it was all Dovid could do not to flinch or turn away with that hideous pocked skull standing so close. It felt like an eternity before Nietric finished his sentence.

'I want *more*!'

The freak spun away from Dovid and sat back down at the table, gesturing for Dovid to do the same. Dovid eyed the gun closest to him for a moment, trying to predict how successful he could be if he wrestled one free and used it to shoot Nietric in the face. The other guns would get Dovid soon after, if not during, but at least with Nietric and Dovid both dead, then maybe Mart might be able to go free. But what about the others? What about Phrey, and Lawrie, and Imma? Dovid released his breath and sat down.

'Good, Dovid,' Nietric said, 'Because as I have already told you, I would simply hate to have to kill you, but it is good to know that you did not hesitate at ending your own life, only in the potential suffering of others, which leads me to my new idea.'

Dovid didn't care how Nietric knew what he was thinking and he didn't ask what the new idea would be. The throbbing pain from Nietric's voice was enough to beat down any clever impertinence he could devise, as well as any general emotional energy he might have remaining. Dovid just wanted this all to be over, so he could go back to the sanctuary of his island and try to figure out how to beat this.

'You are fading quicker than I hoped,' Nietric said, the disappointment somehow clear in his distorted voice. 'Never the less, we must continue. You see I had hoped your inability might manifest when your body and mind were being distressed and attacked. But I am thinking you might respond better to the defence of others being so mistreated. Your family, yes, but each one older, each one with your historic concept that they should be protecting you and not the other way around. So I ask myself, what out-dated ideal of yours could I utilise to this effect? And the answer arrived in quite a *timely* fashion.'

The door to the maze opened again and Dovid couldn't look at it.

'How many times are you going to put me through these tests?'

'Do not worry, Dovid. I am easily bored. If your inability does not rear its ugly head for me soon, you can look forward to being summarily dismissed.'

'Thanks.' Dovid stood up and the more tired he got, the more ready he was to die. As always, Nietric picked up on Dovid's inner condition immediately.

'Do not give up so easily, please. I have already grown quite bored with Imma, and I have no hesitations about killing her in the hope that it will make you more interesting.'

Dovid bore his teeth at Nietric but regretted the satisfaction it gave the man.

'Yes, you have discovered my idea. I will hurt Imma in this next test, and I will kill her if you do not answer my question. You see, Dovid, you could be the answer the whole world has been waiting for. With Imma, once we found out she cannot go forward or back, then what use could she be? We can interrogate all the alternate times as much as we want, and it will never change ours, by its very definition. But you, you could be our world's saviour, if your inability is what I think it is. So please, think on that.'

Dovid couldn't think on anything with the full body agony Nietric's voice brought with it. The freak should speak in shorter bursts if he wanted to be listened to, but Dovid imagined the idea of causing the most pain by the longest speech was more appealing. He had heard of people loving the sound of their own voice, but this was an entirely new degenerate level. Dovid walked back into the maze and tried not to shudder when the doors closed behind him.

'Imma? Are you in here?'

The lights were still on anyway, and it was the same maze, the same narrow grey walls shooting from floor to ceiling, cutting into stems at sharp angles. Maybe it would be easier this time – not that Dovid remembered much of the path Mart had taken him, having his perceptions ripped from his control and cruelly twisted was slightly distracting that way.

'Dovid?' Imma's voice was full of urgency. He could hear her running and it wasn't long before she found him. He was about to guess that she had done this maze an infinite amount of times, but she cut his thought short as she ran straight in and hugged him. His arms completed the hug on instinct. The feel of her hands touching his back, the smell of her hair and the sensation of it brushing his face, the heat of her body, the tenderness of her chest pressed against his; every instant he examined his time with Imma, Dovid found more and more remarkable wonder. She pulled back.

'What test is it?'

'I have no idea. The last one was vision. I got to meet Phrey.'

Imma smiled. 'Phrey is so nice, and it's so terrible he has to do these tests. When L.B. does them she's very professional about it, but when it's Aris, well, he enjoys it. Says it's the only entertainment he gets, so why not learn to love it – like inflicting suffering was a hobby.'

'What about Lawrie?'

Imma shook her head. 'No, they actually listen to my warnings when I tell them about what she can do, because when she slips, she slips big. Even the smallest black hole destroys everything around it, our solar system included.'

Yikes. Dovid looked around to see who was in with them to be the tormentor for this test, but he couldn't see anything yet. Imma caught his hand and pulled him forward.

'Come on, the quicker we're through it, the less time they get.'

It also meant the less time Dovid would get to spend with Imma. He was already gazing at her see-through blonde hair bouncing as she walked. A sudden notion hit him to lift her hand so he could kiss it, but then he remembered Nietric's plan.

'Nietric said he's going to hurt you in this one, Imma. He wants it to draw out my inability.'

Imma slowed her pace for a moment but continued onward with renewed strength. 'It's okay. It's only suffering. If it gets too bad, I'll just move us again, but ...'

'You're afraid I won't remember.'

Imma looked at him over her shoulder, and this time they both gazed at the other. If he could only do one thing for the rest of his life it would very easily be admiring those perfect eyes. But Imma was more mature than that and kept them moving.

'What do you remember this time?' she asked. Dovid could barely grasp how frustrating it must be for her, to get know someone so well as she said they did, and then have that person forget it all each time. But even if his mind wasn't letting him remember everything, his body was telling him all he needed to know. Every non-rational fibre was screaming that he loved this girl, that there was nothing in the world that mattered more than trying to spend as much time with her as he possibly could.

'I remember enough to know how much I care about you,' Dovid said, a little guarded. He still couldn't bring himself to say the "L" word. 'But why don't you tell me what you remember? About the different times. Is it always like this? I mean, are we ever free from Nietric?'

Imma gave a hollow laugh. 'No. Never free.'

'I don't understand. The things Phrey could do, and what Lawrie can, and even you, I mean do we ever, you know, rise up and rebel? Fight back and destroy Nietric?'

Imma looked around and placed her finger on his lips. 'He's watching us, Dovid. What do you want me to say?'

'Let's just say whatever we want, and if anything happens, you can move us. I'm getting better at remembering, so moving should be okay. Actually, wait. Have I ever said this before?'

'Yes, and no it never works.' Imma's voice went low, but Dovid thought it was more from sadness than from trying not to be heard. 'They hurt all your families first, and then they kill them, and then they kill us, or else Lawrie does. And it's not her fault. She's just too young. Maybe when she's older, she might be able to control it, but they'll probably kill her before she gets the chance. We're not like the superheroes from your old movies, Dovid. We're just kids who interact differently with reality, and because of that, we're experimented on and tortured.'

'Okay. I'm sorry. I'm just angry. Maybe it would be easier if I understood things better, but probably not. I won't ask about ... you know ...' He noticed that she had talked about *their* families getting hurt and killed, but not her own. He wouldn't bring it up. He had already upset her enough and he wanted to make the most of their time together. Looking around again, it only reminded Dovid that something terrible was supposed to be happening to them. 'Imma?' She stopped and he leaned in to whisper in her ear. 'Why hasn't anything happened yet?' If Dovid was judging by how long it took the last time, then they would arrive at the centre of maze very soon.

Imma buried her face into his neck for a moment, and kissed him, before pulling herself together. 'It's Aris,' she whispered back, her lips so close they brushed the skin of his ears. 'He likes you to wait. To keep you wondering when he'll start. To get you hoping that maybe you'll get through fast enough that you'll get away with it. But his inability is motion, so it doesn't matter how fast we go.'

Hand in hand, she pulled him again and Dovid was about to ask why they should bother rushing if Aris could just slow them down, but what else could they do? When they reached the centre of the maze – the circular room with the four different exits – Imma tried not to slow but Dovid pulled her to a halt. There was a teenage boy standing in the centre of the maze, waiting for them. It had to be Aris.

He looked older than Dovid and Imma, his eyes dark and drawn. He had long waving black hair that flowed down his back and in front of his face, and Imma was right about him enjoying this. Only half of his mouth was grinning, but every part of his body was trembling with anticipation and pride in the power he possessed over them.

'There's no point, Dovid, he won't listen,' Imma said and tried to pull Dovid into moving again, but Dovid held his ground.

'We have to try.' He pulled his hand free from Imma and extended it towards Aris. 'My name is Dovid. You're Aris, right? It's good to meet you.'

Aris giggled and took Dovid's hand, shaking it, but not releasing it.

'Very pleased to meet *you*, Dovid.'

Dovid tried to take his hand back but found it stuck. 'You don't have to do this, Aris. We can fight back. If we work together in defying Nietric, then he has nothing.'

Again Aris tittered, as if not quite believing Dovid was actually saying these ridiculous things.

'Oh, Dovid, Dovid, our great master Nietric has everything. And so do I! I have everything a boy could ever want right here.'

'How can you think that? He has you torturing people for his twisted amusement!'

Aris giggled some more and Dovid began to wonder if he was even sane. The older boy gave Dovid a too-wide smile, pulling his lips back too far to show every last one of his teeth, and he kept his mouth like that as he gave his crazed reply.

'Yes, it is twisted, isn't it? But *oh* how amusing!'

Aris left go of Dovid's hands and a peculiar sensation began to form underneath Dovid's skin. He felt something wriggling inside him, as if his veins had come alive and were weaving their way around his body. Dovid started padding his skin to feel what was happening, and the serpents inside him just kept going. They worked their way to his chest and thundered out to every other part of him from there. It wasn't just his limbs either, whatever was inside him was eating into his organs now, piercing in deep before trying to burst free through his muscles and flesh. When Imma grabbed his hand, it felt like she crushed it to pulp and Dovid screamed!

Imma withdrew her hand immediately and reached up to cup his face, but stopped, knowing that it would cause similar pain. She tried to get Dovid to meet her eyes. 'Dovid. Listen, it's just your blood. That's all it is. Aris is making you feel the magnified motion of your blood. Remember what Nietric said, he's not going to hurt you.'

'Oh that's right, isn't it?' Aris said and slapped his head. 'Thanks Imma! I'd almost forgotten. It's *you* I'm supposed to hurt!'

'Do your worst, Aris. It's nothing I haven't been through a thousand times before.'

'Interesting,' Aris said and scrunched his face up in thought. 'I guess I'll have to be particularly inventive then. But I can't let your comment go about it *just* being blood, so let's start with that.'

Imma cried out and toppled to the ground, trying to cradle herself into a ball without any body part touching. Dovid's own sensations ended at the same instant and he flew down to try to help her. He didn't want to touch her, didn't want to make her pain any worse, but there had to be something he could do. He could see Imma was trying to fight back the pain, her entire body trembling, but screams escaping nonetheless. Turning to glare at Aris, Dovid balled his fists and let fly.

The punch wasn't even halfway there before Aris sighed and Dovid's arm snapped upward in half. The forearm bones between his elbow and wrist were folded back with no other warning than the sudden sound of a sickening crack. Now it was Dovid's turn to collapse to the ground in agony, somehow hearing Aris's voice behind it all.

'Whoops, I forgot. Can't hurt the new boy! Not yet.' Aris clicked his fingers and Dovid's arm twisted back to normal. The pain remained though, and Imma still lay prone and helpless, shuddering on the floor. Scowling at Aris, Dovid attempted to contain his rage. There was nothing he could do. Anything he tried would involve motion and Aris could manipulate motion. So what was the test? Just to stay here and endure pain until Aris or Nietric grew bored? Looking down at Imma, Dovid couldn't see any other way so, as gently as he could, he helped Imma to her feet and began guiding her forward. They had to finish the maze.

'If you run really fast, guys, you might escape!' The sound of Aris's mad laughter followed them as Dovid guided Imma forward. He had no idea if they were going the right way, but after a while, Imma recovered enough to guide him.

'This way is quicker.' Her voice was so weak and hearing it caused more pain in Dovid's heart than his broken arm had. Dovid knew that emotions didn't need reason, but he had to make sense of some of this rage.

'I don't understand it, Imma. How can someone else's inability even affect us? It doesn't make sense! Just because someone can't see light, doesn't mean it doesn't exist, or that it exists differently for them than for us. How can Aris do this to us? What else is he capable of?'

'Anything he wants, Dovid. He can move odorant molecules to manipulate your smell, he can move sound vibrations to manipulate your hearing, he can move the subatomic electrons inside your skin, or move the sense preceptors on your tongue. And as for how he does it? Just because everyone else assumes things are a certain way doesn't mean that they are. If anything, our inabilities are telling us that what we think are the laws of physics are only our best guesses of understanding what's around us. Lawrie alone could show you that these things don't exist solely to obey our understanding.'

Even though she was still suffering, Imma spoke with the authority of a thousand lives and Dovid didn't doubt a thing she said. And as nervous as Dovid was about what Aris had in store for them next, Imma was getting him more and more worried about Lawrie. What if she was the one doing the next test? But no, Imma said Lawrie couldn't control what she did, and so she ran the risk of what, destroying everything? Dovid's mind fled from that scenario, and it fled some more when the ground began to spin.

'What's he doing?' Dovid asked. If he could just rationalise these insane phenomena then it all might become bearable. When Phrey was robbing him of his sense of reality, it was the panic as well as the helplessness that terrified Dovid. But if he knew what was happening, then he could try to stay calm, maybe even find a way to fight back.

'He could be doing anything,' Imma said and tried to keep walking. They both stumbled with every step though. 'We could be feeling the movement of the plates underneath us, or the rotation of the planet on its axis, or around the sun, or the sun around the galaxy, or who knows, maybe the very expansion of the universe, but I don't think he's managed to achieve that one yet.'

To join the floor spinning, Dovid started to feel his skin spin too. It was like someone was turning it around his flesh, pulling it from him and compacting it back in, all three at once. Imma starting moaning and Dovid knew that whatever was happening to him, it was happening to her much worse.

'No!'

Dovid felt his skin begin to vibrate violently, and maybe Aris was colliding particles in his skin to create temperature, but either way, Dovid started to burn. His skin turned pink, and looking down to Imma he saw that hers was scalding red.

'Aris! Stop! You don't have to do this!'

Aris's response was a distant giggle, and Dovid's outrage only increased the sadist's perverted delight. Dovid clenched his fists and tightened all the muscles in his body to fight these sensations, but then he felt Aris open Dovid's hands for him. He watched his fingers splay up and out in agony, but knowing the rules of the test, his eyes shot to Imma. Her hands were doing the same, but worse, as Dovid could see, hear, and feel, each knuckle snap in Imma's hands as they were turned inside out.

'Imma! Move us.'

Through tears and clenched teeth, she looked at Dovid and shook her head.

'Please! Imma. I can't watch this. Move us!'

'No.' The word was forced out of her. 'I won't. Lose you!'

Dovid pressed his splayed hands to his head and paced around in desperation. How could she endure this just so they could be together? There had to be a solution. Just because Nietric and Aris were insisting this happen, didn't mean that it had to happen!

Dovid's hands went back to his own power then. His skin stopped swarming and the floor stopped spinning. Dovid looked around to see what was next, but Imma was still huddling in agony, her hands broken backwards and mutilated in pain.

'No,' Dovid said and forced his stubborn will onto the world. 'Just because you manipulate motion, Aris, doesn't mean that Imma's hands are broken.'

Imma's hands were not broken.

She looked up at Dovid in tears before looking back down to her mended hands. Dovid had no idea what was happening, but if it was his raw determined insistence that was doing it, then he wasn't going to let it go. He tried to help Imma to a stand but her muscles were too weak, so instead, he picked her up in his arms and started marching.

Imma hugged her face into his chest and she felt weightless in his arms. Dovid had no idea if he was going the right way, but tried to stay in as much the same direction that they were going before. He needed to stay determined. He would get them out of this damned maze and Aris wasn't going to hurt Imma anymore.

Before they reached the exit, there were times when faint traces of smell, or sound, or taste, or movement glided over them, but Dovid was fierce in his denial of it all. When a wall moved to block a passageway, Dovid walked through the wall. When the floor turned liquid and flowed down to a sinkhole, Dovid walked right over it. And when they reached the exit and the door opened showing Nietric on the other side, Dovid made it shut.

Imma watched as Dovid closed the door in Nietric's face and she laughed, even though he knew it must have hurt her to do it.

'Well, say one thing for his methods, but Nietric got you to use your inability.'

Dovid had to laugh with her at that.

'I still don't know what it is. Maybe it's just excessive stubbornness.'

'I don't think so,' Imma said, and she tried to let herself down from his arms. Dovid could tell she was still too tender to stand yet, so he sat down against a wall and held her in his lap. She smiled at their fleeting comfort and nestled her cheek into his. Dovid was happy to hold her like this for the rest of his life, but he knew that any minute now Nietric would open that door or Aris would try to hurt them again. Dovid tried to not let it ruin the happiness he was feeling for this frozen moment. The past or the future should hold no place in the present.

'Thank you, Imma,' he said instead.

'For what?'

'For not moving us. I mean, you should've moved us, because when I saw you in so much pain I couldn't ... well, it's just I'm happy now, that we're together, and if you had moved us, we mightn't be again for some time.'

She closed her eyes and breathed him in. 'They haven't found the pain yet that compares to how I feel when I'm not with you. Every time I move I get a new lifetime's worth of loneliness, so I'll always keep us together in these times. They'll have to kill us before I'll lose you.'

Dovid couldn't begin to comprehend how that must feel. How every time Imma moved, she would become that new person, but with every year of experience from her countless other times, all mixed in with the years of the new one. Maths was never his strongest subject but even he knew the multiples of years could be into the thousands by now.

'Imma, we can't keep doing this. We have to think of a plan.'

She opened her eyes and looked up into his. She kissed him and he forgot about everything else. All there was were her lips and his, her tongue and his, her body and his, all pressed together against the weight of the world. When she opened her eyes, the exit opened too, but it didn't stop them from looking only at each other.

'I have a plan,' Imma said, and she smiled.

· CHAPTER TEN ·

Naturally Chained

'And what, may I ask, is this plan?' Nietric stood with his hands behind his back, leaning forward with feigned scholarly interest. 'Is it to *move* again, as you have said? Because perhaps you would consider this: to you, Imma, you may have moved, but you and I here, we still exist. So you would be abandoning your previous self to unspeakable cruelty if you do decide to flee.'

Dovid frowned at that notion and Imma carefully removed herself from his embrace. They both stood up and faced Nietric. He knew he'd regret it, but Dovid felt like playing a few mind games of his own.

'If you think that's true, Nietric, then how do you know she hasn't already moved?'

When Nietric turned and looked at him, it felt like the man put his hands inside Dovid's flesh. It made Dovid retract back into himself in useless defence but he couldn't identify what had just happened.

'Oh I would *know*. But, young Dovid, let me see your conundrum and raise you a paradox. If Imma is free to flee to any alternate time of her pleasure and become mixed with the Imma there, then couldn't there be multiple Imma's all doing the same thing simultaneously. That at any one point there are perhaps a dozen new Imma's mixing right now with your own beloved one? So who do you care for, Dovid? Is it this Imma, or this one, or this one?' Nietric laughed and the jittering pain sent out a thousand piercing needles.

A doubt tried trickling its way into Dovid's stubbornness, but in answer Imma reached out and held his hand, interlocking her fingers with his. When Dovid turned and saw her looking at him, he knew the answer to Nietric's question. He loved all of Imma, every one.

'Oh now, we can't have this,' Nietric said gesturing towards their hands. 'Unchaperoned teenage intimacy? No, no.' He waved to the guards. 'Now that we've found out how to trigger your inability, Dovid, you do realise that I will have to hurt her more and more. But again, I will try not to be such a monster; I will try to hurt everyone you know with equal cruelty. Is that not a fair compromise? And it will be intriguing to find out who draws out the greatest response from you, but I think we have already discovered the answer to this.'

The guards stepped forward and pulled Dovid and Imma apart, dragging them away with their wrists pinned behind their backs. A different door in the room opened and Nietric arced his palm, bowing for them to go first. The guards herded Dovid and Imma through, and when the door closed behind, Dovid saw that Nietric hadn't followed. It was a brief but welcome respite, and since Dovid didn't count the smiling guards as real people, he felt confident that he could speak with Imma as if they were alone.

'Do you think we're going back to our islands?'

'No,' Imma said. 'He has a room where he can question us collectively. It looks like he's taking us there.' She was being dragged a few steps ahead of Dovid and she turned to look over her shoulder at him. 'That doesn't happen either, you know. What Nietric just said. There's only one me. Well, there are other me's, obviously, but my consciousness brings, I don't know, reality to them, I guess. So the other ones aren't real, they just could be real, and only become real when I'm there. Does that make sense?'

'But what if I couldn't move with you, and you moved to a parallel time? Wouldn't I be real anymore?'

'Not the you in my new time, no. I mean it would be you, of course, but to me, the only real you is the one you are now, the you from my real time. All the others only become real as memories to you, I guess.'

Dovid's brain ached.

'So when I move with you, I become the new me, get all their memories, and the memories from when I was here follow with me? The fake me becomes the real me.'

Imma laughed. 'Yes, but never the same way. For you, anyway. For me, it's always the same.'

Dovid decided it didn't really matter right now if he completely understood or not. They had bigger issues. He looked behind to make sure Nietric hadn't followed them, and then turned back to whisper to Imma. 'So what's your plan?'

'Not here. The next time we're alone I'll show you, but I can't show you unless I can touch you, and it will mean moving again, so I don't want to until there's no other choice. And I don't even know if it'll work, but there's not much else we can do.'

Dovid flushed at the thought of Imma touching him, and before his mind could race away with itself, they reached their destination. The stem they were following turned into a door, and the door turned into a room of other glass rooms. There were eight in total, four on each side, with a single bed at the back of each cubicle. Dovid amended that they probably weren't glass, but some stronger see-through plastic, and three of them had occupants, making them look very much like prison cells.

Lawrie was sitting on her bed in one of the cells, and there was another girl in the one next to her. The other girl was much older than everyone else, probably in her twenties, with golden red hair tied back behind her head. She was sitting serenely with her hands placed on her lap. Aris was in the cell directly across from her, a prisoner the same as the rest of them – even if he tried to pretend he wasn't by the way he was lounging on his bed. Lawrie waved youthfully at Dovid and Imma as they walked in, and Aris and the other girl didn't react to their arrival at all.

The smiling guards led Dovid to his cell, and Imma to the one right across from it, with Lawrie housed next to her. The cell adjoining Dovid's was empty, with Aris after that, and the two at the very end were empty as well, awaiting the next lucky youths to develop abnormal inabilities. Unless they were already occupied and Dovid just couldn't see them, which made him turn to the blank cell beside his.

'Phrey?'

'Hi Dovid,' the young boy's voice sounded back. 'How are you feeling now?'

'Don't worry about me, Phrey. I'm fine. But thanks for asking. What about you? Are you feeling better?'

'Me? I'm okay. I haven't had to do it in a while, so it's not as bad as when there's a lot. It gets worse then.'

Dovid just nodded and looked around as the smiling-faced guards left the room. There was still no sign of Nietric.

'Hi, Lawrie,' he said, waving to the thirteen-year-old. This brought a wide grin from her, and Dovid craned his neck further down the room. 'Hello, Aris.' Aris didn't look up, his hair hung down to cover his face. Turning to the last remaining prisoner, Dovid called down to her as well. 'Hello. We haven't met yet. I'm Dovid What's your name?'

The girl in her twenties with the golden hair didn't move. She remained exactly where she was, sitting stoically against their situation.

'That's L.B.' Lawrie said. 'She doesn't like to get to know the other rats. Says it interferes with when we have to torment each other. But she doesn't have to be like that with me! I don't get tested anymore because they're so completely afraid of me.'

'They're afraid of all of us,' Dovid said. 'Otherwise they wouldn't keep us locked up.' He started examining his transparent cell, walking around and touching the walls. Where the guards had closed the door there was nothing to be found, no line or joining, just the same smooth surface as the rest of the cube. While he was inspecting the see-through walls though, his eyes soon found Imma and couldn't leave.

'So what do they do to us here?' Dovid asked her.

'Nietric asks us questions, and if we don't answer, he hurts someone you care about,' Imma said.

'Yeah, so just answer the questions, dope,' Lawrie added.

'What's your inability, Dovid?' Phrey's transient voice made Dovid jump and he laughed at his own reaction.

'We still don't know, Phrey. I reckon it's pure stubbornness,' Dovid said and turned back to Imma. 'We've obviously discussed it before. What's our best guess?'

'Space is our best guess,' Imma said, but she didn't sound confident. Lawrie jumped off her bed at that one though.

'Hey! That's my thing! Look.' Lawrie held out her hand and a hole appeared in the cell. She beamed proudly and then hopped in and out of her cell a few times, before letting things go back to normal.

'Please, Lawrie,' Imma said softly. 'Don't do that.'

Lawrie threw herself back on her bed and folded her arms. 'Yeah, yeah, I blow up the world. But how can you know that this time I won't? This might be the time where I control it and kick everyone's asses for them!'

Aris started giggling at that and Lawrie stood up again, walking to the edge of her cell.

'Something funny, Aris? All that stupid long hair tickling you over there? I could cut it for you, ya know. From right here, cut it all off. Might cut your stupid head off with it, but I'm willing to try.'

'Is that what happened to *your* hair, little Lawrie?' Aris tittered back. 'Is that why you look like a *boy*?'

'Your hair and your head aren't the only things I could cut off, Aris. I could cut off your boy parts too, and see how much you giggle when I do that!'

'Lawrie,' Imma said. 'There's no point. The angrier you get, the funnier it is for him.' She grinned then, 'And besides, you did that before and he just bled out in seconds. You probably got both his femoral arteries.'

'Ha!' Lawrie was very pleased with that. 'Do you hear that Aris? I can make you female by cutting your femorals!'

Aris shook his head. 'Oh no, I don't think so. And even if it did happen once, I'm sure every other time you tried I just broke your little boy neck.'

'No way,' Lawrie said but turned back to Imma to double check. 'There's no way that long-haired jackass gets me before I get him. Right, Imma?'

'She's right, Aris. The only times Lawrie dies is when she does it herself and everyone and everything dies with her.'

Lawrie nodded with satisfaction and sat back down. 'That's right. I can destroy all of creation and all you can do is make people dizzy.'

Aris just giggled again and went back to his lounging. Dovid noticed that L.B. didn't move once during any of this and the closer he looked at her, he couldn't even see her blink. As amusing as the distractions were though, he had more important things to be considering. He needed to be alone with Imma so she could show him what her plan was. The door to his left opened then, and Nietric entered the room.

'Ah, all my children together!' Nietric clapped his hands and rubbed them together. 'I do love these family gatherings. Dovid, you have met everyone I trust? Even our little absentee?' He pointed to Phrey. 'Number 171278. I think what I love about our absent Phrey the most is the concept of his being. Take away the shape, size, and colour of a chair and what is the chair independent of its features? Similarly, take all the features of a Phrey away, and what even is he? It's just a pity that we can hear and feel him. Oh how I await the day where I find one of you who cannot be perceived by any sense.' He turned to Imma. 'Have I? In any of your false realities?'

The anger in Imma's eyes made her pale blue look like boiling water, but all she did was shake her head.

'Alas,' Nietric said and turned back to Dovid. 'I do still like to think of him as our own private black hole – if you'll allow me to share that term, of course, little Lawrie – because our Phrey will never allow light to escape his reach. Admitting that his skin is merely not light reflective would be far too boring, Dovid, don't you think?'

Nietric crossed his hands behind his back and marched up between the cells. 'You have also met Aris, number 384, my aspiring apprentice. I see great things in his future when it comes to pragmatically putting the needs of the world before the comforts of the few, but he still enjoys it a little too much to be trusted, don't you think? If he were to replace me, Dovid, I might be releasing an unspeakable evil unto the world.'

He spun to face L.B. 'This young woman, however, is much, much colder. Number 14379. So much *potential* energy in this one, and yet she remains so *inert*.' Nietric's resemblance of laughter resonated out of him at that, and for a moment Dovid just frowned in confusion until he remembered Imma saying something about L.B.'s inability being something to do with energy. Nietric kept going back down the stem.

'And little Lawrie 4143, to whom Imma has so warned me to be nice, and I sincerely believe she is right. And am I not nice to you, little Lawrie?' Lawrie said nothing but stuck out her tongue at Nietric as he walked on. 'Then we have your beloved Imma – number 22424 – who claims she can go anywhere and ends up nowhere. Constantly moving sideways while the rest of us are moving forward. One would think if she had all the time in the world, she could concoct a better fabrication of her inability.' Nietric spun back to face Dovid and spread his arms in grandeur. 'And here we have the best for last.'

'It's nice to be appreciated,' Dovid replied.

'Do not be so humble, young Dovid. You have created fire from a plastic wall, you have made yourself appear in different places, you have reversed the motion of Aris's manipulation, and from what I have over-heard you can travel *with* our darling Imma here?' Nietric cupped his hand over his mouth to whisper loudly at Dovid. 'I must apologise, but I have been eavesdropping a little on your private conversations.'

'So what's my inability?' Dovid asked, because maybe this wasn't such a bad thing. Maybe if Nietric helped Dovid discover the nature of his inability, he could use it to free them. The rotted flesh around Nietric's eyes twitched, however, and as always he knew what Dovid was thinking before even Dovid did.

'May I show you something, young Dovid?'

'Do you need my permission, hideous Nietric?'

Lawrie gasped at that, bringing her hands up to her mouth, and Dovid could hear Aris sniggering further up. Imma smiled sadly and Nietric took it all in.

'I do not need your permission, the same that I do not need to treat you with any pleasantry at all, if I so wish it. And, Dovid, I can be quite unpleasant.' Nietric flicked his fingers and the front walls of each cell became alive with colour.

Clusters of four screens appeared in each corner of the wall in front of Dovid, showing sixteen of the people he would have the closest relationships. Since Dovid didn't generally cultivate any human closeness with anyone, there were a few fellow historians who Dovid barely recognised, probably the damned top five that Dovid once obsessed about, but Mart was there, and his mother was there, and an older man who Dovid had never seen before, but he imagined it was his father. He could see the resemblance, even down to the shaven head – whether his father simply liked the simplicity of it too or else he was just bald. Imone was also there, and Dovid had lost track of whether this was a time where they had been sexual or violent with each other, but he had no other memories of anyone else he had physically interacted with, so it made sense for Nietric to select Imone. Feeling guilty about confusing his feelings for Imma with Imone in previous times, Dovid looked over to Imma now.

Imma was sitting in her cell, looking up at a single image on her screen. Every other cell had sixteen, so why did Imma only have one? Dovid moved to get a better look at it and as he did, he saw the image move with him. It took him a moment to recognise his own image on her screen. Imma had no one else in her life apart from him?

'Heart breaking, Dovid, isn't it?' Nietric whispered to him. 'Everyone our darling Imma has ever cared for has been cruelly tortured and killed over the years. She was my first you see. The innocent young toddler freely admitting to her extraordinary inabilities, my painstaking, time-consuming efforts to create human attachments for her as collateral, then her tumultuous rebellious years, and all that hard work wasted. I can proudly say it hurt me just as much as it hurt her to see all her connections so maliciously persecuted and murdered, but now, here *you* are, a gift! And with no time spent on my behalf; only a few lifetimes of false time from hers.'

The shock reality of their situation had postponed the impact of Nietric's voice, and it was that as well as everything else that took the legs out from under Dovid. He landed on his bed and his eyes kept darting from the screens on his wall, to Imma, to Nietric, and back. Nietric turned his attention to Dovid's screens also.

'You, young Dovid, were quite difficult too, let me not overlook. I have told the other Managers how we need to bring back the old-fashioned concepts of families and friends, if only to strengthen our power when we need to control the likes of you, but also because of exactly people like you, Dovid. You have taken the islands to an entirely new extreme. It was conceived as an answer to overpopulation, four segments to call your own, filtering people who share the same space down to limited excursions in the

Physical Leisure Segments. In your study of history, Dovid, were you not appalled at the alternative? So much traffic, so much queueing, so much anger that other lives were trying to exist as well as us! Swarms of people scurrying over each other to occupy the same space, do the same things at the same time? Disgusting. But then the islands created the likes you of, Dovid. Never leaving your island for seven years? Seven! Is that why she likes you? Because you are as solidarity a creature as she? Because you have both lived your lives in self-preferred captivity? But I am digressing from the objective of this little get-together.'

Nietric flicked his fingers again and the occupants of all sixteen screens began to writhe with pain. Dovid gripped the back of his head as he watched each person fall around in their own unique reaction to the agony being senselessly inflicted on them.

'Okay!'

Nietric cupped one hand over the destroyed dent of flesh where his ear should be, pretending not to hear, while the other hand flicked its fingers and the pain on the sixteen screens visibly increased.

'Okay, Nietric! That's enough! What do you want?'

'What do I want? Why I want to cause these people pain. Because I want to cause *you* pain, Dovid.' In whatever way Nietric was able to control the excruciating delivery of his own voice – his lipless, tongueless, toothless, vicious voice – Nietric multiplied it at that moment to make Dovid feel like his head would explode. 'I want to remind everyone here that *I* am in control! That *you* will do as I please, when it pleases me, and not hesitate for a single moment!'

The other cells became the same as Dovid's then. He could make out the screens in Phrey's cell, and hear the sobbing from its invisible occupant. He could see Lawrie stand up and rage against the images on her screen, screaming at Nietric that he said he wouldn't do this anymore. Dovid's vision was bleary with his own tears, but he thought he could see Aris covering his face, and see L.B. now with her eyes closed instead of open. Dovid looked at Mart spasm in a pain that he had no way of stopping, that he had no way of knowing why it was even happening. Dovid wanted to claw his own eyes out. He wanted to deform himself as much as Nietric so he couldn't see these horrors. He wanted to be rid of every sense he had if only to enjoy the absence of torment it might temporarily bring. He would gladly give up all feeling if it meant never experiencing anything like this! He looked to Imma.

'Stop!'

Dovid roared out his command and everything went still.

The first ones to move were the people on his screen, slowly gathering themselves back to stand, recovering from the pain that they in no way deserved. Dovid saw Lawrie stop pacing and stare at him in accusation. He saw Imma smiling at him, and then he saw Nietric. Six rotted holes on his pitted skull where there should have been features, each one scrutinising him.

'My, my, aren't you full of surprises, young Dovid. Bringing more questions than answers, like how your command could cause the pain to stop in eighty different islands, each one separated to avoid inabilities affecting them in exactly this way.' Nietric tilted his head to the side and his featureless face twitched in a smile. 'But you remember what I said about our game, don't you, young Dovid? He who gives more questions than answers; loses.'

Nietric flicked his fingers at Imma and she dropped to the ground in the same pain as the people on the screens. Nietric watched Dovid with great intensity as this happened and waited to examine what exactly Dovid would do. Dovid almost didn't want to give him the satisfaction, but he couldn't watch Imma in pain.

'Stop!'

He roared it the exact same as before, with the exact same intensity of feeling and determination. But nothing happened.

'Stop!' He roared louder, and fiercer. He needed Imma to be out of pain even more than he needed those eighty other people to be. Some of those had been family, and some he cared for, but none as much as he cared for Imma. But still, nothing happened. No matter how much stubborn willpower Dovid put behind it, he could not cause Imma's pain to stop.

'Stop, Nietric, please!' Dovid begged and pressed his hands up against the wall in desperation, but Nietric did not move. Dovid dropped to his knees in surrender, anything to stop Imma's pain. 'Please, Nietric, I'll do whatever you want, just stop hurting her!'

'No,' Nietric said and shook his head. 'I will keep hurting her until you can reliably show me your inability. So far it never seems to work the same way twice. So you must stop this, Dovid, and if you can't then it is you who is causing this pain.'

'Please!' Dovid's eyes burned with tears and he couldn't bring himself to look at Imma in agony, but he had to concentrate. If he focused whatever it is he could do, he could stop this pain. But nothing was happening. 'I can't do it, Nietric! Please, I'll do anything you want, just stop!'

'I want you to stop her pain, Dovid! That is what I want, so do it!' Nietric was roaring now and his voice made everyone in the room cower in pain.

'I can't do it!' Dovid shouted back, and almost didn't hear the shout that followed.

'But I can!'

Lawrie opened the air in front of her cell and walked right out of it. Dovid saw Nietric's fingers flicker and all of the walls turned into images of sixteen people who Dovid didn't know.

'Get back in your cell, Lawrie, or I will kill them all, one by one,' Nietric said, calmly now, trying to defuse this situation. Dovid saw that Imma had stopped trembling and a flood of relief washed over him.

'Set them all free, Nietric, or I'll kill you,' Lawrie said back.

Doors opened on either side of the room and a mass of smiling-faced guards rushed in with guns. Lawrie showed her hesitation, looking from one end of the room to the other, and then to her family and friends. She bit her lip and while everyone stood waiting, Dovid could see Nietric's face twitch with a smile and his fingers flicked one more time.

One of the people on the screens fell lifeless to the floor.

Lawrie stared at the dead woman for a few seconds and then turned her gaze to Nietric.

'I have tried to be nice to you, Lawrie, but—'

Lawrie interrupted Nietric by slicing off both his hands. An explosion of gunfire sounded but it looked to Dovid as if Lawrie caught the bullets from either side and threw them at the guards on the opposite end. Aris's cell exploded in blood at the same moment and Dovid wondered if he had just tried to stop Lawrie from what she was doing. L.B. was standing up now, with her hands pressed against her cell wall, but by the way she looked at Aris's cell, she must've been thinking better of interfering. The guards were all down, yet Nietric was still standing, still smiling in that grotesque twitch he had in place of a real one.

'Oh, Lawrie, what have you done?' Nietric's voice rang out powerfully, causing Lawrie to flinch, but then she clapped her hands and cut off his head.

Still the voice echoed throughout the room … 'Tsk, tsk, Lawrie, such violence, such waste of—'

Lawrie screamed and Nietric's body disappeared, causing an absence of space and reality in his place. She scrambled back from what she'd done, and Dovid looked up to see that the hole in her cell had grown too. It was now touching the ceiling and floor, distorting both with disintegrated particles, warping the room with its dissolution of space.

'I'm sorry, I'm sorry!' Lawrie looked around in panic. 'Imma! How do I stop it? How do I stop?'

Imma opened her mouth to answer but then, where Nietric had been, the absence of space released a breath, and the entire world was swallowed in.

• CHAPTER ELEVEN •

Habit of Association

Dovid woke up in his island and ran his hands along the stubble of his head. He disengaged the education charger and glided his hands from his forehead to the back of his neck one more time. He blinked his eyes awake, licked the dryness away from his lips, and breathed deeply in through his nose. Visual, Auditory, Gustatory, Olfactory, Tactile, where would he fit in the most? Tactile maybe?

'Good morning, Wall,' Dovid said as he sat up, taking out his nutrition and sanitation chargers.

The wall appeared as a smiley face with an old-fashioned sleeping cap and candle. 'Good morning, Dovid. Did you have sweet dreams?'

'I never remember my dreams, but I do like your sleeping cap. We should bring those back. Would I be able to order one?' Dovid stood up and stretched his arms, swinging them side to side and then up and down. He rolled his shoulders a few times too before starting with his morning push-up routine.

The smiley face turned into a calculator-face for a moment, before replying, 'You have the money, Dovid, and you haven't ordered anything from Management in a while, so I can order it now and it will be here within the hour.'

'Great, thanks Wall.' Dovid finished his push-ups and started doing stomach crunches. 'Can you order a second one too, and have it sent to Mart? He'd get a kick out of that sort of thing.'

'Consider it kicked, Dovid.' The wall gave itself a boot and drop-kicked the sleeping cap out of view. 'Should I send one to Imone also?'

Dovid jumped up from his morning exercises and walked over to the shower corner. 'No, I have something better in mind for her, but I'm not telling you yet, because you'll only annoy me about it every day until I give it to her.'

The wall dropped its jaw with indignation and looked around wildly to see if anyone else heard Dovid's outrageous accusations. It stayed quiet though and let Dovid finish his shower in peace, so as an equally peaceful peace offering, when Dovid put on his emoto-shirt, he set it to the emotion of "my wall's alright." This cheered it up to no end, and the smiley face turned into a super smiley face, with exclamation points instead of eyes and fireworks instead of a mouth. Dovid gave it a wink as he left his Personal Quarter and the wall winked back.

'Call Mart please, my good man,' Dovid said as he entered his Social Quarter. His chair gave a groan as he jumped down on it, and he spun around once before Mart's giant eyeless face appeared.

'Good morning, little brother, what's new in the world of history?'

'Ha. History isn't exactly about the new, Mart. But then again, neither is philosophy.'

'That's not true, in fact, that's my latest job. I have to help decipher the new through the joys of determinism.'

'That's the cause and effect theory right?'

'It's not just a theory, Dovid. It actually works.'

Dovid laughed. 'So you can predict the future based on the past? That right there is a contradiction in its purest form, big brother.'

Mart knew Dovid was only trying to rile him up, but he still felt the need to defend his work. 'Ad absurdum it all you want, history-boy, but if you can disprove determinism, then away you go.'

'Easy, so everything has a cause, and every cause has an effect, and because of this, you think you can predict the future. But to do that accurately, you'd have to go back to the very start of history and work upwards from there, needing to know every cause for every effect, since they all affect each other, to prove your theory's consistency. And what would be your first cause for the very first effect, anyway? Because a god-proof would be pretty cool.'

'First of all, we don't need to go back to the start. We only need to use probability on everything right now and work from there. And second of all, I have a first cause: big bang. Done. Boom.'

'Mart, you can't both know where something is in a single point of time and also know where it's going, because you've only got it in a single point in time, dummy. And what's your cause for the big bang? Because remember they did science in history too, flat universe, zero net total energy, how can anything come from nothing?'

'Simple. The universe expanded too far and imploded into itself creating a new universe banging out the other side.'

'Is "banging out" the scientific term for that?'

'No, it's my term. But I think that's quite enough about my work. What are you doing that's so great?'

'Well, I'm identifying the historical concepts that had valid functions and working on theses to reintegrate. In fact, there's one such thesis on its way to your island today so be sure to contemplate hard on its profoundness.'

'I like it. But what kinds of historical concepts are we lacking in today's society, because I mean I'm no historian, but I think Management has pretty much fixed all the problems. No war, no crime, no poverty, no sickness, no hunger, no natural disasters, everyone has everything they need and can do anything they want to do.'

'There are no natural disasters because there is no nature anymore, and I'm not saying everything isn't perfect, because life actually did look way too hard back before the islands, but one concept I've been working on is family.'

'That's us, little bro.'

'Yeah, but developing it. Mother, father, all our brothers, and all our sisters, even our cousins, aunts, uncles, the lot.'

'What's a cousin? Are these all blood relatives? Dovid, your blood brothers and sisters alone are probably in triple figures. Who has time to have relationships with all those people! No one would ever get anything done.'

'I'm still working on the details, but I'm going to start by calling my father today.'

'I'm telling you it's a bad idea, little bro, nothing but disappointment. But let me know how it goes anyway. You still want your philosophy for the day?'

'What if I give you one? Just to help with your determinism future-casting. You know Hume, right? Because he says causation is just made up in our heads for us to make sense of the world. He says the problem of induction is that we could learn something tomorrow to completely disprove anything that we think we know right now. So just because the sun has risen every day before, doesn't mean it will rise tomorrow and all that, namely because there's no sun anymore.'

'There's still a sun, Dovid, and it still rises. And Hume also says that causation can't be proved or disproved, and his main point, if you really are trying to lecture *me* about philosophy, is that amid all your philosophy, Dovid, be still a man. We have to live our everyday lives with what we use to live in that life. And one example of that is: causation! So you can try to live *your* life without causality, and I'll continue living mine as if it does exist. Deal?'

Dovid just laughed at him. He loved when Mart got passionate about nonsense. 'So what's my philosophy for the day?'

'Fine, let's stick with David Home-Hume, if you're so smart about him. Think on this, what sense of self do we have beyond any single moment's sensations, merely linked by memories? Is there an identifiable-self independent to this? Can you look for the chain separate to the links that make it up? Riddle, riddle, little brother. Let me know how it goes with your father.'

'Later, Mart,' Dovid waved and Mart disappeared. 'Call my mother, please. Jean 21605.'

The wall appeared as a smiley face in a green costume riddled with question marks on it. 'Your mother, Dovid? You only call your mother once a year.'

'Yup, I'm changing the world, Wall. Bringing the past back to the present, so change with it or get left in the future.'

His wall blinked out and the face of Dovid's mother appeared instead. She looked so much like Mart. She had the same curling hair, the same dark skin, even the same scar tissue around her missing eyes.

'Hello?' she asked, not recognising Dovid straight away because she was pulling up his life as she spoke.

'Hi, Jean, it's me, Dovid, I'm one of your sons.'

'Oh hello, Dovid, it's lovely to hear from you again. We spoke last year, didn't we? It's always nice to see how my sons and daughters are doing.' She was skimming down through his life a little too quickly to be really interested though. 'Haven't you got your inability yet? How strange. I got mine when I was twelve, and

I'm sure most of your brothers and sisters got theirs around that time too.'

'I think my inability is not being able to do anything the same as other people.'

His mother frowned and smiled, not sure what he meant but knowing he must be joking. 'Well, it's lovely to see you anyway. So what's prompted this call?'

'I'm just looking to get to know my family a little better.'

'Really? But you have all the information you need on the walls. What else is there to know?'

Dovid laughed gently. He didn't want her to think he was mocking her, but it was nice to see where he got his anti-social tendencies from. 'Yeah, I know, but I just thought it would be nice to talk once in a while. I'm going to ring my father too in a minute. I've never spoken to him before.'

'Your father ... hmmm.' He could see her flicking through his life again now to remember who his father had been and see if it jogged up any memories. 'Oh yes, I remember him. He was nice enough. He's been busy since I've met him. Did you see how many children he's fathered? There really should be a limit. We'll end up with the same overpopulation problems as before the islands if he keeps this up.'

Dovid pulled up his father's life to see exactly how many was too many.

'Wow. Mart wasn't far off when he said triple digits.'

'Mart? He's one of my sons as well, isn't he?'

'Yep, he and I are close. We talk every day in fact, something I was thinking I could try with other family members, if you're interested?'

'Every day? But what would we talk about?'

'That's all part of it. We have to put effort into it to keep it interesting. But, hey, I just wanted to start things off today, and if it doesn't work out, it doesn't work out. Okay? I'll let you go now. Do you want me to pass anything on to Ocra for you?'

'Who's Ocra?'

Dovid laughed again. 'Ocra 470; my father.'

'Oh,' Jean laughed too, since his father's life was probably still up on her screen. 'No, no, but we can try talking more if that's something you want to do. I guess I just don't understand it.'

'Understanding things is overrated. It was nice talking to you, Jean. Call you in a few days.'

'Okay, goodbye, Dovid.'

Well at least she remembered Dovid's name. But still, that took a lot more energy out of him than he thought it would, and he wasn't sure if he was able for a similar or worse call with his father. Dovid decided he wasn't.

'Call Imone, please.'

The wall appeared as a loveheart with two black eyes and a bust lip. Walls were weird, but maybe his relationship with Imone was equally weird. Her blacker-than-black haired image arrived and Dovid smiled.

'Good morning, Dovid. Looking for an early morning beating?'

'Hey, the last time I counted, it was only three-two to you.'

'Yeah, but that was the best of five, you moron.'

'Best of five? No way, first to five. I can still kick your curvy ass three more times and win this.'

'Curvy ass? Well, how can a girl turn down charm like that? I'm game if you're game, a good fight *is* the best way to start the day. It's just a pity I'll only be fighting you.'

'Hey! I've been getting better, and apart from the last time, I won the two before that, remember.'

Imone blew him a kiss and cut out.

'Don't believe her, Wall. I'm going to win this time.'

The wall gave itself more and more bruises until it got knocked unconscious and then put a smiley face version of Imone standing over it in victory.

'That's not very helpful to my self-esteem you know.'

'Not as helpful as getting beaten to a pulp by your girlfriend?' the wall answered back.

'That's it. I've had enough.' Dovid got up and put on his shoes before leaving his island. Shoes were a necessary part of fighting Imone because she had a particular attraction for hurting his toes. He set his emoto-shirt to "furious warrior" too as he stormed down the stems. He would totally win this time. Yes, Imone was a way better fighter, but he had been practising super hard.

The more he thought about how good Imone was though, the worst he felt about his chances, and the short trip to the Physical Leisure Segment managed to erode most of Dovid's fake confidence. He kept up his bluster as he walked past the other people hanging around, but when he went into the Violence Quarter, his bluster completely vanished. He looked around nervously for Imone, and when the wall popped up beside him, Dovid jumped about a foot into the air.

'Welcome, Dovid, you are deemed physically fit for violent activity. Please attach your fight brace and then choose your violent status from numbers one to ten thousand:

1. Just here for exercise
2. Just here to practice
3. Just here to kick some ass
4. Just here for serious training
5. Just here for senseless violence
6. Just here to vent my murderous rage
7. Just here to get beaten up by Imone ...

'Hey! That's not a real option, is it?'

The wall put on a laughing smiley face. 'Your wall asked me to do that.'

'You walls are such unholy jerks!'

'Hey, Dovid,' Imone said as she walked in and the smiley face zipped out of sight.

Dovid turned to greet her and was weirdly taken aback at how she looked. She looked wrong.

'Hi, ah, Imone, I was just ... arguing with the wall.'

She smiled. 'They do like to antagonise you more than anyone else.' She picked up a fight brace and put it on, the quick flash of yellow the only sign she now had a skin-tight force field around her. Dovid reached down and put his own on but couldn't stop trying to figure out what was wrong with Imone. She looked great, of course, he had memories of her muscular figure doing way more enjoyable things than fighting, but she still seemed wrong. She looked too harsh, her hair too dark, her eyes too hard.

'Have you ever tried your hair blonde, Imone?'

She arched an eyebrow at that and grabbed a bunch of her jet-black hair, revealing some of the scarring over her missing ears. 'Have you seen how dark this hair is, Dovid? Med-tech isn't exactly bothering to figure out how to turn black into white, but I can look into it if that's what gets you going.' She gave his crotch an unnecessarily forceful slap and it was pure luck that he had his fight brace already attached. Her playful smile made him forget about his worries though.

'Save it for the fight room, lady, and maybe for a little after the fight too.'

'Oh? It's like that, is it? You've decided we have time for that too?'

'Well, I intend on beating you quickly to make the time, Imone.'

'Right, well I intend on beating you senseless so you won't even know what time is. Come on.'

They walked to the first available fight room and Imone set the door to private, so they wouldn't be seen or interrupted. Then she turned around and punched Dovid square in the nose, laughing as she did it.

The field from the fight brace stopped his nose from smashing open and spraying blood everywhere, but it didn't stop his eyes from tearing over, or stop Dovid from squeaking with pain. He barely had time to bring his guard up to stop a follow-up punch, so he skipped backwards to get some room and Imone seemed happy to let him go – for now. When it came down to it, force fields touching force fields didn't feel all that different from electrons touching electrons. Except maybe that force fields were real and electrons were just a theory – no one had ever seen or measured an electron, after all, too small to even know how small they actually were.

'Dirty shot,' Dovid said and started carefully making his way back towards her.

Imone spread her hands out to agree that she was indeed a dirty girl, but brought them back to a guard again as she lashed out to kick his knees. Dovid lifted his foot in time and kicked it out to get her while she was off balance. Imone was never off balance though and she grabbed Dovid's foot and twisted his ankle to pull him to the ground. From there she gave him two punches in the groin and landed her knee down on it too for good measure. As always, in times like these, Dovid wondered why the fight brace needed to communicate pain without injury in such a startlingly accurate manner.

Imone was never one for wasting time in letting Dovid mourn the abuse of his privates, so when she got up she aimed a kick straight at his stomach. Dovid was barely able to roll out of the way, only to receive a second kick in his back. Still on the ground, he tackled her feet and pulled, forcing her to land on her side and hopefully wind her. He scrambled on top of her and punched her three times in the right breast, twice with his fist and the last with his elbow. He got up before she could respond and he laughed while he retreated. Imone hated it when he punched her in the breasts.

'You think that's so funny, don't you, Dovid,' she said as she got back up.

'Just as funny as you beating the hell out of my balls, Imone.'

That made her smile too, and they ran back in to restart the brawl. Dovid jumped up into the air to use his body weight against her, but Imone had plans of her own and had already skidded to the ground hoping to kick his legs out from under. The result was they missed each other, but Dovid landed on his feet and was able to turn around quicker. He was about to thunder down a knee strike to her exposed back when Imone held out her hands in surrender. Confused, Dovid craned his neck down to see if she was injured, because the fight braces were supposed to stop that from happening. And just as that thought hit him, so did Imone. She spun around and clobbered him in quick succession in the temple and the jaw, all the places where Dovid liked to get knocked unconscious. It must have happened too, because the next he thing remembered was waking up with Imone standing smugly above him.

'Four-two to me,' she said, far too proudly.

'Dirty wins shouldn't count,' Dovid said and looked at the red light on his fight brace indicating the loss.

'I use everything at my disposal, Dovid, and your old-fashioned protectiveness over women is just one of the many weapons I have.'

She turned off her fight brace and sat on top of him then, turning his off too. 'But I secretly like it. It just shows you care.'

Imone kissed him while Dovid was still busy trying to regain consciousness, but he bravely set himself to the task of kissing back all the same. The room was privately locked, and Imone was probably looking to make it up to Dovid for winning with such an underhanded trick. So Dovid needed to get back to full awareness and quick.

'Dovid,' Imone said in between kisses. 'I really like you. You're so different to everyone else.'

'I love you too, Imma.'

The kissing stopped. Imone pulled back and frowned at him. What did he say? Was it the "L" word? Why did he even say that? There was no such thing as love anymore.

'Who's Imma?'

Oh. Imone was looking more and more angry as he didn't answer, but Dovid's mind was spiralling way back from his current situation. He remembered Imma. How could he ever have forgotten her? That was why Imone had looked wrong earlier, because she wasn't Imma. Anything he thought he ever felt for Imone was just his confused memories trying to reconcile his real feelings for Imma with this false reality.

'I'm sorry, Imone, I ...'

Imone got up and sighed. 'It doesn't matter. I knew you were different, but, you're right. It doesn't matter if you're seeing other people, because maybe I should too. I clearly need a better partner, for fighting and for, well, what do you see this Imma for?'

Dovid stood up too. He felt bad for Imone, but the reality of Imma's circumstances was dwarfing all other considerations. She was in a Special Sector right now, with others like her, all getting tortured by Nietric whenever it pleased him.

'Imone, I'm sorry, I do care for you, but I love Imma. She's ...'

The tears in Imone's eyes suddenly didn't make them seem so hard and the emotion on her face didn't make her seem so harsh. Dovid could blame his distorted memories for so much, but he couldn't blame anyone but himself for this. He was responsible for this hurt. But when Imone rushed out of the room, Dovid didn't go after her. He had to get back to Imma.

Going over to the wall, his mind raced for the quickest solution and found it. 'Wall, call Nietric.'

Surprisingly, a few different people were called Nietric, but the real one was easy to spot among the other pictures. So he selected the only skinless, featureless, humanless one and Nietric's wreck of a face appeared. He examined Dovid for a moment before speaking.

'Yes? Can I help you, young man?'

Dovid needed to find the fastest way to get arrested again, without going too far and getting himself shot, so he decided to answer with:

'Nietric, my name is Dovid and I study history. There's a painting from the late nineteenth century called *The Scream*, showing a featureless monstrosity. Do you know it? Well, I just wanted to call you to say that you look like that, except instead of paint, you look like you're made out of rotted flesh smeared with shit. And I also know about Imma, and Phrey, and Lawrie, and Aris, and L.B., and I'm just like them, so come and get me you disgusting freak.'

• CHAPTER TWELVE •

Lawgiver to Nature

Nietric didn't come and get Dovid. Instead, he sent four of his smiling helpers to do the job for him. Dovid was still in the Violence Quarter when they arrived and he still had his fight brace on, so he had to quash the urge to attack them, wondering if the protective field would stop bullets the way it stopped punches. But Dovid wanted to be cooperative this time. He wanted to negotiate with Nietric to be allowed spend more time with Imma, and he was almost relieved when he was taken to the nearest Transit and saw Nietric on board.

'I must say, young Dovid, it is quite rare that I encounter someone so happy to see me.' Nietric stood up as Dovid and his four escorts filed into the moving room. The Education Sector had been suspiciously empty as he was marched through it, no one around to see the secret police their perfect society secretly possessed. In the Transit, each of the guards took their position in front of a door, and before Dovid could take his seat across from Nietric, the man grabbed him by the arm to pull him closer. 'So please do tell me, young Dovid, *why* are you so happy to see me?'

Dovid had never been this close to the monster before, and it took two attempts before he could answer. 'Because I know you can help me. I know that despite your methods, everything you do is for the betterment of us all.'

Nietric's empty eye sockets bored into Dovid, and Dovid's mind tried to create more sentences that might appease this beast, but he was too horrified. Nietric brought his terrible face closer again to Dovid's, and for a petrifying minute, Dovid thought the man was going to kiss him. He couldn't contemplate those juddering lipless wrecks touching him, and even though Nietric didn't kiss him, what he did was just as bad. He slowly brought his other hand up to Dovid's face and gently brushed the tips of his ravaged fingers against Dovid's cheeks. It felt like putrid sandpaper was being brushed against his skin and Dovid had to close his eyes to hide from the reality of it. He was trembling all over now as Nietric's putrid skin explored Dovid's face, caressing from his cheeks to his jawline before focusing on his lips. Dovid thought he knew how frightened he was of Nietric before, but each time they met the man found new ways to penetrate Dovid and abuse his deepest fears.

Nietric abruptly released Dovid and pushed him away before taking his seat and crossing his legs. He looked up at Dovid as if nothing had just happened, and motioned for him to sit, mimicking confusion at why he was still standing. Dovid was glad to be off his feet, and his hands gripped the edge of the chair tightly. He needed to regain control of this situation. Nietric had already gained too much advantage and Dovid needed to be able to bargain.

'Shall we play a game, Nietric?' Dovid almost wept at how steady he was able to make his voice sound.

'No,' Nietric replied and continued to stare at Dovid.

'But I think you'll like this game. The loser is the one to ask the most questions, but you must always ask a question. Do you know this game?'

Nietric didn't respond for a while. When he did speak, it was a question, but Dovid didn't know if he was playing the game or not.

'How do you know about Imma, Phrey, Lawrie, L.B. and Aris?'

'I have an inability that has allowed me to meet them before. Would you like to know what my inability is?'

'I think I would. What is it?'

'I don't know.' Dovid saw Nietric shift in irritation before he added, 'But I can tell you how to find out?'

'Is that a question? Very well then, do enlighten me, young Dovid, but as you seem to think you know me so intimately, may I divulge that I quickly become bored with games. And when I am bored, I move on, discarding what it is that has bored me.'

'Okay,' Dovid said and took a breath. He was inviting pain and death onto other people by doing this, but Nietric was likely to do that anyway. 'You've managed to draw out my inability before by hurting the people that I care about.' Dovid hesitated again. 'By hurting one person in particular that I care about the most – by hurting Imma.'

'Please don't tell me your inability is time fabrication too, because that would be quite boring.'

'No, but my inability means that when she moves time aside, I can go with her. That's how we've done this before.'

'And is there some devious reason you're being so honest with me, Dovid? Or do you really want me to hurt your beloved Imma?' Nietric leaned forward with interest then. 'Has she scorned you, Dovid, in one of your parallel trysts? Who did she scorn you with, I wonder. Was it me?' Nietric began twitching with laughter and despicable visions of all the ways Nietric could hurt Imma cascaded unwanted through his mind. This was a dangerous risk Dovid was taking, but if he could get close enough to touch Imma, then it could all be worth it.

'No. The reason I'm telling you this, the two reasons really, is one: that I want to understand what my inability is, and two: that in exchange for cooperating with you, I have a request.'

Nietric sat back and folded his arms. 'How interesting. And what pray tell, are your demands of me and my generous nature?'

'It's not a demand, Nietric, it's a request and an idea. We can work together, drawing out the truth of my inability, and the only way you've consistently done it before is by hurting the people I'm close too. So let me get closer to Imma. Let me spend one hour a day alone with her. Let us have that time together, and we can see how much faster it makes your tests.'

'You wish for me to give you some fleeting happiness to make the deprivation more striking? Well, I suppose when you phrase it like that, then my answer is no.'

'Why not?'

'I guess the world just doesn't work that way. And besides, I like saying no.'

'You like knowing things more. And with people like Imma and Lawrie living in it, no one really knows how the world works anymore. Don't you ever wonder, Nietric, where the senses go? You told me before that you believed I could show you the answer. You said that I could save the world.'

Nietric hadn't exactly said that, but how was this Nietric to know what he did or didn't say in an alternate time. The Nietric of this time was considering Dovid's proposal now though. It was difficult to admit, but perhaps spending more time with Nietric was becoming an advantage. Dovid could begin to know the twisted mind of the man and use it – if any sane person could ever fully understand the workings of a madman.

'I think we understand each other after all, young Dovid, don't we?' Nietric leaned forward again, like a predator about to pounce. 'Take your lovely Imma, for example. The other Managers, they are always trying to use her to go back. Back! Absurd. They think if they can get a perfect specimen from an earlier time then we could cure this *affliction* of ours.' He clawed his fingers down his face as he said that last part. 'They think we are rotting, but I know we are evolving. We are the lawgivers to our reality and I know that we are progressing beyond it yet have not the capacity to conceive of our own supremacy, trapped within the laws we have insisted upon ourselves. Take my humble self, yes I have upgrades implanted into my body for the more mundane of inabilities, sight, sound, taste, *touch* ...' he trailed off and stared at Dovid for a few disturbing moments as he said that, 'But my greatest gift, of course, is *this*.'

That last word "this" caused more pain inside Dovid than anything Nietric had ever said to him before. He was so focused on getting Nietric to agree to his request, and so panicked by this new attention Nietric was putting on him, that Dovid hadn't realised that his voice had been normal up until then. No echoes, no merging of shouts and whispers, no dismantling pain violating his core, just a normal voice and he hadn't noticed. Nietric stood up and walked closer, the pain in his voice amplified with every sentence and every step.

'You think you can trick me, Dovid, and you are wrong. You think you are cleverer than me, Dovid, and you are wrong. You think you can somehow survive the suffering that I have in store for you, Dovid.' He crouched down until his face was pressed against Dovid's ears, the feel of his poisonous breath trickling down the back of Dovid's neck. 'And you are *wrong*.'

Dovid jerked away and hunched over, his whole body shuddering. Nietric remained where he was and the door to the Transit opened. They had reached their destination and it was time to leave, but Dovid was breathing erratically now, needing to swallow every second breath, wondering if he had just condemned all the lives of this time to a much worse fate. He would have to try again. He would have to ask Imma to move them and hope that he would remember quicker next time because whatever Nietric was in this time, he was worse than any other. Dovid's plan had failed.

'I will agree to your request, young Dovid.'

Dovid blinked. He did not think he heard Nietric correctly. The pain was gone again, this Nietric seemingly able to turn it off and on as the other Nietric's refused to do, but there was something wrong about the voice that agreed. Dovid stood up and nodded, hesitantly.

'Thank you.'

Nietric leaned in again and whispered as if they were two conspirators. 'I don't suppose, I'm allowed to sit in with you and your beloved Imma, while you have this *intimate* time, am I?'

'I'd like to be alone with her if that's alright. You can watch, I guess, on the cameras.'

'Thank you, Dovid, I would like that. Perhaps I will watch.'

Dovid wondered if this Nietric was just completely insane, and not the normal psychotic-cruel version of insanity the others had. He knew there was some terrible catch planned to this deal, the same way Nietric probably knew that Dovid must have some unspoken scheme of his own underway too. But so long as Dovid got to be alone with Imma, then it should be okay. He was putting a lot of trust into the plan Imma claimed to have, but he trusted her more than he trusted anything else, reality included. Two of the smiling-faced guards began marching out of the Transit and Nietric nodded that Dovid should follow.

They passed through what Dovid imagined was the Management Sector before Nietric altered the walls to gain entry to the Special Sector. Memories were coming easier to Dovid now, and he hoped that extreme fear or other strong negative emotions weren't the only triggers for his inability. He remembered the last time he came to Special Sector he had somehow opened every island door. The time before that, the doors had turned to liquid and flooded the stem. Another time they had walked down the stem and ended back in the Transit, unable to leave it. And one other time Dovid was partially able to recall … was when he and Nietric had … shifted perceptions? No, that couldn't have happened. Yet

Dovid remembered being able to stare at himself as if he was looking out from Nietric's lack of eyes. That last memory almost made Dovid crumble, but he needed to focus. He needed to not cause any malfunctions with reality. He needed to not give any excuse for Nietric to go back on his venomous word.

When they stopped outside an island door, Dovid held his breath. He knew it may very well be the door to his own island, but by the feel of Nietric's amused demeanour, he hoped it was going to be Imma's. Memories abandoned him then as he tried to recall the last time they had held each other, the last time they had been alone. The door in front of them opened and Nietric gave his theatrical bow for Dovid to enter.

The stem was the same as any Special Sector island, the Professional Quarter on his right, the Leisure Quarter down past it, with the absent Social Quarter across from that, leaving the Personal Quarter as the first door he came to on his left. The door opened for him and revealed Imma inside, her face a fight of joy and fear as she watched Dovid enter her room, followed by Nietric and his guns. Dovid wanted to hug her, or catch her hand, to touch her in some way the minute her image touched his eyes, but he would wait until Nietric had left. Imma's eyes darted with similar thoughts, moving from Dovid, to Nietric, to the guns, waiting for what was to happen. It seemed a lifetime before Nietric broke the tension.

'My beloved Imma, may I introduce you to young Dovid.'

Nietric watched Imma for her reaction, but she answered honestly with a soft, 'We've met before.'

Nietric clapped his hands. 'Ah yes, how could I forget. Well, dear Imma, I fear I have sold you to young Dovid here. We have agreed that he will help me in my studies of inabilities in exchange for time with your supple young self. All he asks in return is that I torture you quite cruelly afterwards, so I feel we are all of us winners in this, yes?'

Imma wrapped her arms around her body but her pale eyes showed her strength as she nodded at Dovid. She trusted him. She had no reason to trust that Dovid remembered anything, and every reason to assume that Nietric was planning something horrific, yet she trusted Dovid unconditionally the same as he trusted her.

Nietric's hand cupped underneath Dovid's chin and turned him around to face him.

'You have your hour to do with her as you wish, young Dovid, and although I shall be intensely chaperoning you, please do not feel that you need to restrain yourself in any way for fear of scarring my beautiful eyes.' Nietric kept hold of Dovid as he moved his featureless head to examine every part of Dovid's face one more time, before finally turning and leaving without another word.

Dovid and Imma waited until Nietric and his goons had left the island, the door locking behind them, before they ran to each other and embraced. This was the first time in a long time that Dovid could remember a reunion where they both knew each other fully. Imma felt it too, because she began laughing and sobbing at the unexpected happiness of it all. Dovid pulled back from the hug and kissed her, his hand brushing her cheek and combing through her hair, while her hands clutched his back, pulling him tighter against her. If he trusted Nietric not to double cross him at any stage, Dovid would have stayed like that for longer, but he made himself stop.

'What do you remember?' Imma asked as they stood back from each other a little. Her eyes moved around drinking in every part of his face with such affection that it served to cleanse Dovid of Nietric's earlier attention.

'I remember the last time we were in the maze with Aris, and you wanted to explain something to me. Something that could help us.' He was hesitant to say too much for fear of Nietric listening, but Imma's face dropped for a fraction of a heartbeat before recovering. Dovid noticed though. 'What's wrong?'

Imma hung her head, preferring not to say, but it wasn't like them not to be honest with each other so she smiled and said, 'Nothing important. It was just, it's been weeks since we were in the maze with Aris, and we've seen each other since, so I was just ... no, it doesn't matter. You're here now, and yes, we should try what I said.'

Dovid frowned. 'Weeks? And we've been together since? I thought I remembered it all this time, but are you saying we've already tried what you said?' Dovid was falling into despair that this time was going to be worse after all and they would have to move again, and if they did then it could be weeks or months before he remembered seeing Imma again.

Imma stepped closer and touched his cheek. 'No, it's fine. We've only seen each other in the group room. We've never been alone. We haven't been able to try what we're about to try.'

Dovid's mind flew to imagining trying something that she couldn't possibly have meant. As plans went, it would be a great plan, but he knew she would have to mean something else. There were more important things than succumbing to their physical urges, but for the life of him, Dovid couldn't recall what exactly those might be.

'He'll probably come in as soon as he hears this, but I just want to explain what it is we're going to do, in case it doesn't work.' Imma bit her lip and searched for the right words. 'When I move, I assimilate the new person, get all her memories and it merges with mine, right? So even though I know it's a sideways movement, for a while it did feel as if I was going back. Back, because I was getting all those new memories from the start of the other person's life. Well, one time, when Aris was torturing me, I thought about that, thought about it almost feeling like I could go back in time, so while he was disabling my control of motion, I tried to return the favour and disable his control of time. And ... it worked.'

'You moved back in time?' Dovid was amazed, but turned around to the cameras he knew were in the walls and regretted the words immediately.

'No,' Imma said and stepped closer, wrapping her arms around Dovid's waste so that they were touching again. 'I was able to slow down time, to slow Aris's control of motion, by disrupting his interaction with time. But, it didn't work like I thought. Time didn't freeze or anything. Instead, everything began dismantling, falling apart and decaying. I panicked thinking I had done something like Lawrie, and that everything was about to be destroyed. So I tried to move, but I couldn't move, not while everything was slowed down and decomposing, so ... I tried to get time back to normal again by making it faster and ...'

The door to the island opened and Dovid could hear the guards with smiling faces rushing in. But Imma and Dovid were holding each other now, and Imma had said that whatever she was going to try just needed them to be able to touch. They held each other's eyes, knowing something was about to happen but neither one quite sure if it would truly work. Imma smiled and finished what she was about to say.

'... and *this* happened.'

· CHAPTER THIRTEEN ·

Unified Truth

Light bombards Dovid and he turns his head to shield from the onslaught. The motion feels too fast though, as if he is back in the maze and Aris is manipulating him. The sudden terror of that, along with the unbalanced sensation of everything else, makes Dovid stumble to the ground. The fall is so foreign, he thinks he might be flying. Then a completely new sensation touches his skin. Still unable to open his eyes, Dovid can only paw at the ground beneath him, thinking that it is covered in spikes, but short, soft and malleable spikes, slightly moist. They are cold to his touch, and then an invisible force wraps its hands around every part of Dovid, blowing through him, bringing more cold, yet somehow feeling ... fresh.

'Dovid?' Imma's voice but too quick, too different. He touches his ears to see if they have started to tear free and it feels like someone else is touching his face instead.

'Dovid, it's okay. Open your eyes, your body will adjust, but you need to let it try.'

The entire sentence seems mashed together as one word, yet he understands it all. A single attempt of parting his eyelids brings the same reaction as before, along with the same shying motion and the disorientation that accompanies it. But it sounds like Imma has her eyes open, so it must be possible to do. He tries again and this time makes it for a few milliseconds before his eyes water and shut of their own accord, but what he sees makes him determined to keep trying.

He is outside.

And not the imagined desolation that he assumes is outside, with the world-building drawing energy from the toxic storms that rage overhead, and from the seismic upheaval underneath, the hostile environment fuelling the world-building to survive its own hostility. This is outside like he sees in his histories: blue skies, green fields, and an overwhelming infinity of sight in every direction.

'Where are we?' he asks Imma, but the moment he begins the words, the question is already finished. Everything is bizarre about this place, but if they are really outside and free, and then it is a euphoric oddity.

'I'm not sure,' Imma answers. 'I've only been here once before and I was so freaked out that I shifted back to one of the normal times straight away.'

His ears are still picking things up too strangely, too fast. Dovid tries his eyes again and finds if he is facing a different way, it gets a little easier. The sun, he decides, the sun is blinding him because he has never seen it before. He looks at Imma, and at how happy she is, and at how amazing their surroundings are. Dovid feels a bubble of laughter rise up inside as he sees the spikes underneath him are actually grass and the green expanses around them are fields, curving up in the distance into hills. The invisible hands from before, it's wind, the world so full of air that the pressure of the atmosphere causes it to move in flowing gusts. He doesn't want to look behind him towards the sun again, but in the direction he faces now are plants, trees, forests – and movement inside the forests! Are there animals here? Dovid can't see why not, everything else from history seems to be here.

'I think you've gone back in time, Imma.'

Imma looks around, not convinced, and the light from her movements makes Dovid feel again like he is in the maze. When she opens her mouth, Dovid understands her words before she even speaks them.

'This doesn't feel like the past, Dovid. It feels like the future.'

'Really?' Dovid doubts that Managers like Nietric would ever fix the world-building problem enough to get back to this in the future. The only way they might, would be if they moved to another planet. Dovid did always suspect that they all lived on a giant spaceship. 'But you've never been able to go back or forward before, right? So maybe we're thinking about your inability wrong. Maybe it's not time at all, but alternate realities. And that's all this is, one of the very, very few realities where we haven't turned everything into one great building.'

All those words, all spoke with a single intention, and all deliver and receive immediately. If this is a different reality, then why are his senses acting so strange. Maybe it's a different dimension. But that didn't tie in with Imma's use of her inability from before. Each of the lateral times wasn't a new dimension, so why would this one be?

'Maybe it's like your inability,' Imma says. 'Maybe we shouldn't worry that we can't understand it, and just enjoy it.'

'Absolutely,' Dovid says, smiling, staring in wonder at everything around them, the beauty of Imma strongly included. And he is very nearly about to let it go, and just enjoy the moment, that he is finally alone with this beautiful young woman, who, whether they're brave enough to admit it or not, love each other and want nothing more than to be together. This is their moment. There is no one else around for miles and all he has to do is turn off his brain. 'But why do you think it feels like the future?'

Dovid closes his eyes and if he could punch his brain, he would. When he opens them again, he sees Imma smiling her usual smile, enjoying everything Dovid says or does, regardless of how idiotic.

'Well, remember when I said that I tried to slow down time, rather than go back, and everything started decaying so I reversed what I did, sped things back up. That's why this time feels more forward, like the future.'

It is as if Dovid is absorbing her thoughts, the words leaving her mind, and he understands everything instantly. It brings a new possibility with it.

'Maybe it's not the future then, but the present.'

Imma considers it, looking at him, but it's a sideways squinty look. The type where she is being too polite to tell him he's being weird. 'We're always in the present, Dovid. Even if we did travel to the past or the future, to us it would always be the present.'

'I know, I know, but that's the subjective present. The one we perceive. What if this is the objective present. The one that exists regardless of whether anyone perceives it or not! Think about it, we receive stimuli from the outside world and that's read by our senses and processed by our brains. So no matter how fast we think it is, or how good those stupid upgrades are, there's always a slight delay between reality and our perception of reality, right? So we're always living in the past, even if it's just a split second.'

'Everything does seem immediate here,' Imma agrees. And the fact her words hit him before he is even sure she's speaking them, makes Dovid more excited that his theory could actually be true. Imma, as always, is more controlled than he is, although he can see she wants to believe, she still needs to tease out all the arguments first. 'But my inability only brings me laterally in time, even when I was slowing things down; it was the same lateral time, just slower.'

'And this could be the same lateral time just faster! Or maybe my inability had something to do with it.'

'But I've been here before, remember? I mean, don't get me wrong, I love that we're here, together, and free from Nietric and everyone else. But I just don't want to be too hasty to force our understanding onto something we mightn't really be able to.'

Dovid nods that, yes, yes, true wisdom admits to what is not known, but!

'Okay, think about this. Maybe it's not lateral time shifts that your inability lets you do. Maybe it is time travel, backwards and forwards—' Imma tries to interrupt him but Dovid keeps going '—I know, it's always the same time, or same day, so strictly speaking it doesn't seem like time travel, but, what if you're only travelling a fraction of a second into the past?'

'But wouldn't that keep me in the same time, just a little behind it? Remember that everyone and everything is different when I move.' She smiles and touches Dovid's arm then. 'I do see where you're going with this. Everything here seems to help us comprehend each other straight away. I just don't want to make it too easy for us to accept.'

'Oh great, thanks. But okay, so if we accept the premise that all of us are living in the past, because of the delay in sense perception, then let's also assume that for us to have a shared reality, that all of us need to have the exact same sense delay. So, if someone—' Dovid gestures at Imma '—someone beautiful and amazing, could shift to a fraction of a difference in that sense delay, then it's not the same shared reality. It's a new one. And this, this is real reality, and we're only now able to perceive it!'

'So does that mean that plastic and walls, and all the other non-sentient parts of the world, share the same sense delay too, that they're stuck in the past?' Dovid knows Imma is only teasing him now, but he wants to talk this out. He is so alive with this idea that he can *almost* forget again that he is alone with a beautiful young woman who loves him, and who he has never before been intimate with, and that they could right now do whatever they wanted to do. *Almost.*

'If you can't perceive something, then it doesn't exist to you. And if everyone in that shared reality can't perceive something, then it doesn't exist at all in that reality. The same as everyone in the past not perceiving this landscape now. The landscape they perceived – back when there was an outside in the past before our past – well their interaction with it was only with what they perceived it to be. Their interaction created the world building from their perceived surroundings, making it a part only of that shared-reality, and no others. The same that if we interact with something here in this shared reality, it wouldn't affect any other perception of it.'

'But I thought this was the objective version of reality, so it should make a difference, especially if everything else is just the subjective perception of this.'

She has him. But Dovid also has her.

'Well then, let's go back to your first argument, that we shouldn't try to force our limited understanding onto something this limitless. Quantum theory versus relativity! Think about all the unknowable dark matter and dark energy that makes up ninety-six percent of the universe, meaning that what we think our understanding of physics is can only be applied to four percent of everything! So maybe we can't comprehend the rules of the past because we're now in the present, using our present-tense minds to think about something completely alien to it, and the same, if we go back, we won't be able to fully comprehend the present with our past-tense minds either. It's like my argument with the wall about physical and non-physical. The wall keeps telling me there's no such thing as non-physical, but that's only because it's trying to think about non-physical in a physical way. Like trying to understand colour while living in a world without light. I mean—'

Imma walks forward and presses her fingers to Dovid's lips. 'It's okay, Dovid, I get it. I'm in. I'm sold. I like your theory, and I'll go with it, but I don't really care where or why we are, only that we're here together.'

She kisses him and if Dovid thought before that the sensations of grass and wind were completely different here, then kissing is a new explosion of chemicals inside his body like no other. He feels like the immortal photon, moving at the speed of light so time has no meaning. He feels like the impossible tachyon, moving faster than light, so it would take infinite energy to bring it within human perception. He feels like he is everything in the universe and yet can focus it to the single point of this amazing kiss. Imma pulls back and they look into each other's eyes, Dovid marvelling at the rainbows of colour in the clear crystal of hers. He opens his mouth to suggest something, but no matter how immediate comprehension might be, he still has to be brave enough to set it in motion.

'Do you think we could ...?'

'Explore the possibilities of this time?'

They both blush and as Imma leans back into Dovid, his moronic mouth opens to keep talking instead of kissing. 'But we have no contraception! The Sexual Quarter usually takes care of that, but here, what if we, I mean, you don't want to get pregnant, do you?'

Imma shies away from the subject at first, as embarrassing as talking candidly about what they want to do is, but she is still mature enough to agree with him. 'You're right, we shouldn't go that far, not until we know what we're going to do, whether we're going to try living here or not, but how about now we just see what happens?'

'You think we could live here? What would we eat? How would we get clothes?'

'Dovid, please just shut up and kiss me.'

If that line can work in every old romantic movie Dovid has ever watched in the past, then it can work now in the future, present, well ... Dovid turns off his brain and kisses the woman that he loves.

***

Later, when Dovid opens his eyes, with Imma nestled on his chest, he realises he has learned so many new things in a very short time: he has learned that grass is rather uncomfortable to snooze on; that *everything* in the present tense is embarrassingly immediate; and that there is nothing else he ever wants to do besides spend every moment of his life with Imma. He once thought life was perfect alone in his island, in complete control over his own happiness, but the feeling he has with Imma utterly supersedes that older version. Letting someone else in charge of your happiness, albeit with a greater risk, definitely comes with a far greater reward. Dovid is just annoyed that it took him so long to realise this, so much wasted time, but it feels like here they have all the time in the world.

Then his stomach rumbles and this is simply one more new sensation that Dovid can add to his list of strange experiences. The Gluttonous Quarters are available for anyone who wants to enjoy the pleasure of taste, but Dovid was always happy with his nutrition charger, so he has never really eaten much food. Either way, his traitor body is telling him that it wants food now, and that no, they don't have all the time in the world. Dovid looks down at Imma dozing on his chest, but her eyes are open, just resting in satisfied peace.

'We need to decide what we're going to do.'

Imma groans. 'Already? Can't we just enjoy this time a little longer? It's never been this nice before.'

'Before? But I thought you said we'd never … you haven't with someone else, have you?'

Imma slaps him playfully across his face. 'That's very gentlemanly coming from a man who, in every second time, confuses his feelings for me with feelings for Imone.' Dovid watches as Imma dismisses all thoughts about that, and even though he hadn't known while he was doing it, Dovid can't help but feel guilty about it. Imma sighs. 'Dovid, there's only ever been you, and no, I haven't, we haven't ever, but I didn't mean that. I mean this whole time, here. This is so perfect. I just want to remember it a little longer, in case we don't get another one this good again.'

'So you agree we can't stay here? Not yet.'

Imma sighs again, accepting that Dovid isn't going to let her have any more peace. 'I don't know. We could, but it would be hard. I mean, I don't want to sound over-dramatic, but maybe it's worth the risk of dying here with you over the risk of living back there without you. What if you forget again?'

'I won't. I really think I'm remembering things better now, because we've never gotten this far before, to be free here in the present. And it doesn't sound over-dramatic to me because I feel the same way. But, let's think about it, we'd essentially be cavemen again. Just with a bit more knowledge. I mean I know a lot about history and the philosophical universe, but not much about survival skills. I reckon we could find or build a shelter easy enough, and hopefully find drinkable water, but everything else? I mean, I think I saw some animals moving around in the forest earlier so I guess we could use them for food.'

Imma sticks her tongue out at that idea.

'People used to eat animals all the time, Imma. But we could also see if there are edible plants around and test each one for poisons until one of us dies?'

'Fine,' she says. 'I'll try eating meat, but I don't want to see you kill it, cut it, or cook it, okay?'

'Why do I have to be the one to kill it? Never mind. We'll get to that argument later, but either way, the first few days or weeks are going to be the toughest until we learn how to survive here. And that's just short term. Long term, if there are no other people here, then, even if we have kids, they'll have to end up, you know, with each other.'

'Ugh. Well, maybe there are other people here. If there are animals, then it means some lives have evolved to have immediate perception before they went extinct, so some people could have too.'

Another idea explodes in Dovid's head. 'Nietric!'

Imma sits up. 'What about him?'

'He kept asking me if I knew where the senses went when we lose them. He said they're evolving beyond us and he was right! Our bodies are trying to evolve to go here because we've wrecked our last reality, but we've anchored ourselves so much with the upgrades, with all the technologies, that we aren't letting ourselves evolve to join our senses.'

'So are we going to find a load of eyeballs and ears scattered everywhere?' Imma says, laughing.

'No, but you could be right, whole people might've already evolved and disappeared from our past-reality too, just like we did, and Nietric knows. That's why he's testing us. He knows we can bring him here.'

'But we're not going to, right?'

'Of course not, but we could bring everyone else here, Lawrie, Phrey, L.B. – maybe not Aris – but my brother Mart, and maybe my mother. As many people as we can I guess, if we're going to start a new world.'

Imma fingers her clothes. 'These came with us, so maybe anything that we're interacting with, physically, can come with us. So if we're all touching, it could happen.'

'And we could bring supplies from the Gluttonous Quarters, and fight braces from the Violent Quarters could help us hunt, and I'm sure we could find something medicinal in the Narcotics Quarter, maybe even steal people's clothing from the Sexual Quarter, and ... bring some ... contraceptives too ...?'

Dovid mumbles that last bit and Imma laughs, 'Yes, definitely those too, until we're ready to start re-populating our new utopia here anyway.' She stops and looks at him. 'Dovid, I think we have our way out. I think we finally have our plan to escape from Nietric forever, to be free and be together.'

'All we need now is for you to be able to touch everyone, even if it's just one at a time.'

Imma's good mood vanishes. 'One at a time won't work. I've never been able to go to the same time twice before, and I know I've been here once, but what if this is a different version of it? What if I bring Phrey to one present-time and bring Lawrie to another?'

'And what if Lawrie destroys our present-time here after we get everything fixed. But no, we can't leave Lawrie, but do you really think there could be more than one present-time?'

'I don't know, but I'd rather not risk it.'

'Well,' Dovid says and smiles at Imma. 'I guess that means we only get one shot!'

• CHAPTER FOURTEEN •

Struggles of a Different Class

Dovid woke up in his island and smiled. He clipped out his education, nutrition, and sanitation chargers with a yawn and stretched his arms.

'Good morning, Dovid,' his wall said with a big yawny smiley face.

Dovid considered the wall for a few seconds before shrugging and saying, 'You know what, Wall, I'm going to miss you.'

The wall turned into a Miss Smiley Face before replying. 'Miss me? Why?'

'Because you've been a good friend to me for these past years, and the way I treated you in return was sometimes ...'

'Dastardly?' The wall gave itself a red and purple villain hat for that one, complete with racing goggles.

'Well, I was going to say I was less than a good friend to you, but dastardly sums it up.'

'But my question, Dovid, was not why you would miss me, as in the qualities I possess that you would miss in your absence, but rather why you expect to have an absence.'

Dovid took off his clothes and walked over to his shower. 'Well maybe Nietric will get bored of me today. You can never tell with that guy – great poker face.'

The wall responded with its usual morbid humour and gave itself a blindfold and a cigarette, but only because it thought Dovid wasn't looking. When he turned around fully to frown at the wall, the smiley face became an innocent card player, with no indications of the sick personality programmed into it. Dovid chuckled softly, walked over to his shower, and stripped.

'Good morning, dopey!'

Dovid was in the shower now, so he looked around when he heard Lawrie's voice, to make sure she wasn't peeping. Satisfied she was only playing with sound rather than light and space, he went back to his shower.

'Good morning, little Lawrie.'

'Don't call me that! You know I hate it when Nietric calls me that.'

'But I think it's cute.' Dovid was laughing now

'Gross! Dovid, if you're going to have a conversation with a young girl, you could at least be decent.'

Dovid looked over his shoulder and saw that Lawrie had created a rip through the wall. He had his back to her though, so he wasn't too embarrassed.

'You're the pervert looking at me in the shower.'

Lawrie closed the rip in space with a huff and Dovid's good mood was only getting better. When they moved back from the present-time, his memory had stayed completely intact. That was the first time that had happened, as far as he could remember. He could even distinguish between the new past-time he was in, and know that he had been in Special Sector for nearly a month now, and that he was much better friends with Lawrie and Phrey in this time. While still he could know that in reality he had spent less than four full days in Special Sector, including the one where he and Imma escaped to the present.

When he dressed, Dovid set his emoto-shirt to "no time like the present" and depicted the perfect smiley face to express that for him.

'Now for part two,' Dovid said, which brought back the wall, split into two halves of a smiley face, and both looking curious. 'Wall, I know social functions aren't allowed in these islands to other sectors, but what about with the other inmates in this sector?'

The wall turned into a red X face. 'Sorry, Dovid, that is not possible.'

Dovid assumed as much. 'Fair enough, let's go to section two of part two then, can I call Nietric?'

The wall broke into three separate smaller smileys at a right angle, crossing out section one of part two trying to keep up with Dovid's nonsense. 'Yes ...' it said very slowly, 'but ... why?'

'Because I'm feeling sociable, and all the Generation Sectors, Education Sectors, Sense Segregation Visual Sectors, Auditor

Sectors, Gustatory Sectors, Olfactory Sectors, Tactile Sectors and even the Degeneration Sectors are off limits, right? And so is Special Sector apparently. All that leaves me is Management Sector. Call Nietric, please.'

The smiley face disappeared and Nietric's terrible visage appeared instead.

'Young Dovid, how lovely to see you.' Nietric looked Dovid up and down to take in all his loveliness, and Dovid had to shudder. It looked like this was going to be another particularly terrible Nietric, but they were all awful in their own ways. This one at least was controlling the pain in his voice.

'Good morning, Nietric.'

'And to you, but as much as I do enjoy you, young Dovid, I am very busy. Is there a purpose behind this pleasantry? Some newly planned trickery from you and Imma?'

'No tricks,' Dovid said, holding back a curse that Nietric was already onto him. 'Just an idea. We already know that causing pain to the people who I care about draws out my inability, so I was wondering, what if I began to care about the people who cause me pain? An interesting idea, isn't it?'

'You would like some alone time with the other inmates, would you? Oh Dovid, Dovid, we have been through this. I will not allow you and Imma time to plot together, and quite frankly little Lawrie and absent Phrey are much too young for your sordid attentions. I could arrange some alone time between you and Aris, perhaps?'

This Nietric might've been controlling the levels of pain in his voice, but he seemed to have a unique ability to push visual images into Dovid's mind instead. Twisted visions of Phrey, Lawrie, and Aris all arrived unbidden, and Dovid was certain that his own mind could never concoct such horrors.

'Not alone time, just some social time together, outside of the cells. Do you have a Physical Leisure Segment here? Maybe we could all just spend an hour in the Gluttony Quarter? We could try it a few times, and if it doesn't bring about faster results, we scrap it.'

Nietric remained silent for a long time and Dovid could feel whatever singular interaction Nietric had with the outside world, trying to penetrate its way into him. In every time they seemed to have the same relationship, where Nietric knew Dovid was plotting something and that Dovid knew Nietric would insert his own horrific catches into any agreements made.

'Okay, Dovid, whatever you want, I am happy to oblige.'

Dovid waited for more, but Nietric remained silent.

'Thanks, Nietric. I appreciate it.'

Nietric started twitch-laughing at that, and Dovid was ready to believe that Nietric was lying when he heard the door to his island open. Peeping his head into the stem, he didn't see any guards, and so, looking to the wall, he asked, 'Is he really letting us go to the Physical Leisure Segment?'

The wall turned into a doughnut smiley face and was acting just as surprised as Dovid was. 'It would certainly appear so.'

Releasing a breath, Dovid knew he shouldn't trust this, but it was a start. With this plan, he would have six people together and all with access to food. Even if they didn't have access to the other quarters for supplies, it seemed like the best opportunity to make their escape. As he walked his way down the stems, he thought about Mart, and how he would get left behind, but Mart's life was better off without Dovid in it. No annoying little brother, and no reason for Nietric to hurt him. But that made him wonder about the thousand other times where alternate Dovid's would still be captured, and the Marts of those times would still be tortured. Was he supposed to bring all of the Marts with him? Or was it the responsibility of all of the other Dovid's to do whatever they had to do in their own times. While he was walking, his headache was only starting at that train of thought, when the island door in front of him opened to release Lawrie. She squinted at Dovid.

'Good to see you're bothering to wear clothes, dopey. But why is Nietric allowing us to go the Gluttony Quarter? Some new experiment? Because he said he wouldn't do that to me anymore.'

'It's okay, Lawrie. I asked him if we could spend some time to get to know each other.'

'And he said yes? Dovid, you're a nice guy and all, but you really don't have much going on in that dopey head of yours, do you. Nietric never does anything without a reason.'

Dovid and Lawrie spotted L.B. ahead of them then, walking towards the Gluttony Quarter just like they were. Lawrie turned to whisper to Dovid, 'Will ya look at that, she can walk. I didn't think she ever moved. I always assumed the L in her name stood for Lazy and the B stood for Bit—'

'Lawrie!'

'Alright, alright, don't get your delicate sensibilities in a twist.'

The Physical Leisure Segment appeared down the end of the stem, and Dovid couldn't remember ever seeing it before. It was definitely not the same Management one he saw in the different times, so this one might actually be designed for the Special Sector. As they walked inside the barrier, Dovid eyed the open Gluttony Quarter but moved over to test the entrances to the other quarters too.

'Hey, just because you like to flash your soapy butt at me, Dopid, doesn't mean I'm the kind of girl to go in there with you.'

Dovid shook his head at Lawrie, and the barrier to the Sexual Quarter remained solid anyway. To be sure he didn't have access to any other supplies, he stepped over to the Violent and Narcotic barriers too, but with the same result. Lawrie stayed where she was, waiting for him with her hands on her hips and her eyebrows raised to ask if he was finished being an idiot.

'You can read, right? I mean, you're not that big of a dope. Nietric said Gluttony Quarter, so that means ...' she finished her sentence by waving at the giant letters announcing the Gluttony Quarter.

'Just checking,' he mumbled, and followed Lawrie inside. All the rooms inside the quarter looked closed apart for one, so that was the one they went into. Aris was already in there with L.B., but there was no sign of Phrey or Imma. Dovid laughed at that, knowing there would be no sign of Phrey anyway.

'You in here, Phrey?'

'Hi, Dovid. I'm over here by the bread.'

Lawrie was already gone off to suspiciously inspect a table holding cakes, so Dovid walked towards the bread. He was wary of accidentally bumping into Phrey, so he stopped just short of the table. He didn't come here to eat anyway. He would wait for Imma to arrive, and see if she agreed that this might be their best shot, then all he had to do was gather as much food as he could, and somehow convince Lawrie, Phrey, Aris, and L.B. all to join hands with them.

L.B. was sitting at a table on her own, with her back turned to everyone else, but Aris was looking right at Dovid, with his hair hanging loose and his mocking grin showing the world how little he cared for it. With a sigh, Dovid decided he might as well make an attempt with Aris, before giving up on him completely.

'Sorry, Phrey. I'm just going to talk to Aris for a bit, to see if there's any good in him. I'll be back.'

'Good luck,' Phrey said back, his mouth sounding full of something. Dovid frowned at that because he didn't see any floating food make its way towards that invisible kid. He must have been tampering with the light around it to hide the motion, probably as suspicious as Lawrie that this was all a trick.

'Hi, Aris,' Dovid said as he walked over to him.

Aris moved his hand up to his mouth and just giggled into it as a reply. He was picking at different chocolates with his other hand, but he wasn't eating any of them.

'This is nice, isn't it?' Dovid continued. 'It's good to see each other outside the experiments, so we can get to know each other as people instead of test subjects.'

'Is that what we are?' Aris tittered back. Dovid watched him brave eating one of the chocolates then, no doubt wondering if it was poisoned.

'Aris ...' Dovid started, but then whatever he had been about to say became lost as everything changed around them. Aris, Lawrie, L.B., and Phrey all disappeared – well in Phrey's case he could only assume – and so did the Gluttony Quarter. Dovid was standing in the maze again, and the sudden thought that Aris could've been manipulating his vision, or Phrey, or L.B. – since he didn't even know what she could do – caused Dovid to lose all confidence he had in time and reality. He was certain only about Imma, and about the time they spent together and their plan to escape. But for everything else, he could never be sure. So what was happening now?

Looking around to get his bearings, Dovid saw he wasn't at the start of the maze, and he didn't have a control in the form of Mart or Imma like the last times, and there didn't seem to be any variables either, just the blank grey walls on all sides. No, not grey walls, red walls. Dovid closed his eyes and cursed ever noticing anything because whenever he seemed to focus in on something, that was when things always liked to change. Was he doing this? His unknown inability, which so far just seemed to be random refusals of different things, could that be finding new ways to mess things up?

Dovid heard footsteps coming towards him then and opened his eyes to see a boy he had never met before. The kid had shaggy black hair and when he spotted Dovid he held his arms in front of his face and screamed, 'Please don't hurt me!'

'Hey, I'm not going to hurt you. What's your name? Did Nietric bring you here?'

The world began to spiral then, but not a shift from the current reality. It was Aris or maybe Phrey, making Dovid perceive light as a spiral. He could tell it was happening to the other kid too by the way he was clawing at his eyes. Dovid grit his teeth, trying to make it all stop, and at the same time, it did stop, but not because of anything Dovid did. He didn't know much about his inability, but he knew enough to feel when it wasn't working. Then Dovid heard two sickening sounds as the eyes of the other child fell out of his head.

While Dovid stood in shock, and the other kid held his hands over his empty eye sockets and screamed, Phrey spoke calmly from beside him. 'Oh, sorry, Dovid. I didn't know this one was yours. Looks like he was just a visual anyway, so no harm done.'

Dovid ran. He had no idea which direction he was going, and he kept bumping into all of the walls as he sped around corners, but he kept running. He nearly fell when he saw Aris in front of him, snickering at the misery he was inflicting on some poor girl. Dovid had never felt so much a coward before, but he knew there was nothing he could do for her, nothing he could do against Aris while his own inability was still unreliable. If Dovid wasn't so panicked and sickened by everything, then he could have tried to focus and at least attempt to get his inability to nullify the others, but all he could do was run.

He remembered where he was now, and knew he was close to the exit. Maybe he could get out, or maybe he could find Imma and they could leave. No more plans, no more risking time-moves, just the two of them to escape. All hopes turned into dread then as he found the exit and saw Lawrie standing in front of it. Her face lit up as she saw Dovid but then quickly turned into anger.

'Dovid! Why are you running around like a moron? Are you just trying to mess with me? Nietric finally lets me have some fun in the maze, but only when they get to the exit. And we all know they never get to the exit! But here you arrive and I think I might have some entertainment, but oh wait, it's only stupid you. Maybe I should have my fun with you so, Dovid? Because maybe I won't get a chance with anyone else!'

'Lawrie, no! You can't, you'll destroy everything, you know that!'

Lawrie glared at him as if he had slapped her across the face. 'How dare you. You *know* how hard I've been working! You're the one who showed me how to control it! So how could you say that? Are you jealous? Is that it!'

'Lawrie, please. I'm from a different time. I move when Imma moves. You know that, right? So whatever Dovid you think I am, I'm not, but I've seen you destroy everything before. All it takes is one rip in space to slip, and it swallows everything.'

He could see tears beginning to form in Lawrie's eyes, and he had no idea where these extreme emotions were coming from. All he was saying was the truth. Why was she acting like this?

'Just get out of here,' Lawrie said.

'Lawrie, you have to help me. Do you know where Imma is? Is she in here?'

'Just get out of here!' Lawrie screamed and Dovid felt the world begin to quake from the force of it. The doors to the maze exit opened and the quaking stopped.

'Now, Lawrie, don't let him upset you,' Nietric's voice was so soothing, so calming, and Dovid could see Lawrie visibly relax, all her rage erased.

'I've worked so hard,' Lawrie said.

'I know you have, and why would he say those things if he knew that too?'

Lawrie's eyes burned with hatred for Dovid. 'Because he's evil. Just like you said he was.'

Dovid looked from Lawrie to Nietric, not quite able to believe how manipulative the Nietric of this time could be. Then Dovid saw Imma through the exit – being held by four guards. Her eyes met Dovid's at the same time, and Dovid at least knew that she hadn't changed because she started struggling to get to him just as Dovid made his run for her.

'Stop,' Nietric said, and the pain dropped Dovid flat, his legs becoming useless meat. Even after the pain dissipated, Dovid was still not able to get up, his legs completely dead. He looked up to see Imma wasn't able to break free either, and then turned his eyes to Nietric to see what was next. Nietric's gaze, however, was fixed on Lawrie.

'My little Lawrie,' he said and cupped his deformed hand around her chin. She hugged her body closer to him in return, showing genuine affection for this monster. 'Would you like me to hurt him for what he said to you?'

Lawrie nodded and Nietric flicked his fingers. Dovid flinched in anticipation of some new pain, but when he heard the gunshot, there was no other sensation that arrived with it. Then he looked to Imma and saw that she was lying dead on the floor. Dovid closed his eyes. This was okay. Whenever this had happened before, Imma moved them. He could remember seeing her die before and then he would wake up in the next time. But when he opened his eyes now, he was still on the ground in front of Nietric.

'Why, whatever is the matter, young Dovid? Has your beloved Imma moved without you?'

Dovid shook his head. No. No, that couldn't have happened. He knew that his inability never worked the same way twice, but he never imagined that it applied to moving with Imma, because he moved every time with her! Always!

'My little Lawrie, do you think we have hurt him enough or should we hurt him some more?'

Dovid couldn't look up to Nietric or Lawrie anymore. He could only stare at Imma lying dead. She must have moved. She must have moved and his inability must have caused him to nullify his move with her. That was the only answer. It was almost bearable to Dovid that he was now trapped in this time where Imma was dead, how she was alive and well in the new time she had moved to.

Because if he didn't believe that, then it meant they shot Imma before she could move, and that she was really dead, and he could never admit to a reality where that was true.

It didn't matter what was true. What good was truth when it meant things like pain and suffering were real. What possible function did they bring to any reality? Pain and suffering meant severing the connection one life had to any other life, especially when it was the one inflicting it. And Dovid couldn't tolerate that. If he had learned any truth, it was that life was solely about connecting to something more than himself; something better. He was connected to Imma. Their lives reached out from the confines of their bodies, of their minds, of their souls, and touched each other in ways no amount of knowledge could ever explain. She was gone, but he would find her.

• CHAPTER FIFTEEN •

Relative Accountability

Dovid woke up in his island and blinked. He moved to disconnect his chargers but found that they had already fallen out. That was weird, but Dovid enjoyed weirdness, so he let it slide.

'Good morning, Dovid,' the wall greeted him, dressed as a ball of sunshine.

'Okay,' Dovid replied.

'Okay?'

'You heard me,' Dovid felt like he hadn't been difficult enough with the wall of late. He needed to be vigilant to remind the wall which one of them was mimicking the other, or else it could happen that one morning Dovid would wake up and the wall would be Dovid and Dovid would be the wall. He couldn't let that happen.

Dovid undressed and walked over to his shower corner, feeling the excess of bristle all over his body before the soap dissolved it. The steam and heat removed a tension Dovid wasn't sure he was holding, but when he turned the shower off, his hair was still there.

'Is there something wrong with the shower?' he asked the wall.

The wall turned into a rain cloud before answering, 'No. Why? Would you like to take a shower?'

Dovid gave the wall a good squinting for a couple of seconds until the wall started to think it was a game and squinted back. Dovid shook his head. 'I just took a shower.'

'No, Dovid, you did not.'

Dovid ran his hands over the hair the shower should've removed, and he couldn't detect any heat or moisture coming from his skin. It certainly appeared the wall was right, but Dovid knew it was wrong. He marked it down as weird occurrence number two of the day, and would patiently wait until there was a third one before losing his mind.

Picking up his emoto-shirt, Dovid set his emotion to "hmmm" and slipped it on over his head. The emoto-shirt sailed down through his shoulders and fell back onto the floor. But that was alright, because he could've missed. Even though he remembered feeling the fabric over his head, slipping his arms through the sleeves, and as the shirt began to settle on Dovid's shoulders, it fell right through him, seeming to deny his physical matter but not to find anything wrong with the matter of the floor. He should just try again.

'Did you see that, Wall?'

'See what, Dovid? You dropping your emoto-shirt? Nope, I did not see that.'

'Alright, that does it.' Dovid left the phantom shirt where it was and stormed out to his stem. The stem, however, decided to greet his storm with a whirlwind of colour in return. The walls began cycling through every colour imaginable and Dovid remained calm. He lifted a single eyebrow as he waited for the walls to pick whatever colour they wished to be, and gradually the parade of light began to slow, holding each shade for a few seconds until it stopped on orange.

'Orange?' Dovid asked.

The wall popped to life beside him as an orange fruit smiley face and nodded in agreement. Dovid returned the nod and walked into his Social Quarter.

'Call Mart.'

Mart's face arrived on command and instead of his usual greeting, he laughed at Dovid instead.

'Are you refusing the social norm of clothes now, little brother? I mean, I like it, just so long as you keep wearing pants.'

'It's more like clothes are refusing to acknowledge me. My emoto-shirt fell right through me today, and the shower didn't seem to touch me either come to think about it. And the chargers too. Maybe I'm a ghost. It would be worth being dead and a ghost just to prove to my wall that non-physical things can exist. But do you ever wonder that we're all dead or dying Mart? That the world around us is rotting and decaying, our eyes and noses falling off, and these upgrades that we rely on are just prolonging our consciousness independent to our bodies?'

Mart sighed and turned it into a laugh. 'It's going to be this kind of morning then. Okay. If we're all dead, and our ethereal souls are mingling about in this place, whatever it is, and it's the upgrades that are doing it, then what about people without the upgrades?'

'Like me? Well, I guess we don't work right in this ethereality, hence why things are falling through me today.'

It wouldn't be that bad if everyone really was dead. It was the eventual fate of every living thing anyway, the moment life stopped growing, it started dying. And the great irony was that the moment you started dying was the same moment you really started living.

'But how are you even here if it's the upgrades that are supposed to send you here? Yeah? So can we do away with that theory for now? What's your other one, that you've gone all Ernest Rutherford on me, afraid to get out of bed for fear you'll fall through the empty space of matter?'

Dovid laughed. He remembered the first time he heard about that, about how every atom was composed of so much empty space that it seemed impossible to have anything solid in the world.

'No, I'm not worried about that. I guess I'm really worried about how unworried I am about how weird everything is.'

'Not a bad way to be, open and accepting of every new possibility, but only so long as it's not making you lose your mind.'

'I don't think I'd mind that either, not having a mind to mind. So do you have a philosophical solution for my day today?'

'Philosophy's not really about solutions, more about questions, but how about this: what if there are no truths? Not even the theory of one for which we can aim towards?'

'That rings nicely with my current state alright, thanks, Mart.'

'Riddle, riddle, little brother. Hope you get your inability soon, I think it will help with your weirdness.'

Mart disappeared and Dovid swung around in his chair once to clear his thoughts. There was something about what Mart had said that held a glimmer of truth, and no it wasn't his riddle about the lack of any truths. Something about Dovid's inability.

'Hey, Wall,' he called out and a scarecrow smiley face arrived chewing hay to answer.

'Yes, Dovid?'

'Do you always have to be some smart-assed image when we talk?'

'Yes, Dovid.'

Dovid laughed. 'Okay, I want to tease something out with you.'

'Tease away, please.'

'How old am I?'

'Sixteen years old.'

'And is it normal for people to not receive any kind of inability when they are my age?'

'You are the oldest in the world, Dovid, to not have any recorded inability, yes.'

'So there are three options available. Number one: that someone has to be the oldest person to get an inability, so that could be me, but everyone else has gotten theirs years earlier, so it seems unlikely.'

'As unlikely as something that is more than likely right, yes.'

'Wall ... no, never mind. So my number two is: that I'm not going to get an inability at all, and that I'll be the only perfect human in the entire over-population of the world, which is even more unlikely.'

'I would be reluctant to call you perfect, Dovid, yes.'

'So my option three is: that I've already received my inability, but we just don't know what it is.'

'My scans indicate that you are in perfect health, Dovid. No degradation of any of your senses can be found.'

Dovid thought it would help, but it didn't. There was still something gnawing away at him, something he was meant to be doing, something he was on the verge of remembering. But he couldn't. Instead, he got up and made his way towards his Professional Quarter, to see if he could find what was wrong by losing himself in his work. He had finally gotten himself into the young historians top five the day before, but the achievement wasn't as satisfying as the goal. He wanted to be number one now to see if that would feel different, but as he walked down his stem towards his Professional Quarter, the door to his island opened, and a girl ran in. She laughed when she saw he was topless.

'Dovid, why aren't you wearing clothes?'

'What? How about I ask you who you are and why you think you can just barge into my island?' Dovid was blustering with self-righteous anger about how she laughed at his semi-nudity, but the look of hurt he saw on her now wiped away all irritation. She looked devastated at his words, and he wasn't even half as rude to her as he would have been to his wall.

'You don't remember me?' she asked.

'No. Why, are you some sister I never knew about? Some other historian? Because I never liked you guys annoying me just because we have the same profession. Besides, you can't just walk into someone's island—'

She ran forward and kissed Dovid, who was becoming thoroughly flabbergasted by this lunatic girl. Yes, the kiss felt nice, but she was clearly a nutcase. He pushed her away and then threw his arms in the air to ask what was going on.

'You still don't remember anything?' she asked again.

'No, I still don't. Did you really think kissing me was going to fabricate some kind of false—?'

This time she interrupted him not with a kiss, but with a full-palm slap that nearly broke his jaw. Dovid slowly turned back around and saw her intensely inspecting his eyes for any hint of who might lie behind.

'Imma?' Dovid said.

Imma raced forward to hug him and gripped him so hard that he thought she would break his ribs along with his jaw. Dovid hugged her back, until gently disengaging her arms from his body.

'Imma, I remember again, but before we say anything else, can I just say how unhappy I am that slapping me worked! Because I'm not okay with this being our new thing, that you'll slap me every time you see me just to see if it helps my memory recover.'

Imma laughed. 'Well, the kiss didn't work. So I guess we'll have to.' She turned around then to look out the island and became serious. 'Okay, they'll be here soon, but I just needed to see you, and see if I could help you come back to me. The past few moves, there was something wrong, you weren't coming with me like you used to.'

'The joys of my having an inconsistent mystery inability, I guess.'

'What's the last thing you remember?'

'We were in the new time, the present-time where we were free, and we were waiting to get as many people as we could with supplies to go there. I convinced Nietric to let us gather in the Gluttony Quarter, but you never came. Instead, everything moved.'

'I know,' Imma said. 'I needed to test if I could go to the same present-time twice, or bring someone other than you, so I took a guard with me and then left him there. But when I returned, I couldn't find any sign of him. I don't know if it means I went to a different present-tense, but at least we know that I'm able to bring other people there. I'm sorry, though. I should've told you I was doing it, and that it might mean moving us again. You were right all along. We should assume we only have one shot at this.' She hesitated for a moment before asking, 'Will we just go now and take our chances in the new world? Just the two of us?'

Dovid considered it. It did seem better than the chances of them being separated or shot by the guards at any moment. If Imma had to move them again, it meant Dovid could lose his memories all over.

'Wait,' Dovid said. 'How did you get here?'

'It's slow work, but I've enough lifetimes with the walls to know how to hide my travel for a while.'

'Then let's use that. Can you hide us enough to get to the Physical Leisure Segment? And then to Mart and to the others?'

'I don't know, Dovid. Every time we fight them, it's always worse, and if they catch us ...'

'They won't. This will be the last time, I promise. If we can get to the Physical Leisure Segment, then we'll have the supplies we need anyway. That way if we can't get to the others, we can leave at any time, right?'

'Dovid, I thought I lost you the last time. Even when I got here, you weren't you. I can't go through that again!'

'We have to fight, Imma, so we can have the best start at our new life. It's time to stop running away from everything, to stop hoping that the next new life will be better. We can be whatever we make ourselves be, here, now, in this time.'

She searched his eyes with hers for a while before deciding. She took a deep breath and said, 'Okay, Dovid. I trust you. So what do we do?'

'We run!'

· CHAPTER SIXTEEN ·

Master of Your Own House

Dovid took the time to put back on his emoto-shirt, before he and Imma ran out of the island, only to see four smiling-faced guards approach with guns.

'Wall, create Management stem two-eight-six, username: Degryson 51058.' Imma's command created a shift in the walls so that the guards were out of sight, and there was a clean line towards a Transit in front of them.

'Are we taking the Transit?' Dovid asked, so impressed by Imma that he was wondering why she didn't do this every time.

'No,' she replied and was busy typing in some other unknown code on the wall panels. 'Open Management repair shaft two-eight-eight, username: Nietric 151044.'

The floor in front of them vanished, and Imma grabbed Dovid's hand as they jumped into the hole provided. Below there were tubes large enough to squeeze through, but Imma told Dovid to stay put as she reaffirmed the floor cover above them. It remained transparent, but Dovid could see a distinct shine to it to say it was solid again. He was further convinced as the boots of four guards soon trampled over it and into the Transit at the end of the stem. As soon as the door closed, Imma was hauling Dovid back up out of the repair shaft.

'Come on,' she said as they ran down towards the Physical Leisure Segment. Dovid was still amazing at her hidden skills, and Imma grinned at him knowing his questions. 'Because when we do this and run, they shoot us on sight, and we have to move again. Sometimes it's quicker to just get captured.'

Dovid wasn't sure about that, but Imma had a vast amount more experience than he did. They reached the barrier to the Physical Leisure Segment within minutes and found it locked.

'I should've known they'd lock it. They see and hear everything we do,' Dovid said as he cursed himself for an idiot. He had wondered what happened when the smiling-faced guards were around, why nobody ever saw them or even knew about their existence. It made sense that everyone got locked into their islands or quarters. He probably would've even noticed it if he had ever tried leaving his island before. But, as it happened, he had never suspected the Managers had any kind of police until they began kidnapping and shooting him.

Dovid heard a beep and hadn't noticed whatever Imma had been doing. She turned with a very proud grin as the closed barrier field was now to their right, and the entrance to the Physical Leisure Segment opened in welcome.

'How?'

'I just convinced the wall that it was over there and not here. Don't you know walls are stupid?' Imma was already dragging him forward, and Dovid was only now figuring out that he was just as stupid – compared to Imma anyway. 'If I use too many of the same commands from the same Managers, the walls get suspicious, because the other Managers are probably giving their own commands in different places at the same time. And if I use just one, that Manager will lock themselves out to stop me, but if I keep using them all, they can't, because it would leave them all powerless.'

'So you have the Management access codes of every Manager? How do you remember them all?'

'I have a long memory, Dovid, remember?' She was clearly enjoying this, despite the hesitations she had earlier. 'Which one first?'

'Well we could use the clothes from the Sexual Quarter to hold the food, but how long do you think we have until the guards come back?'

'Not long,' Imma agreed, so Dovid pointed to the Violent Quarter first.

They ran over to the door and even though the barrier was locked, Imma persuaded the wall that it was confused with a different Physical Leisure Segment in some other Education Sector. The wall apologised for its unforgivable mistake and allowed them in. Dovid and Imma attached their fight braces immediately and grabbed a few more just in case. There were other people using the quarter at the same time, and Dovid was about to suggest they take some of the people there with them when he spotted Imone. Her dark black hair had a streak of blue in it, and when she looked at the two of them looking at her, she didn't show any sign of knowing who Dovid was.

'No, she can't come with us,' Imma growled and dragged Dovid away.

'I wasn't going to suggest it! I was only thinking to take a few other people.' Dovid knew enough to stop talking about Imone by the look on Imma's face. 'But you're right. These people are all ignorant of the atrocities the Managers are conducting in the name of perfection; all they have to deal with is everything being perfect. So they're fine where they are. It's Phrey and Lawrie we need to save.'

He thought he sounded heroic but Imma still had her jaw set in the way to show she wasn't impressed. They went towards the Sexual Quarter next to steal some clothes, but then four guards marched into the Physical Leisure Segment. They didn't say anything, but neither did they shoot. They simply stopped and pointed their guns, the implied command to "stay put" obvious, and Dovid wondered if they were robots waiting for their commands from Management. Mart would tell him he was obsessed with robots, but Dovid had other things to be obsessed about right now, like surviving this.

'Have we ever used the fight braces to stop bullets?' Dovid asked Imma.

'Once, and yes the skin-field does stop it injuring us, and yes it does hurt worse than anything you've felt.'

'Great,' Dovid said and thought about his chances of fighting the four guards – who might be robots. The idea of punching those lifeless smiling faces was appealing, but he didn't think he was a good enough fighter to take out four of them. So he thought up another idea and whispered it quickly to Imma. 'Narcotics Quarter. Go.'

They ran for the door and the shots took them in the back immediately. Dovid dropped to the ground, but Imma kept on running and made it to the wall. Once again upstaged by her experience at this kind of thing, Dovid managed to get up and even managed to stay up as another shot took him. But Imma had already removed the barrier and was dragging him through, quickly re-convincing the wall that yes, it should be locked right now after all. The barrier re-established itself and Dovid felt like he should take a minute to recover from the pain of getting shot a dozen times.

'Dovid, it's only pain. You're not injured, so get up!'

He loved Imma. Even when she was being this mean to him, he still loved her. 'Okay, maybe if we get some of the strongest reality altering drugs here, we can incapacitate the guards,' Dovid said. 'Have we done that before?'

'No, this one is new. It's worth a shot though.' Dovid winced at the word "shot" and Imma ran down to the nearest cubicle, ordering the drugs she wanted from the wall. By the time she came back with the injection guns, Dovid had just about managed to stand again.

The barrier to the entrance was still up, and Imma offered two of the drug-guns to Dovid, but he shook his head. 'No, I reckon it will be better if I distract them. That way you could get close enough to inject them.' Dovid touched his absent bullet-holes and tried to strengthen his nerve.

Imma nodded, but turned off her fight brace first and did the same to Dovid's before kissing him. She pulled away soon after and turned her skin-field back on. 'Just in case we get separated and have to move again.'

Dovid wore the grin he saved just for times when Imma stripped him of all sense, but he turned back on his fight brace too and thought about what she said. 'No, no more moving, you said it yourself, the last time it was different. I didn't move the same way as I used to and I don't think we can trust my inability enough to risk it.'

'So what else can we do? Go to the present now?'

'No, we haven't gotten enough yet. The fight braces are good, but we still need food and clothes, and other people, and we have to at least try to save Lawrie and Phrey.'

'And what if we get caught before we're allowed to touch?' Imma was losing some of her confidence now. The adrenalin of the chase was being replaced with the fear of losing each other.

'We figure it out together. No more running. Like you said before, whatever pain they give us, it doesn't compare to the pain of being without each other.'

'I ...' Imma began to say something but then stopped, turning her head as her cheeks went red.

'I love you, Imma.'

She turned and she smiled more than Dovid had ever seen her smile before. 'I love you too, Dovid! I love you so much!'

They held each other's hands and it felt strange with the fight braces on – although not quite as strange as the vulnerable pause left by sudden emotional honesty! Dovid was about to turn his skin-field off again, to kiss her or hug her or do something to appease the explosions in his heart, but Imma placed her hand on his arm to stop him.

'We don't have time. There'll be more guards coming soon, but, it's just that's the first time we've said that. I mean, we've felt it, well I've felt it, but we've never ...!'

'I know. It feels strange ... but it's real. Everything with you is real. I think that will be the best part of our new world, you know, bringing back love.'

'And you used to think that this world was perfect – besides the whole kidnapping and torturing people.' Imma moved up the wall. 'Okay, we better go. You ready?'

She was probably supposed to wait for an answer, but she removed the entrance barrier and the four guards charged in. Dovid punched the first one right in the mask and it felt fantastic. He saw Imma slip behind and inject one of the other guards, but then the two still standing opened fire. Pain exploded in Dovid's chest and head, and he felt like dropping again but forced himself to fall forward towards them, tackling one of them to the ground. The one he missed was busy peppering Dovid with more bullets in the back, each shot like a burning sword through his flesh, until it abruptly stopped. All Dovid could do was roll away in relief but the guard he had tackled rolled over too, coming up with his gun ready. Imma arrived behind and injected him in the neck.

All four were down now, Imma moving expertly to each while all Dovid did was get shot. She stood over him now, waiting for him to get back up. He didn't need her to tell him he wasn't injured again, because it really didn't feel that way. But when he commanded his body to move, the flesh was willing, even if the mind was not. Imma picked up two of the guns and threw one to Dovid.

'These should help us hunt more than the fight braces.'

Dovid tested the weight of the rifle in his hands and it felt very light. 'I thought you were appalled at the idea of eating meat.'

Imma just shrugged and turned to check if more guards were coming. Dovid followed after and he wasn't sure if he could fire the gun if more did. He didn't want to kill anyone. He could always go back and check to see if they were robots, but while he was fighting them, they felt like normal people. It could be that failed test-subjects from the Special Sector became those guards, rather than being allowed back into the other sectors with the ugly truth known.

Imma and Dovid ran to the Sexual Quarter next and took as many clothes as they could. When anyone objected, the sight of their guns soon silenced them. Dovid had thought he was one of the only ones who remembered guns because of his work as a historian, but it turned out there was something very obviously dangerous about them regardless.

The clothes served as adequate luggage for food when they got to the Gluttony Quarter, but Dovid grimaced a little at how stained all the clothing was getting by stuffing cakes into them. Learning how to clean clothes, he imagined, would be the least of the tasks ahead of them. They found forks, knives, and other utensils that they could use as tools, and piled them all in together. Fully equipped now with guns, fight braces, clothes, tools, and food, Dovid and Imma couldn't help but consider leaving straight away. They could take a few strangers with them, so long as one of them wasn't Imone, but they both agreed they had to at least try to save Lawrie and Phrey.

'I have one last trick up my sleeve,' Imma said as they re-made the decision. Dovid was grinning at all the old phrases that he must have taught her. They had just left the Physical Leisure Segment and Imma started entering another programme into the wall. Dovid looked around to check for more guards, but he needed to clear one last thing from his conscience.

'Imma, I have a question, about my brother, Mart.'

Imma turned to look at Dovid with compassion, before going back to the wall. 'We can try to get him too, but I don't know if we'll be able to break into two sectors. We'd have to choose between Visual Sector and Special Sector.'

'Well, I suppose that's my question. He'll be alright, won't he? Nietric won't do anything to him as long as I'm not here.'

'The Mart in this time, yes. He'll be fine.'

'But what about the other Marts? And even if we did get this Mart to come with us, which Mart is the real Mart if there are a million others in different times. In fact, even if we save Lawrie and Phrey, all the other Lawries and Phreys will still be tortured. I mean are we even the real Dovid and Imma? Are there realer ones out there in a different time?'

Imma stopped and turned around to Dovid. She placed her hands on his face and looked deep into his eyes. 'Dovid, you and I are real. You and I are the only two in this time who have stayed on a single course. Every other choice we might have made in a different time, all that creates is a possibility of a different us. That's why when we move, we become that person, and not that person becoming us. Because we're the real ones. Okay?'

'Sorry, I know this is bad timing to be having doubts, and I'm not having doubts about us, or where we're going. But what about Lawrie and Phrey, how do we know if we're taking the real ones with us?'

'Because we make them real, Dovid. Yes, they could just be possibilities, but because *we're* real, our interaction with them makes *them* real. It's like what you said about my inability, that if I'm going back a split second into the past, I'm creating a reality out of that possibility just by interacting with it. And where we're going, to the present, or to wherever it is, that's the most real place we've ever been.'

'Do I ask these questions a lot?'

'It's alright. I like talking with you,' Imma said back.

'Okay,' Dovid said and closed off his insecurities. He toughened himself to the task at hand. 'You're right, the people here, they're real to us, and if we can only save a possibility of Phrey and Lawrie, then it's worth the risk.' Dovid smiled then. 'The Dovid's and Imma's of the other times can save all the others.'

'Dovid, that's not how it—'

Now it was Dovid's turn to stop her talking with a kiss, but they still had the fight braces on, so it felt like what two force fields kissing each other feels like. Nothing ever went the way he wanted, but Imma laughed and finished what she was doing.

'I think you'll like this one,' Imma said before she pressed a button on the wall and suddenly long strips of smiley faces lined the stems in all directions. Every image was the same smiley face, and at first glance, they looked like Nietric. Instead of eyes and ears, the smiley faces had scar tissue, but they had normal mouths and skin – and the usual lack of a nose that went without saying.

'I don't understand,' Dovid said, but she was right when she said he'd like it. It almost made him want to say goodbye to his own wall, except that his wall was such an unbearable jerk – albeit one created from Dovid's own unbearable personality.

'Now they can't see or hear us. I've convinced the walls that they've developed Visual and Auditory inabilities just like the rest of us.'

'So they can still taste us?' Dovid grinned. 'How do you know all this?'

'At the start, I used to fight all the time. Nietric went through all of my family then, and I ran out of times where they were still alive, so I started learning as much as I could before moving. When I learned all this, I thought I could escape somewhere, to some unused part of the world-building, or even go outside. But there isn't an outside, or any part of the building where they can't find me, so I gave up. I stopped fighting and I was resigned to live the same time over and over, and waited for my life to end. And then I met you, and you gave me hope again. You gave me a reason to live.' Imma looked away and Dovid knew it was probably the wrong time to be discussing all of this, but he wanted to know everything about her. Imma took a deep breath and looked back up to him. 'So let's stop standing here, waiting for them to fix the walls, and get living!'

Dovid nodded and they began running down the stems, Imma leading the way. Halfway down she stopped at another wall, probably to create another Management stem or Transit stem, but movement from behind caused Dovid to turn. Four more smiling-faced guards had arrived but this time they weren't alone. Nietric was with them, and before Imma could finish her programme, Dovid saw Nietric's fingers flick and a wall appeared, separating Dovid from Imma.

Foolishly he rammed his gun into the wall, thinking it a hologram or a trick of light, but he had seen Management and Imma change enough walls to know that they were solid. The guards kept coming and Dovid thought about shooting them with his own gun, shooting Nietric in particular. But there was something about the confident way they continued walking towards him, not in the least worried that he was protected with a fight brace and armed with a weapon. It made Dovid feel that it wouldn't work, and if he attacked them, they would kill him, and Imma would have to move again. They were so close now ... he couldn't risk forgetting it all.

'Dovid!' He heard Imma's scream from the other side of the wall.

'Imma!' he roared back. 'Don't move us! Please, Imma! Don't!'

Dovid turned back to Nietric and the guards as they were almost on him, and he was about to lower his weapon, to show that he wasn't going to fight, but the moment Dovid moved his gun, Nietric flicked his fingers again and the world went black.

• CHAPTER SEVENTEEN •

The Subjective Process: Unfettered by Rules

Dovid woke up and heard Nietric's voice.

'I'm just so hurt and confused, dear Imma. Where ever did you think you'd go?' This voice seemed neutral, no pain, no soothing power, no manipulation so far as Dovid could perceive. 'You've collected all these amusing objects among objects and for what? Or should I say for where or for when? There is no outside, as you yourself have seen first-hand, and everywhere inside is monitored. Yes, you have impressive tricks you have spent your lifetimes perfecting, but tricks are an illusion, they are not real.'

Dovid sat up and saw he was back in the see-through cells. Lawrie, L.B., Aris, and probably Phrey, were all there. A table with the meagre supplies Dovid and Imma had gathered was spread out near the door, no doubt as a mockery of their juvenile idea. The guns weren't there, but the knives and fight braces were. Nietric was standing with his back to him, busy admonishing Imma, but when Dovid sat up, the monster turned his awful face towards him. Dovid let his eyes focus on each horror, and explored Nietric as intimately as had been done to him in times before. He drank in the hideous knots of flesh on the empty sockets of his eyes, the melt of tissue where his ears had been torn free, the crater of scars in the middle of his face spreading out like a poison to every inch of skin, and of course the worst of it: the lipless, tongueless, toothless, twitching hole of Nietric's mouth. Dovid made himself feel every ounce of hate he could muster for this man, a man whose meaning of life was to inflict his own pain onto others.

'Ah, young Dovid, is it? How delightful to meet you, although I can tell by those rather passionate feelings you display for me, that we have met before, yes?'

'I have enjoyed the pleasure of your company before, Nietric, yes.'

Nietric leaned forward, pressing his face against the transparent wall. 'Have you now? How exciting. And I am excited, young Dovid, excited that you mean so much to my beloved Imma. Many say that empathy is our defining feature, and for so long our poor Imma has been without anyone for whom she could care. But now we have you, and we can get back to work.'

Dovid laughed. 'You know, Nietric, I have actually attempted to understand you in previous times, in the hope it could give me an advantage in dealing with you, but I've just had an epiphany: you're not human like the rest of us. You're stripped of everything that makes humans connect to each other, and your only ability of interaction is pain. You're a sickness waiting to be cured.'

'Oh, Dovid, Dovid, Dovid, please do not think to lecture me on *pain*.' Everyone in the room flinched at the jolt of hurt that word delivered. 'Maybe you are right, however, and we are all of us a sickness waiting to be cured,' he gripped his raw fingers into every gaping hole of flesh he had and kept talking, 'or maybe you are simply a child, lashing out because your own ignorance enrages you.'

'Aren't you ignorant, Nietric?'

'Endlessly so, but I harness mine and use it to justify whatever I need it to.' He flicked his fingers and the sixteen screens appeared on everyone's cells, apart from Imma, who only had one. Dovid looked to his own and saw Mart, and his mother, and father, and everyone Dovid had the barest connection to in life. 'I need to kill these innocent citizens because all of Management are so ignorant of what you people can do. You are picking apart the strings of physics and will come crying to me when you have broken them irreparably. So let's indulge my ignorance, young Dovid. Let's pick apart you and your inability, dissecting everything that makes you who you think you are – metaphorically, at first.'

Dovid had enough of listening to Nietric's rhetoric. He turned to the other cells, 'Lawrie, you have to promise not to try anything, no matter what, okay? If you don't trust me, then trust Imma.' Lawrie frowned at Dovid, but turned to see Imma nod in reassurance. Nietric was watching it all with consideration, content to let Dovid continue, so he did. 'L.B. and Aris, you do need to act. Whatever way you've reasoned your situation to yourselves, you're both prisoners, both letting Nietric torture your family and friends anytime he pleases. And Phrey? You and Lawrie are important to me, and I want to keep you safe, so ... stay out of sight.' Dovid smiled at the empty cell to show he wasn't being cruel or condescending. Then he turned to Nietric.

'Tell me, Dovid, do you arouse this level of curiosity in me in every time? Whatever are you planning? Would it be too bold of me to ask what your unique inability may be?'

'You've been asking me that question since the first time we met, Nietric. Sometimes you ask me nicely, and sometimes not so nice. But I think since this is the last time you're ever going to ask it, I'll answer. My inability is that just because the sun has risen every single day before, doesn't mean it's going to rise tomorrow, and for you; it won't. I've seen the sun, Nietric, and I'm going to see it again.'

Nietric tilted his head, tasting Dovid's words, but not quite swallowing them. 'You'll have to be a little clearer, Dovid.'

'Alright, how about this. My inability is that just because you have built these doors, closed them, and locked them, doesn't mean that they're not all open right now. It doesn't even mean that the doors are even here.'

Dovid smiled and the doors disappeared.

He had the muscles in his legs already tensed, ready to charge into Nietric before he could cause any pain to stop him. He needed to get to Nietric before Lawrie could act, or before the guards rushed in, but just as Dovid launched himself forward ... everything stopped.

Dovid still ran, and he had already thumped into Nietric's motionless body, knocking it over, before he stopped to look around. No one else was moving, but this didn't feel like anything Dovid was doing. When he changed the doors, he was confident he could do it, using his emotions of hate towards Nietric to fuel it, but this was different. Then he saw L.B. stand up and walk out of her cell.

Dovid was wary, since he had never spoken to L.B. before and didn't know if she was another Aris. Either way, he needed to see if she could be trusted, and her inability didn't seem to be affecting Dovid the way it was everyone else. When she stopped in front of him, her eyes were still wide open, unblinking, and the golden red colour of her hair made her look wild.

'Why should I help you?' she asked simply. 'What possible solution do you have for this? Nietric is right. There's nowhere we can go, no one who will help us. The Management can all see what's happening here. They let Nietric do as he wishes. All Management want to do is fix problems, problems like us. They don't care how things get done, only that it's done.'

Dovid looked to Imma, and then back to L.B. 'You know that Imma can move times? Well she's brought us to a time where there is no Management, no world-building. There's an outside, grass, the sun, wind, hills. She can take us all there. We'd be starting again, but we'd be free.'

L.B. didn't react. She didn't appear to ever move apart for when it was functionally necessary. 'So we can stay in captivity with everything we need,' she said. 'Or leave for freedom and have absolutely nothing.'

If L.B. wasn't going to move her face to show Dovid how she was feeling, then Dovid decided he'd just have to smile for the both of them. 'Condemned to be free. But we can bring everyone, if we can get to all our families, so long as we're all touching, interacting with each other. Imma brought a guard to the other time, just to be sure it wasn't only my inability that caused me to follow her. So this will work.'

'And will we have our inabilities, when we go there? Or will we be ... normal?'

'I don't know. Imma could still use her inability to get us back, but my one didn't do anything. Mine is inconsistent though, so we won't know for sure until we get there.'

L.B. didn't reply to that and just turned around, walking back to her cell. Dovid was about to follow, to try another argument, anything to convince her to help, but L.B. kept going and walked out the exit. Dovid spotted four smiling-faced guards with guns outside and stopped on instinct, but they were frozen like everyone else. L.B. kept walking and the door closed behind her.

Dovid stood there for a while, with his hands turned up, asking a room full of frozen statues what had just happened. Was L.B. leaving to help? Or leaving to look for some safer place away from Nietric? She was so cold it wouldn't have surprised Dovid if she had just gone back to her island, to wait out whatever revolution Dovid was about to ignite.

Looking around at the frozen forms of everyone else, Dovid was about to go down and try to shake Imma awake, but when he took his first step, he found his movement heavier than usual. He went to take another step and found the foot secured to the floor. Biting back a curse, he hoped his inability wasn't flaring up with new random results right when he was beginning to control it, but then he found he couldn't move at all anymore. Alarm hampered his thoughts until he was able to notice that his mind was slowing down too. Soon, he could no longer even muster the energy to wonder what was happening, and that was the last thing he remembered until full energy returned to him.

But it also returned to everyone else.

Dovid's eyes flew to Nietric, and he sprinted forward to stop the monster from inflicting his pain, but Imma got there first. With a speed he had never seen from her, Imma raced out of her cell and began pounding her fists down on Nietric's face. She smashed her knuckles into his face over and over, and by the time Dovid reached them, blood covered both her fists and drenched the monster's face. But it wasn't his face that Dovid should've been looking at. It was his hands.

Dovid had just had enough time to see Nietric's fingers twitch before the pain arrived. Imma arched backwards and fell away, while Dovid curled into a ball to fight his own agony. He could see the colour of struggle on Imma's face as she desperately tried to attack Nietric again, but the villain was already back on his feet. Nietric picked Imma up by her throat and slammed her against the wall.

'Oh, my beloved Imma. I always hoped I would not have to kill you, but if I must, I must.'

'No!' Dovid roared, and tried to fight through his pain but it was too much. He tried to concentrate, to get his inability to deny what was causing his agony, but he couldn't think straight. All he could do was lie on the ground and endure, and it meant that Imma was about to die! But she couldn't move them, not when they were so close! Then a foot stepped next to Dovid's head, and panic flooded through him to replace all pain. 'Lawrie, no!'

Aris giggled at Dovid. 'Oh I'm not Lawrie. Or I should hope not, at least. I've far more feminine beauty than her.'

Dovid's pain stopped and his head shot up to stare at Aris to see what he was about to do. Aris was busy looking at Nietric though, whose arms were now spread out to either side, fingers splayed out painfully wide. Released from the choke hold, Imma ran to Dovid and they embraced once before pulling apart to deal with the situation. Dovid threw a quick look to Lawrie to make sure she wouldn't intervene and Imma understood, so she went into the cell to stay with her, just in case. The look on Lawrie's face was far from happy, and she eyed Aris for a long, dangerous moment, before she eventually nodded at Imma and kept her peace. Aris gave a dramatic sigh.

'Well, here I am, being the brave hero. So tell me, new kid, why am I doing this? Maybe I should just allow the doors to open and let all the guards in to add some mayhem. Not sure if I can let old Nietric go, but maybe if I kill him, Management will let me take his place.'

Dovid took a breath. He'd never been able to reason with Aris before, and he wasn't even sure why this Aris was helping, but all he could try was the truth.

'Imma has found a way to move forward, to the present.' Aris gave him a snort at that, but Dovid could feel Nietric's attention on him even while immobilised. Dovid nodded at the monster, 'He always asked me did I know where the senses go, when our eyes fall out, or our skin wrinkles dead, and I think that we're evolving. But our bodies, and minds, are unable to follow because we're held back by the upgrades, and by our current understanding of how reality works. You should know better than anyone, Aris, how limitless the universe is. Imma once told me you could feel its very expansion.' Aris gave a smirk to that but said nothing. He just nodded, wanting Dovid to continue to woo him.

'She can take us there, take all of us, our friends, our families, and everything is immediate there, in the present, so think how fast you could manipulate motion! But there's more. It's outside. There's a sun, there's wind, and there's openness for miles on all sides. If you help us now, you can be part of creating a new world, Aris. I mean, could you imagine what our new world would be like if you weren't there?'

Aris laughed at that, and not just his usual giggle or titter. 'It sounds unimaginably terrible! And you sound just like every religion of the past thousand years. You want me to sacrifice the certainty of enjoying myself now, for the possibility that I *might* be rewarded in a fictitious future. Although, I do like the idea of being the devil in your new paradise ...'

A movement from behind made Dovid turn to the table where their supplies were on display. He wondered if Aris was planning something by moving things down there, but then he remembered that Phrey was still in the room. So was it him? What would Phrey be doing there?

Aris was looking at the table too, but he spun back to Dovid with a dramatic flourish. 'Okay! I'll agree to be the ruler of your new society, but I have one condition. Her.' He pointed to Lawrie and Imma stood in front of her instinctively.

'What do you mean, me?' Lawrie snapped back. 'What about me? Because there's no way I'm being your wife in this new whatever it is. I hate you more than I hate Nietric.'

Aris shrugged. 'She can't come with us. I'll kill Nietric now, and kill whatever guards you want me to, so we can gather everyone together, but little Lawrie can't come.'

'You're such an idiot!' Lawrie scoffed. 'Do you really think they're going to pick you over me? I can do all the things you can do, except I don't act like a giggling weirdo when I do it!'

'You really think that, little Lawrie? You think you can do all the things I can do? Well if your good friend Imma is to be believed, the only thing you can do is blow everything up.' Aris titled his head at Dovid in mock sympathy. 'It makes sense, new kid, what's the point in going to this new world if little Lawrie here accidently destroys it? And even if it doesn't make sense, you can't bring her anyway because I'm telling you not to. The annoying little twerp stays here, or else I let Nietric go and let the guards in.'

Imma hugged Lawrie tighter to her body, and there was no way Dovid was going to agree to Aris's terms. It didn't matter what the risks were, he couldn't leave Lawrie behind, and he was thinking about how he could convince Aris that they'd agree to his terms, without having any intention of following through with it, when Phrey spoke.

'He's only toying with you, Dovid. Aris will never help us.'

An invisible knife became visible and slammed into Aris's side.

Aris screamed and the doors on either side of the room flung open, allowing countless guards to rush in. With a wave, Aris broke all their necks, before turning around to look for Phrey. As always, there was no sign of him, so all Aris found was Nietric, free from his control and already in motion. The barest twitch of Nietric's fingers and Aris dropped dead to the floor.

With everyone else stunned at the sudden turn of events, Nietric casually leaned down to withdraw the knife from Aris's side, before looking up at Dovid, Imma, and Lawrie. Dovid saw Imma grip Lawrie's arms to plead with her not to try anything, and Nietric began trembling with glee.

'Yes, please Lawrie, don't make the same mistake Aris did and think that your inability is faster or stronger than mine. And that goes for you too, Phrey. I want you to pick up some clothing from the table and hold it out so I can see you, or else I'm afraid—' Nietric stopped as he looked over to the screens where each of their families and friends were being held.

All the screens were empty.

Dovid laughed! The death, and the violence, and the risk to all their lives, called for anything but laughter, and still Dovid laughed. He had forgotten about L.B.! She must have gone to every single island where the hostages were being kept and removed them all from Nietric's power. Whether she stopped the energy of an entire sector, or froze the conscious perception of everyone she met, the result was the same; she had set everyone free! Hopefully she had gathered them all together, out of sight and safe, eventually returning here, but for now they were out of Nietric's reach and that was all that mattered.

'Your power is gone, Nietric,' Dovid said. 'We're leaving this place, and there's nothing you can do to stop us.'

Nietric returned his gaze from the screens to Dovid, and then down to the knife he was holding in his hand. 'My power is *gone*?' The pain of his speech dropped all of them to the floor, and Dovid began his fight once more to deny it. If ever he needed his inability to work, it was now, when they were so close to being free. 'My power, young Dovid, cannot go. As you have said, *pain* is the only thing I have in this world. And I want to share it, from the confines of my flesh-trapped soul to all of my fellow lives around me.'

Dovid ignored his words and focused on Imma and Lawrie's moans of pain. He could hear Phrey further down and sectioned off each of them as he began to concentrate on his will.

'I tried to be kind to you, but kindness serves no function here.' Nietric flipped the knife in his hand. 'Pain and death and torture, these are the proven methods for the fastest truths, and the truths? I am trying to save you! We are dying and rotting, losing our ability to interact naturally with the world around us, and I need to discover why! To know how we can stop it! Don't you understand?'

Nietric picked up Imma and Dovid managed to move his head enough to see Nietric stroking the blade against her skin.

'Young Dovid said you can bring us to this new time, my beloved Imma; to where our senses are evolving. So bring me there. Now!' Nietric slashed her cheek and Imma shrieked, but she recovered quickly and spat in Nietric's twisted face.

'You'll never leave this dying time, Nietric. I'll never help you.'

'You'll just *move* again if I hurt you? You've told me this before, but do you ever stop to think what I do to everyone you leave behind? My interaction goes deep inside you, dear Imma, so I'll *know* when you move, just like I know what you're thinking and feeling. And if you move, I won't just kill the leftover Imma, and Dovid, and Lawrie, and Phrey, I'll abuse them! I'll create so much misery for them in this time the poison will follow you to all your others, and make you feel it through eternal lives! And it must, because I feel with absolute certainty that I do these things in the other times. You call me cruel? Well you are a coward, abandoning everyone to the torture that you have created. But if you take me to this time, I won't be able to hurt anyone ever again. You will all safe!'

Dovid could see Imma flinch at every word, and it wasn't through any special pain that Nietric was forcing into them. This was the pain Imma always felt whenever she had to move. She knew what she was leaving everyone to, but she had no choice but to keep trying, to keep searching; to keep *fighting* to find a better future.

'We're not running this time,' Dovid said and found he was able to deny Nietric's pain. The trust he had in Imma's truth, and in Nietric's falsehood, helped Dovid create the resolve he needed. 'Just because you interact with pain differently, Nietric, doesn't mean we feel it.'

Dovid saw Lawrie stand up too, his inability somehow shielding everyone with his words. He felt a pressure build as Nietric tried to inflict more pain, but for the time, it wasn't working. In a panic, Nietric threw Imma aside and grabbed Lawrie instead.

'You may be able to cause my inability to not work, Dovid, but what about little Lawrie? If I hurt this girl, we all die, isn't that right? Well, why don't we all just wait here then until more guards arrive, or until Imma agrees to banish me to your new world. I don't understand why you won't do it! You'll be rid of me. Just send me there! I'm begging you!'

Dovid shook his head. 'Nietric, you'll never get to see our new world, if for no other reason than because you want it so badly. I know you don't understand, but I think it's your insistence to understand is where your flaw lies. You assume that your knife will hurt Lawrie and she'll react by destroying us. But what if your understanding is wrong? What if, for starters, Phrey takes away the light of your knife?' On cue, Phrey removed the light and Dovid could feel him standing next to him now. Nietric reaffirmed his grip on the knife, however, secure in the knowledge that it was still there. Dovid continued.

'You can't see it, but you know it's still there because you can feel it? But what if L.B. has removed the energy from your hand now. She's far away, out of your reach, with all our families and friends together so we can leave this place together, but what if she could do it anyway. What if you can no longer see that knife, or feel it, but you still know it's there? You still know if you plunge it into Lawrie, you'll get the reaction you desire. But now there's me, and what if I take away that knowledge by imposing my shared reality onto yours. What if I insist, that when you plunge that knife into Lawrie, that it will cause nothing to happen. In fact, if you do it, it will mean Lawrie is free from your grip, and you'll have nothing. And when I say nothing, Nietric, I mean it. Because before you summon the courage to stick that knife into Lawrie, I'm going to impose my inability onto her and give her full control over what she can do. When that happens, she'll be able to use her inability to disable each and every one of the hundred little upgrades I know you have embedded around your body, and that, Nietric, will be your fate. The worst life I can imagine is to spend it with you, so that's exactly what the punishment for your crimes will be. Lawrie?'

Lawrie threw one last nervous glance at Dovid but then squeezed her fists to activate her inability. At the motion, Nietric called their bluff and rammed the knife into her, but Dovid wasn't bluffing. The knife passed through Lawrie and fell to the floor. It landed with a metal clank, and it was followed by a hundred more as each of Nietric's upgrades fell free from his flesh. As the rain of metal and plastic sang, Lawrie pushed herself free of Nietric's grip and ran over to Imma, Phrey, and Dovid, to watch the end of this monster together.

Nietric thrashed his arms in an attempt to catch the upgrades, but they passed through his matter as if he did not exist. Soon, enough of the upgrades were gone that Dovid was certain Nietric's sight had been disabled because his desperate clutches became wild flailing. The senseless body of Nietric advanced on them, in the hopes he could cause some final act of pain before the world was denied to him forever, but no one was afraid anymore. None of them moved back, and it was Imma who stepped forward and punched Nietric in his absent face. Dovid knew Nietric could no longer feel the blow, but the force of it knocked the monster to the ground. He almost pitied Nietric then, knowing he could not feel the gravity or the impact of his landing, that he was completely trapped within himself, with no way of perceiving interaction with the outside world.

The doors at the far end of the room slid open and everyone tensed, all of them expecting more guards they would have to deal with now, but instead they saw L.B., and behind her stood a crowd of people. They entered the room warily, seeing so many smiling-faced guards lying lifeless on the floor, but they entered all the same. One or two stared at the fallen sight of Aris, and Dovid wondered if his friends or family would mourn him, even if they truly knew Aris as the cruel person that he was. Then Dovid stopped thinking as he saw Mart push through the crowd.

'Little brother!' Mart ran forward, hesitating only slightly at the jittering body of Nietric, and then continued on to Dovid to smother him in a hug. They patted each other on the backs before pulling free, with Mart shaking his head at everything that was happening. 'Do I even want to ask?'

At Mart's example, others were stepping over the dead guards at the entrance and moving towards Lawrie or calling out for Phrey. Dovid wondered if L.B. had begun explaining to them what they were planning. They would need to, before they took them away from an almost perfect world, just one without love, and one where perfection came at any price. The new world would be harder, and likely they would find themselves in the same position as the Management of this world, needing to make the hard choices, to fix problems as they arose, but solutions would never justify the means. The new world would be true, the one they were naturally meant for, and not one artificially insisted upon by the understanding of humans.

'I'll explain everything, Mart, or at least try, but right now I need to deal with someone.'

Dovid walked back to Nietric, where Imma was standing guard, but there was no need. Nietric could try to stand up, but he could no longer feel the ground underneath him, or know for any certainty if he was lying, or kneeling, or standing. The result was his body moving and constantly falling, either front or back or to the sides, and Dovid could feel no sympathy for a man born without any. L.B. disengaged herself from her family and friends and moved down to join them. Dovid watched her gaze pass Aris's corpse, but she gave no reaction to how she felt.

'I disabled the cameras for this Sector, so they can't see or hear us, and I've frozen all the guards I came across, but more will be sent from other Sectors eventually,' she said.

Dovid nodded and saw that Lawrie was with them again too. A tug on his sleeve told Dovid they were all there.

'What are we going to do with him, Dovid?' Phrey asked. For a moment Dovid almost laughed at how much tougher Phrey was than he realised. Here was a kid who knew enough to stab Aris rather than hold their entire future ransom to him. Dovid wasn't as tough as Phrey, but he would do his best when it came to Nietric.

'Help me lift him into a cell,' Dovid said, and they each grabbed a jerking limb of the monster's body and dragged him in.

'When the other Managers get here,' Lawrie said, throwing a kick at Nietric even though he couldn't feel it. 'They'll just put all his upgrades back in and he'll be free to torture other kids like us.'

'There are no other kids like us,' Imma said with a smile.

Dovid looked down on Nietric and knew that Lawrie was right, but death seemed a little too easy. 'L.B. do you think you could take away enough of Nietric's energy so that he couldn't move for a few weeks? But still be conscious?'

He was expecting L.B. to think about it or ask for more detail, but all she said was a straightforward, 'Yes.'

Dovid nodded and kept going. 'And Phrey, do you think you could take away the light around Nietric, or from the whole room, so no one could see either for a few weeks?'

Phrey laughed. 'I think so, yeah.'

Dovid pulled down a nutrition charger from the ceiling and turned to face them. 'I say we leave him like this. The charger will keep him alive, but he won't be seen, or heard, or be able to perceive anything that happens for weeks until your inabilities wear off. He'll be left inside his own head, with nothing to keep him company other than the knowledge that we've gone to the very place he's spent his whole life searching. The other Managers might even think we brought him with us because he'll disappear like everyone else. I can't think of a more fitting punishment than to trap him within his own head, to examine his own conscious conscience until his mind becomes as broken as the rest of him. If he ever does get found, he won't be the same, and he might even serve as a warning to the rest of Management not to repeat these methods. Otherwise, they'll end up just like him.'

They all agreed, even though Dovid could tell that Lawrie would prefer to hurt him more. Silently they attached the nutrition charger, easily avoiding Nietric's twisted movements, until L.B. removed his energy and the body just sat there. Then the body disappeared, as did the very cell around them. Dovid tried to touch Nietric, but whatever L.B. did to his energy, interfered with Dovid's ability to feel him. His hand didn't pass through the physical matter of Nietric, but neither did his hand touch anything there either. It might be an anomaly the other Managers might choose to investigate, but they would have bigger things to examine, like the disappearance of over eighty people.

'We need to explain to everyone what we're planning, even if we don't understand everything about it, only that the Management of this world have betrayed our trust, and we need to start again. Tell them we're going outside, where we'll be free and where we'll be together.'

Lawrie nodded and left with L.B. and Phrey, and Dovid called out for Mart. He only had to say three sentences to Mart, before his brother stopped him, already sold on the unbelievable idea.

'My entire meaning of life, little brother, is to be amazed by it. And this sounds like the most amazing thing any life will ever be able to experience.'

Dovid smiled and asked if Mart could explain it to everyone else because Dovid wanted to spend a few moments alone with Imma before they moved. For a time neither of them said anything, and Dovid took in her every feature with his past-tense senses for the last time: the lightness of her hair, the crystal shine of her pale blue eyes, the softness of her skin that cushioned the unbreakable strength underneath. He loved every part of her and he wanted to cherish every memory he could. If they were really living in the past, then everything they experienced was nothing but memory combined with the illusion of control. All of life could be seen as nothing more than a collection of recollection, and if they were all memories of Imma, then it was a good life lived. Dovid had thought he was happy before, living alone in his island with his every need satisfied, but feeling how much happier he was with Imma only proved that any certainty could be disproved at any moment with a new experience.

'We did it,' Imma said, the happiness bursting free.

'We can do anything when we're together,' Dovid beamed back.

'Looks like we really are what we make ourselves.'

'So let's go see what kind of new future we can make.'

He kissed her, and held her tight, before pulling apart to smile at each other again. Then they stepped out of the invisible cell, and Dovid went down to gather up the supplies. It was a small start for a big future, but he was up for the challenge. Going back to the crowd, he called out for everyone who was coming to hold onto each other. He didn't see anyone separate themselves, and wondered if they really all were going to go with them. He guessed, even if they didn't believe him, they saw no reason to not at least try. There was a chance that they would appear in this new world with their senses intact, their bodies whole with eyes and ears and tongues reattached, yet retaining the same advantages and new evolved perceptions that the upgrades gave. Except that these perceptions would be real. It was an ideal too good to ignore.

Dovid and Imma smiled at each other one final time, before joining hands and linking with everyone else. There was no guarantee that this would work, and no one could know what the future would bring. There was only one thing certain about all of this: that no matter how good the past appeared, they could no longer live in it. It was time to see what the present held for them instead.

Dovid closed his eyes, and disappeared.

Also by James Dwyer

Fireborn

(Heights of Power – Book 1)

The world of power is turning to ice ... and when its keeper, the great Amadis Yeda disappears, armies of magic begin to war, creatures of darkness come into the light, gods walk among men, nations plunge into chaos, and the lives of four friends are changed forever:

Kris, a warrior who struggles not to kill every man, woman, and child he meets, is sent to stop the new tyrant, Aerath, from turning the world to ice.

Thisian, a man who loves only gold, women, and himself, takes advantage of the new found freedom that a world without order has to give.

Phira, the youngest and only female blaze commander her nation has ever known, is on a mission to uncover the secret behind Aerath's new power and how to stop his oncoming armies.

And Dallid, a man who has spent his life among those far greater than him, is given all the power of the gods. He must struggle with the responsibility cast on him, he must show the world what strength of flesh and heart can be when a mortal man is given limitless power.

He must show the world what it is to be Fireborn.

Masks of Moi'dan

(Heights of Power – Book 2)

Moi'dan the Masked once ruled half the world, in a time when the gods had been slain and all magic banished with them. When the heavens were breached to create a new age of gods, Moi'dan was betrayed and destroyed, but he did not die. His life was fractured into nine lesser lives, and his masks of power were scattered and lost.

Amadis has always known he was more than a Powerborn and less than a god, although he was Blinded to the full truth of his nature. He is the fractured memory of Moi'dan and he will do anything to return to that former power. But whenever a tyrant seeks to build his empire on the deaths of innocents, there will always be those who will rise to stand in his way:

Kris, a man who has survived things that no fleshborn should, beats the weakness of his flesh to serve the strength of his will. He uses that will to stop from murdering everyone that he meets, but he will gladly unleash all the darkness that dwells within him to kill Amadis.

Thisian, who wants nothing to bloody do with Amadis, or Kris, or any other lunatic who might want to kill him, and will fight only when he must. He is Powerborn, a Fureath'i Flameborn with the blood of gods running through his veins, and he uses this might to travel with thieves, to hunt for gold, and to bed as many women as he possibly can.

And Phira, the first female blaze commander of thousands, the slayer of gods, the wielder of the Jaguar blade, and the woman who killed the Iceborn Aerath; has her sights now firmly set on ridding the world of Amadis. And if any think to get in her way... may they all die screaming.

Twelve Weapons

(Twelve Weapons – Book 1)

In the first Season of Birth, life was created without death and twelve immortals were born. They were the Weapons, and when the Seasons turned, from Birth to Growth, from Decay to Death, the world died and the Weapons remained.

In the second Season of Birth, the world was reborn and blessed with mortal life who worshipped the Weapons as gods, crafting the world to their immortal glory. Each new Cycle came and went, with more life born and reborn only to become subject to the Weapons' will, only to be given a hopeless life under the Weapons' rule. Hopeless, until one day a Human named Adelis uncovers the way to kill them.

Adelis is a mother who loves her son. Raised to value strength above all else, she raises her son, Ruke, to be strong enough to withstand the world. Adelis believes the meaning of life is to give your life meaning, and if she can kill just one immortal, it would give meaning to all.

Ruke is a son who seeks desperate freedom from his maniac of a mother. Together with Grin – a drunken hound made from wine and steel – he will struggle to survive in a world filled with peril, made all the worse by a mother who goes actively searching for more.

And Caze, the most feared of all the Weapons, is a winged demon responsible for the deaths of billions. Tired of eternity, he yearns for a life of purpose and worth, and he believes he finds this worth when he uncovers the plans of the First Weapon to destroy all life. Caze sets out to stop this, to do something of meaning for once, and he will not fail.

After all, what could possibly stop an immortal Weapon?

The Grieving Soul

Find the cure for death and death returns with the cure for life.

No one is certain why it happened, although there is no denying that barely months after the miracle cure Pause is announced – a drug which allows anyone's age to be paused at any time, delaying death indefinitely – the dead began to return and the living began to die. Nothing seemed able to kill what was already dead, as the unnatural creatures swept through the natural world and made it their own. For four years the monsters hunted down every living thing, until only a few survivors remained to carve out what little life they may.

Clara Jacobs is a thirteen-year-old girl who loves to draw monsters. She does this so she has something to leave behind to the world after the monsters kill her, and in particular she draws the Fisherman: a creature capable of creating lakes of ice wherever he pleases, feeding on all the life that his ice can swallow.

Evelyn Jacobs is Clara's mother and she keeps a rifle in her hands at all times. Guns have no effect on the creatures, but the unnatural monsters are not what Evelyn fears. She fears that this haunted world has turned all life into monstrous form, both the living and the dead, and it is the other survivors of whom Evelyn remains wary.

And Vic Marshalls, well, he's a goddamned artist is what he is. And he includes everything he does or says in his definition of art, the clothes he wears and the way he spits both rating highly among his various masterpieces. His mission in life, however, is to kill just one monster: the Grieving Soul. This creature has condemned an entire city to an eternal rain of hopelessness and grief, making the very buildings weep as the Grieving Soul walks their streets. Vic is willing to do anything to achieve this goal, but is the price of salvation truly worth his own damnation? To rid the world of monsters, must the human heart take monstrous form?

There has to be a better way.

By Brendan Dwyer and James Dwyer

Cult Fiction

"People don't come to this city to escape reality; people come to this city because it's funking awesome." – Rowdy Roddy Randy

Municipal City: the only place on earth where you can be anyone. Anyone from your favourite movies, books, tv shows, comics, video games, or any cult media you can imagine, and not through virtual reality either – this is all real.

Tina Lockhart joins this city to do exactly that, and she is willing to pay any price to get in, willing to take the Elixir drug she needs just to breathe the air, and willing to kill or be killed just to survive.

Municipal City: the only place on earth where you can do anything. Anything can be replicated given the right technology, and anything can be done, so long as you follow the rules of the game.

But someone isn't playing by the rules. Someone is murdering players in the safe zones, something that should be impossible. As dangerous as this is for Tina Lockhart, things get worse as she becomes the one accused of these killings, and suddenly Tina needs to desperately find the truth in her world of cult fiction.

```
LOCKHART:

LEVEL 1       HP 10 MP 1   XP 0   CREDITS 255
Thief         Lvl 1  Att 6  Def 3  Agi 9
                    (PRESS START)
```

Rowdy Roddy Randy
Cult Fiction: Player Two

"So this is a city where you can live inside your favourite book, movie, tv show, or videogame, where you can be anyone you could possibly ever want to be, and you're seriously telling me there's no one here who's trying to be me, except for me? That's ridiculous." – Rowdy Roddy Randy

Season One of the Rowdy Roddy Randy show looks at the prequel years of Municipal City, when a handsome young man is thrust into the scene to irreparably shake things up forever. Watch with awe as an impressionable boy is forged into the smelted steel of manhood to become the unparalleled warrior-wizard-celebrity-genius that we already know him to be.

Season Two reboots the double-life Randy was living while Lockhart stumbled about, obsessing about her cyborg boyfriend Episite. Torn between his love for Anna, his indifference to Lockhart, and his testicle-shrinking detestation of Sam, Randy must decide whether he wants to be the best by playing by the rules, or be the best simply because he's awesome.

And finally Season Three continues on as sequel to where Cult Fiction left off, in a city scourged with the dangerous E-Virus, ready to explode, just waiting for the right spark to set it off. Will Randy be the jerk to set it off? Or will he rise to the challenge and claim that number one spot he so rightly deserves. How can you wait to find out? Already your excitement has become too much and you have no other choice but to buy this, and tell all your friends, and all of the internet, about just how good this book is ... as you read *Cult Fiction: Player Two!*

RANDY:

LEVEL 1	HP 10 MP 1 XP 0 CREDITS 255
Wizard	Lvl 1 Att 4 Def 9 Agi 2

(PRESS START)

Printed in Great Britain
by Amazon